⬧ P9-CSV-533

THE BAYOU BULLETIN

Mary Delacroix Celebrates Eightieth Birthday!

The Delacroix clan will be pulling out all the stops next week when Mary Delacroix, one of Bayou Beltane's most cherished citizens, celebrates her eightieth birthday. The family has planned an afternoon fete so Mary can receive her guests in the comfort of her own home. The office of Senator Philip Delacroix has confirmed the senator's attendance at the party, despite his busy schedule, and despite the almost certain attendance of his twin brother, Charles. These elder statesmen of Bayou Beltane are rarely seen at the same social events, due to an estrangement that dates back at least fifty years.

Toni Delacroix, current toast of the New Orleans jazz club scene, has also arranged her schedule in order to be present at the celebration. It is not known at this time if Jacqueline Delacroix, Olympic equestrian medalist, will be in town to join the rest of her family, but Delacroix from all over the country will be converging on Bayou Beltane over the next week in order to pay their respects to Mary. Floral arrangements will be handled by Bayou Florists, who are keeping their plans top secret at this time....

If you purchased this book without a cover you should be aware that this book is stolen property. It was reported as "unsold and destroyed" to the publisher, and neither the author nor the publisher has received any payment for this "stripped book."

Jasmine Cresswell is acknowledged
as the author of this work.

ISBN 0-373-82561-7

CONTRACT: PATERNITY

Copyright © 1997 by Harlequin Books S.A.

All rights reserved. Except for use in any review, the reproduction or utilization of this work in whole or in part in any form by any electronic, mechanical or other means, now known or hereafter invented, including xerography, photocopying and recording, or in any information storage or retrieval system, is forbidden without the written permission of the publisher, Harlequin Enterprises Limited, 225 Duncan Mill Road, Don Mills, Ontario, Canada M3B 3K9.

All characters in this book have no existence outside the imagination of the author and have no relation whatsoever to anyone bearing the same name or names. They are not even distantly inspired by any individual known or unknown to the author, and all incidents are pure invention.

This edition published by arrangement with Harlequin Books S.A.

® and TM are trademarks of the publisher. Trademarks indicated with ® are registered in the United States Patent and Trademark Office, the Canadian Trade Marks Office and in other countries.

Printed in U.S.A.

DELTA JUSTICE

Jasmine Cresswell

Contract:
Paternity

Harlequin Books

TORONTO • NEW YORK • LONDON
AMSTERDAM • PARIS • SYDNEY • HAMBURG
STOCKHOLM • ATHENS • TOKYO • MILAN
MADRID • WARSAW • BUDAPEST • AUCKLAND

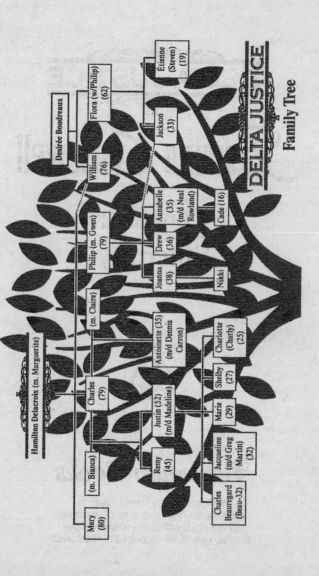

DELTA JUSTICE
Family Tree

CAST OF CHARACTERS

Antoinette Delacroix—jazz singer, owner of *Chanson Triste*, a New Orleans jazz club

Brody Wagner—attorney, a recent addition to the firm of Delacroix and Associates

Justin Delacroix—Antoinette's brother, senior partner in law firm of Delacroix and Associates

Dennis Carron—attorney, ex-husband of Antoinette Delacroix

Mary Delacroix—great-aunt of Antoinette Delacroix

Charles Delacroix—Antoinette's father, semiretired attorney, former head of Delacroix and Associates

Philip Delacroix—Charles's estranged twin brother, a Louisiana state senator

Shelby Delacroix—Justin's daughter, and youngest new attorney at Delacroix and Associates

Maya Johnson—Antoinette's best friend, and mother of Antoinette's godchild

Pudge Johnson—Antoinette's arranger, accompanist and confidant

Fifi—Brody Wagner's favorite four-legged, pedigreed friend

Dear Reader,

One of the tips most writers are given early in their careers is that they should write about things and places that they know well. This always seemed very good advice to me, and since I'm lucky enough to have lived in a lot of interesting places around the world, I'm usually not tempted to set my stories in any city where I haven't spent a lot of time.

So when the editors at Harlequin asked me if I would like to write the first book in an exciting new series about the Delacroix family, who live in a small town near New Orleans, Louisiana, I realized I faced an interesting new challenge. I had visited New Orleans a few times over the years and, like most other visitors, I had fallen in love with its unique charms and intriguing history. However, this didn't seem sufficient background for writing an entire story about a family with roots deep in the Louisiana soil.

Fortunately, this was a problem with a delightful solution. My daughter and son-in-law had recently moved to New Orleans, and my daughter was expecting a baby. What better excuse did I need to spend a month in Louisiana!

My new granddaughter arrived at the end of July. In between admiring how beautiful she was and how fast she was growing, I explored the city. Toni, the heroine of my book, is a singer who owns a nightclub in the French Quarter, and I spent some wonderful evenings with my son-in-law, a jazz lover, sampling some of the fabulous music that New Orleans offers. But the most exciting discovery for me was the rich history and unique ecology of the North Shore region where the DELTA JUSTICE series is set. New and old are meeting head-on in this part of the world, and it was fascinating to write about the inevitable clashes.

I hope you will enjoy *Contract: Paternity*. I can certainly say that doing the research for this book was some of the most fun I've had in a long time!

Sincerely

Jasmine Cresswell

CHAPTER ONE

CHAPTER ONE

WHEN ANTOINETTE DELACROIX agreed to meet her ex-husband for lunch, she was prepared for almost anything—except the possibility that she wouldn't recognize him. Circling the lobby of the Hotel Maison de Ville, she scrutinized half a dozen unaccompanied men and decided that at least three of them might be Dennis Carron. She should have asked him to wear a red carnation or carry a balloon, she thought, and smiled at the mental picture of her uptight, buttoned-down former husband sitting in the lobby of New Orleans' most elegant hotel, clutching a balloon.

"Antoinette? Er...Toni?" A deep, vaguely familiar voice spoke from behind her, and she swung around. A tall man with thick glasses and sparse brown hair gazed at her uncertainly.

"Yes?" Her voice rose in a question. Perhaps Dennis had been delayed, and this man was delivering a message from him.

The man's smile became more confident. "Toni, it really is you. For a minute, seeing you in profile, I wasn't certain. It's been a long time." He cleared his throat and held out his hand. "Thanks for coming at such short notice. I sure do appreciate that. You're looking...great."

"Dennis?" Toni stared at him, too shocked to move or even to murmur a conventional greeting. This nondescript, middle-aged man was *Dennis?*

Basic good manners took over at last, and she finally

reached out to shake his hand, returning his smile with a great deal more warmth than she'd have managed if he hadn't looked so…old. "I'm sorry if I kept you waiting," she said. "I had a meeting out near the airport this morning, and I got hopelessly snarled in traffic coming back. You know what it's like in the Quarter at lunchtime."

"Don't apologize," Dennis said affably. They were both being so polite, Miss Manners could have used them as an example of how divorced couples should behave toward each other. "I expected you to keep me waiting a lot longer than five minutes," he added.

Toni's smile froze, but only for a moment. "These days, I try very hard to be punctual."

"Do you?" Dennis let the question hang between them just long enough to remind her of all the trouble she'd caused during their brief marriage because of her stubborn refusal to arrive anywhere on time. "Well, I'm sure we've both changed a lot in fourteen years," he concluded smoothly.

"I hope so," she said. "Heaven knows, we both had plenty of room for improvement."

He frowned at that, making the fan of lines around his eyes more conspicuous as he considered what she'd said. "You're right," he said finally. "It's amazing how grown up we felt when we were really nothing more than a couple of kids playing house. No wonder we messed up."

His voice was as attractive as she remembered, making the changes in his appearance even more startling by contrast. *He's only forty,* Toni realized. *Five years older than me.*

At the thought, her stomach jumped queasily. She didn't like acknowledging that in three short weeks she'd be thirty-five. These days, it seemed that everywhere she turned she was confronted with yet another reminder of the accelerating tick of her biological clock. She must be one of the few women in the world who would have been quite happy to meet her former husband years after the divorce and find him looking young, dashing and sexy. Instead, Dennis was living proof of how fast time had run away from both of them. Fourteen years since they'd played at marriage under the watchful gaze of her family. Fourteen years since she'd staged her rebellion against the smothering embrace of the Delacroix family. Fourteen years since she'd escaped from Bayou Beltane and launched her fledgling career in New Orleans.

It all seemed a very long time ago. Long enough, perhaps, that she could finally acknowledge that she owed Dennis an apology. She'd married him for the wrong reasons, and then blamed him for every problem in their relationship. The fact that she'd been nineteen when they eloped and twenty-one when they divorced was only a partial excuse for her miserable behavior in between.

"I'm very glad you suggested we should have lunch," Toni said. "It gives me the chance to tell you how much I regret the way I behaved when we were married. It's an apology that's long overdue, Dennis."

He turned away, but not before she saw an unexpected flash of emotion in his eyes. "We already agreed that we both made mistakes."

"Yes, but I'd like you to know how much I regret some of mine." Toni's hand tightened around the strap of her purse. "I was never unfaithful, Dennis, but I deliberately convinced you that I was, and I'm very sorry about that."

Dennis flushed as he bent to pick up his briefcase, the sordid finale to their relationship obviously as vivid in his mind as it was in hers. He cleared his throat. "We both have plenty to apologize for," he said. "The truth is, we should never have gotten married. I was attracted to you because you were a Delacroix, and you were attracted to me because you wanted to stop being a Delacroix. No wonder we couldn't make things work."

Toni was surprised at the stark precision of his assessment. Not because she disagreed, but because he was willing to express it. The Dennis Carron she had known years ago would never have admitted that he'd married her for such a reason, and his newfound honesty was refreshing.

"You've changed, Dennis," she said, and this time she wasn't even thinking about his appearance.

"I hope so. Like you said, there was lots of room for improvement." He started to walk out of the reception area, indicating that the reminiscences were over. "Toni, I'm sure we both have busy schedules this afternoon, so we need to get started."

She fell into step beside him. "Yes—although you never actually said what it is we're supposed to be discussing over lunch. Just that it was important."

He carried on as if she hadn't spoken, a sign that the Dennis Carron she'd married hadn't totally disappeared inside this new, middle-aged person. "We can eat in the restaurant if you wish, but I'm booked into a small suite on the sixth floor and I would prefer to order lunch from room service, if that's all right with you. What I have to say is somewhat confidential, and I believe my suite would be the most convenient place for us to continue this discussion."

For a split second, Toni found herself wishing there was some slight chance that Dennis was attempting to lure her into his suite so that he could seduce her. Not because she wanted to make love to him, even for old times' sake. But it saddened her that she had been married to this man for two years and now there was nothing left between them. Nothing, not even a tiny residual spark of sexual curiosity. She'd expected this meeting to be difficult, she thought ruefully, but it was turning out to be difficult for rather surprising reasons. Seeing Dennis wasn't so much bringing back unpleasant memories as forcing her to confront issues about the present that she'd have preferred to leave buried.

She wasn't ready to delve any further into her subconscious and pursue those issues, although she usually prided herself on being a straightforward person who liked to get such matters out on the table, where they could be examined under a clear light. Yet another reaction to the years of her childhood in Bayou Beltane, where all the most important emotions were forced deep down below the surface, spreading their roots in silent darkness, sending up tentacles that twisted relationships and choked off normal family life.

Wanting to dispel her introspective mood, Toni spoke with calculated briskness. "By all means, let's go up to your suite," she said, returning the wave and smile of an aide from the mayor's office. "You're right, that's the only way to guarantee we won't be interrupted."

Dennis cast a frowning glance at the aide. "I guess you're acquainted with a lot of important people in New Orleans," he said as they headed for the elevators.

"I guess so." She ignored the faint note of resentment in his voice. Dennis had always been ambivalent about the Delacroix family's links to Louisiana's centers of power. She preceded him into the elevator car. "In some ways, New Orleans is still a small town. The old families don't have the stranglehold on commerce and finance that they used to, but in my line of work, you aren't going to succeed unless a few of the right people decide that you will."

"You used to say that talent was all you needed for success."

Toni pulled a face. "I'm sure I did. Isn't it amazing how arrogant we are when we're teenagers? Nowadays, I realize that for a singer, talent is just the basic starting point. Then you've got to have clawing ambition, nerves of steel and an ego the size of Lake Pontchartrain. Most of all, you need a lot of luck.''

''You must have had all of those qualities,'' Dennis said, holding open the elevator door for her once they'd reached his floor. ''Chanson Triste is a huge success, and every guidebook says that no visitor can leave New Orleans without hearing Antoinette, the fabulous blues singer.''

''I'm a local success,'' Toni said and shrugged. ''I had my shot at national stardom, and I blew it.'' The admission no longer hurt as much as it would have done even a year ago.

''You're talking about your national tour three years ago.'' Dennis swiped his card through the lock and pushed open the door to his suite. ''The music critics loved you everywhere you went,'' he said. ''You got rave reviews in New York and in Chicago, too. Those are tough cities to impress.''

She was surprised and oddly touched by this revelation that he'd followed her singing career with such close attention. ''The reviews were great,'' she said wryly. ''But the audiences stayed away in droves. The tour promoters lost money on me, and they're only willing to do that once.''

''I'm sure the low ticket sales had nothing to do with the quality of your singing. I guess jazz and blues are like crawfish. They don't travel well.''

''Thanks for those kind words.'' Laughing, she followed him into the suite. ''Anytime I get depressed thinking about my disastrous national tour, I'll remind myself I'm like crawfish, best sampled in New Orleans.''

He took off his jacket and loosened his tie, turning the air-conditioning to maximum. Summer in New Orleans was an endurance contest between the climate and the miracles of air-conditioning. Today the climate seemed to be winning. Dennis handed Toni a menu and she fanned herself, waiting for a welcome blast of icy air to waft in her direction. "Let's order lunch, and then we can talk while we wait for the food to arrive," he suggested.

Toni ordered Cajun shrimp salad and iced tea; Dennis ordered grilled red snapper and Coke. With lunch taken care of, he seemed anxious to get down to business. He opened his briefcase and drew out two bulky files, which he set on the coffee table in front of them. But once the papers were all spread out, he stared at them in silence, his fingers drumming nervously on the arm of his chair.

"I don't know how to start this conversation," he said, taking off his glasses and rubbing his eyes. "It seemed a hell of a lot easier when I was rehearsing what I planned to say during the drive down from Shreveport."

During the past fourteen years, they hadn't exchanged so much as a postcard or a phone call, except to arrange this luncheon meeting, and Toni couldn't imagine what was left of their relationship to cause him so much anxiety. She squinted at the papers he was fiddling with, trying to read them upside down. They were handwritten in an old-fashioned copperplate, and she could make out nothing beyond the occasional word. "Pretend I'm not here and that you're still rehearsing," she suggested.

He laughed without mirth. "You aren't the sort of woman any man can ignore," he said. "Even a happily married man like me can't help noticing that you still have a body that belongs in a *Playboy* centerfold."

"Actually, it's been in a *Playboy* centerfold," Toni said. She sat up straighter in the chair, uncomfortable beneath her ex-husband's scrutiny, and not at all sure why she'd mentioned a photo shoot that she now deeply regretted. Was she so worried about her approaching birthday that she needed to remind herself that her body had once been youthfully perfect? That until this year, she'd been confident of her choices and quite happy to keep her dreams and ambitions focused exclusively on her career?

Dennis stared at her as if she'd grown two heads. "I can't imagine what your family must have said when they realized you'd allowed yourself to be photographed nude!"

"On the contrary, I'm sure you can imagine exactly what they said. Everyone went predictably ballistic." Toni grimaced. "Those were the pictures that finally persuaded my father I was beyond redemption. He barred me from the family home and didn't speak to me for three years."

Dennis frowned. "I didn't know things got so bad between you and your family. Are you and Charles on speaking terms now?"

"More or less. Dad was seventy-nine last birthday, and he's mellowed a bit in the last few years. He no longer seems quite so obsessive about the precious Delacroix family honor."

Dennis put his glasses on again and got up to walk over to the window. He stared in silence at the uninspired view of the hotel rooftop. "I heard that your brother's been nominated to the federal bench," he said, and she wasn't sure if he'd changed the subject for her benefit or for his own. "Justin must be pleased. He always wanted to be a judge, didn't he?"

"Did he?" It was a sad commentary on her strained relationship with her family that Dennis Carron knew this fundamental fact about her brother and she didn't. "Justin's always found the criminal side of the family's law practice more interesting than the commercial side," she said finally. "But he's so much older than I, we've never talked about his ambitions the way some brothers and sisters might. Why do you ask?''

Dennis hesitated. ''I was approached by somebody who suggested your brother might meet with opposition in getting his appointment confirmed by the Senate Judiciary Committee.''

''Good Lord, why? Justin's devoted his life to the law, and he's the soul of integrity. I can't imagine anyone who'd be more qualified to serve on the bench.''

''There's a lot of politics involved in the appointment of federal judges,'' Dennis said, and lapsed into a brooding silence. After a minute or two, he brought his gaze back to Toni. ''Have you ever thought about how strange your family's situation really is?'' he asked.

''Which particular strange situation are you referring to?'' Toni responded dryly. ''The Delacroix family has so many.''

Dennis didn't smile. ''I'm talking about the feud between your father and your Uncle Philip. They're identical twins, they're both lawyers, they live practically in each other's backyards in a small town where everyone knows everyone else's business, and yet they don't speak to each other.''

Toni shrugged. ''I read an article just the other day that said it's a myth that twins are always close. Sometimes the intensity of the relationship is too much for either twin to handle.''

''Maybe. But if Charles and Philip dislike each other so much, why didn't one of them move away?''

''Well, I don't know. Their roots in Bayou Beltane go deep—''

''That's true. Which only makes it more surprising that the pair of them have lived in the same town their whole lives—and nobody seems to know what they're feuding about!''

"You're right," Toni said. "It's crazy. But what's one more crazy situation among so many? I've never noticed that my family is particularly dedicated to the art of compromise and common sense."

"But there's crazy and then there's crazy," Dennis persisted. "Haven't you ever wondered what caused the rift between Charles and Philip?"

"To be honest, no. Their feud was a fact of life, like alligators in the bayous, or wearing scratchy uniforms to school." Toni got up and paced, uncomfortable as usual when forced to think about Bayou Beltane and the hothouse atmosphere of her upbringing.

"There was always so much tension swirling around in our family," she said. "That was one of the reasons I was so desperate to escape and lead my own life. But I never felt any pressing need to go searching for explanations as to why my father and my uncle don't speak to each other. You lived in Bayou Beltane, so you know the two of them are perfect candidates for starting a feud. I've come to admire the way my father sticks to his principles, but that doesn't mean he's an easy man to get along with. As for my uncle Philip, superficially he seems more approachable than my father, but I've always felt there's a lot going on beneath the surface charm that Philip doesn't want the world to see."

"The fact that Charles and Philip are both stubborn and opinionated doesn't explain why they've barely spoken to each other for almost sixty years."

"I guess not." Toni shrugged. "Does there have to be a good reason? The pair of them could have fought over something as trivial as who got the family car one night, or something as serious as how to interpret the terms of my grandfather's will. In fact, come to think of it, my grandfather's will is probably what started their feud. My grandfather died right before World War II, when Dad and Uncle Philip were in their early twenties, and that's how long they've been feuding.''

"Your grandfather's will is a matter of public record, and there's nothing in it likely to start a family feud. Hamilton Delacroix split his assets very fairly among his children.''

"You've checked out the terms of my grandfather's will?'' Toni stared at him. "You were that curious about what caused the rift between my father and my uncle?''

"I had good reason to be curious,'' Dennis said tightly.

Toni walked over to the window and stood next to her ex-husband. "Dennis, cut to the chase. If these preliminaries are supposed to give me a hint as to what's bothering you, they're not working. You're simply making me nervous. Have you found out what started the feud? Is it something awful? Is that why you wanted to see me today?''

"In a way, this meeting is all about Charles and Philip and their feud. In another way, it's about us.''

She shook her head. "But, Dennis, there is no *us*.''

"Not now,'' he agreed. "Not for the last fourteen years. But in the past...'' Dennis drew in a long, shallow breath. "I was in love with you, Toni, and I knew you didn't love me. That sort of a situation can drive a person crazy.''

Toni didn't know what to say except that she was sorry.

Dennis stopped her apology. "Don't get me wrong,'' he said. "I'm very happy in my current marriage. I love my kids, and Cheryl...my wife...is a good person, In fact, she's the reason I'm here. She persuaded me I couldn't give way to blackmail, just because it might seem the easy way out.''

"Blackmail?'' Toni jerked around so fast that she almost stumbled over a chair. "You're being blackmailed? What about?''

Dennis visibly searched for the right words, but before he could find the answer he wanted, a knock at the door heralded the arrival of lunch. The room service waiter set a table near the window with a starched, peach-colored cloth and napkins and a centerpiece of a fragrant gardenia floating in a small glass bowl. Toni wasn't really hungry, but her meal—true to the traditions of one of New Orleans' finest hotels—looked and smelled wonderful, and for a couple of minutes while the waiter hovered, she and Dennis exchanged pleasantries about the food.

The moment the door closed behind the waiter, Toni resumed their former conversation. "Dennis, please don't keep me in suspense. Why are you being blackmailed, and how in the world does that have anything to do with our marriage? We ended that a lot more gracefully than we started it. There's just nothing about our relationship for a blackmailer to work with."

Dennis twirled his glass around, watching the ice melt. "It's a complicated story, with long roots. The short version is that I'm the guy in the middle, but it's not me the blackmailer is out to get. It's your brother, Justin."

"Justin?" Toni exclaimed, more puzzled than worried. "But that makes no sense. How can you be involved in an attempt to blackmail my brother? The two of you barely know each other."

"We don't know each other well on a personal level. But it so happens we were both working on the same business transaction five years ago. That transaction is what I'm being blackmailed about."

Toni was surprised at how indignant she felt on her brother's behalf. "If there's one thing I know about Justin, it's that he would never be involved in any deal that was professionally dubious."

"Sometimes you don't need to be dishonest to get into trouble, just careless."

Toni drew in a sharp breath. "Are you suggesting Justin was careless?"

Dennis spread his hands in a gesture that wasn't quite a denial. "Five years ago, your brother was involved in a negotiation with one of the major oil exploration companies. The oil company was attempting to buy a hundred acres of land that were crucial to their drilling operations but weren't very important or valuable to the family that owned them. Justin represented the Hendersons, the elderly couple who owned the land. The oil company was working through a subsidiary, a real estate company called Louisiana Properties. The real estate company never actually said they wanted to build houses on the land, but Justin assumed that was their purpose—"

"So in effect, Justin was deceived as to who he was dealing with?" Toni asked.

"In a way. But everything done by Louisiana Properties was totally legal and relatively aboveboard. A couple of hours' research by Justin would have turned up the facts about exactly who wanted to buy his clients' land. And once he knew who wanted the land, he would have known they didn't plan to build houses on it."

Toni didn't much like the direction in which the conversation was heading. "Let me guess. My brother didn't do the necessary research?"

"No, he didn't. Louisiana Properties took advantage of the fact that Justin was busy handling a couple of high-profile criminal cases at the time, and they counted on him to drop the ball. Which he did. He went to the negotiating table without any idea of the potential value of the Henderson land. He sold out for less than half a million dollars, whereas—if they'd been pressed—the oil company would have been prepared to pay five million."

"Are you saying my brother was negligent?" Toni asked.

Dennis hesitated. "Negligent is too strong a word. Like I said, the oil company deliberately organized the negotiations to minimize the chance of Justin finding out who he was dealing with."

"But you think he should have realized what was going on," Toni persisted.

Dennis shrugged. "If it had been a criminal case, I doubt if Justin would have been equally as willing to take everything at face value."

Toni added ice to her tea and stirred mindlessly. "Okay, so Justin dropped the ball and somebody who doesn't like him has found out that he messed up. It's embarrassing, but every potential judge in the United States must have some story like this that could be used against them."

"That's true, and that's where I come in."

"How?"

Dennis gave a smile that held no mirth. "I work as chief-in-house legal counsel for Shoreline Exploration, the oil company that owns Louisiana Properties. Not only that, but I was in charge of the negotiations, although I always sent in somebody else to do the face-to-face bargaining with your brother."

Toni let out a long slow breath. "I see. Or at least I don't see, not yet. But this is obviously heading somewhere nasty."

"Very nasty," Dennis said. "Before Justin's appointment to the Federal bench can be confirmed, the FBI will conduct a routine background check. The check will be very thorough because the White House has gotten tired of reporters discovering scandals the government investigators have missed. Unfortunately, when the FBI turns its attention to Justin's dealings with Shoreline, they'll uncover a major scandal—"

"Not major," Toni protested. "How can a careless error become a major scandal?"

"Easily," Dennis said grimly. "Because Justin's actions won't seem like a mistake. I've been instructed to doctor my records of the transaction to make it look as if your brother walked away from the deal having pocketed two hundred thousand extra dollars for keeping the sale price of the Henderson land so low."

Toni set down her iced tea, aware that she suddenly felt chilled. "And if you don't doctor the books?" she asked.

"Then the FBI will be informed—anonymously, of course—that Justin and I split the payoff and that I've doctored the company records to cover up our crime. Whatever I do, Justin gets screwed. And if I don't cooperate with the blackmailers, I'm screwed, as well."

Toni was silent for almost a full minute, trying to organize her whirling thoughts. Dennis had been right about the seriousness of the situation. "Have you been in touch with my brother?" she asked.

Dennis shook his head. "Not yet. Cheryl and I have been going around and around on whether I should contact Justin and warn him what's happening, or whether that would just make it look as if we're conspiring to cover up what we did."

"It's a good thing you came to me," Toni said. "I can act as an intermediary and warn Justin what's going on."

"Yes, that's what Cheryl and I hoped...."

Toni frowned, deep in thought. "We need to find out who's behind this blackmail attempt, otherwise they'll just try something else if this doesn't work. Do you have any idea who's doing this, Dennis? Any clues at all?"

"No." He spoke firmly, but Toni wasn't at all sure she believed him.

"But who approached you? And how?"

He shook his head. "No one I could identify. And the

note was generic—no way to identify where it came from."

"It must be someone who feels threatened by Justin's appointment," she said.

Dennis gave a short laugh. "Given that your brother has a reputation for being impossible to bribe, that narrows the field of suspects to about one-third of the population of Louisiana."

Toni sent him a searching gaze. "You're not being up front with me, Dennis. You do have an idea who's behind this."

He was silent for a moment or two, then got up and walked over to the coffee table, where he'd originally set out the small collection of file folders. He picked them up, riffling through the pages without looking at them. "I might have some suspicions," he said. "But I have no real proof, and I've no idea why this person would be willing to go to so much trouble to keep Justin off the bench."

"Tell me, anyway."

Dennis laced and unlaced his hands a couple of times before answering. "Philip Delacroix," he said at last.

"Uncle Philip?" Toni was astonished. To her knowledge, the infamous feud between Charles and Philip had never taken an active form, much less spilled over into revenge against another family member. The two brothers had been content simply to ignore each other for almost sixty years, and—as far as she knew—Justin had done absolutely nothing to offend their uncle or expand the feud. On the other hand, Philip had been a state senator for more than twenty years, with political views that differed strongly from her brother's. He might have political reasons for opposing Justin's nomination, but Toni was having a hard time believing that he would resort to such underhanded methods to oppose her brother's nomination.

"Why do you suspect that my uncle might be behind this?" she asked.

"Because the person who's trying to blackmail me knows something about my past that only Philip knows. Or I thought only Philip knew. Of course, in fourteen years, Philip could have told any number of people what I did, which is why I can't prove that it's Philip who's behind this blackmail attempt."

"Wait, you've lost me," Toni said. "Run that by me one more time."

Dennis flushed. "If you must know, the blackmailer is trying to use something I did—something I'm ashamed of—as a weapon to control the way I behave, and I'm going to call his bluff. Whoever is behind this obviously doesn't want me to warn Justin what's going on. To make sure I keep quiet, he's threatened that if Justin finds out about the scheme to discredit him with the FBI, then you'll be told that I stole Hamilton Delacroix's personal files from your father's office."

Toni didn't consider that much of a threat and said so. "Good grief, Dennis, why would anyone care that you'd taken a few musty old legal papers? I thought you were going to confess that you'd done something truly dreadful, like embezzling a poor widow out of her life savings. Taking my grandfather's files, years after he died, doesn't sound like a major crime to me, or even a minor one."

Dennis continued to look grim. "It's more serious than you realize. I stole Hamilton Delacroix's files because your uncle Philip promised me a job with his law firm if I did. He also paid me five thousand dollars as a signing-on bonus for agreeing to switch to his firm from your father's. In other words, he handed over a five-thousand-dollar bribe to persuade me to steal my employer's property."

Her uncle Philip had wanted Hamilton Delacroix's personal papers so badly that he'd bribed Dennis to steal them? What on earth for? And, since he'd stolen them, why hadn't Dennis handed them over? Toni gestured to the documents spread out on the coffee table. "Are those the files my uncle wanted you to steal?"

"Yes. They're your grandfather's personal notes on various important cases he handled during the course of his career. From the haphazard way they're written, I doubt if he ever expected to share them with anyone."

"Why would my uncle Philip want them? Do you have any idea?"

"Maybe." He cleared his throat. "There's information in those files about an old murder case. The one Hamilton Delacroix had been working on right before he died."

"And Philip was curious about this case years after my grandfather died?" Toni looked skeptical. "His interests aren't usually so whimsical."

"I don't believe Philip's interest was whimsical this time, either."

"Then what was it? How could it be practical or profitable to delve into a murder case my grandfather had been working on years and years earlier? He must have defended a dozen murderers during the course of his career." Toni spread her hands. "Help me out, here, Dennis. Stop acting like a lawyer and just say what the problem is, straight out."

Dennis drew in a deep breath. "From the notes Hamilton Delacroix made, it seems as if your father had been friendly...more than friendly...with the woman who got killed. I'm guessing that Philip wanted those files because he'd been trying to dig up some dirt on his brother in regard to this old murder case. Hamilton's notes make it clear that your father had been with the victim only a short while before she was killed."

A knot of anxiety formed in the pit of Toni's stomach.

Her father had once been friendly with the victim in a murder case? It was impossible to visualize Charles Delacroix, rigid moralist and pillar of society, involved even peripherally in something as sordid as murder.

"I don't understand any of this," she said. "Leaving aside the question of what the files contain, why do you still have them, Dennis? You're telling me that at Philip's request, you stole my grandfather's papers—or at least some of them—and found jottings suggesting that my father might know more about an old murder case than he's letting on. Then, you didn't give the files to Philip, you didn't go to work for him—and you kept the files. Why?"

"Philip offered his bribe just a little too late." Dennis had the grace to look embarrassed. "Hamilton's personal papers weren't easy to find. I guess that's why Philip needed an insider like me to do his dirty work. By the time I'd located the files, our marriage had gone from bad to hopeless. At that point, all I wanted was to get out of Bayou Beltane." His mouth twisted. "I also like to think that some remnant of professional integrity kept me from handing the files over to Philip."

"Okay, in that case, why didn't you just put them back where you'd found them?"

"I couldn't do that once the two of us split up. You see, the files weren't stored in the office, they were stored among Charles's personal papers at home—"

"In Riverwood?"

Dennis nodded. "Yes, in your father's study, kept under lock and key. And once you and I separated, I wasn't living there anymore, so I didn't have free access to Riverwood, let alone to your father's study."

Toni felt a surge of relief. "Well, if my father had Hamilton's files stored in his study, they can't contain anything very incriminating, can they? Otherwise, he would have destroyed them."

"In fact, I often wondered why he didn't destroy the files." Dennis cleared his throat nervously. "I even considered destroying them myself."

"Why didn't you?"

Dull color stained Dennis's cheeks. "Heck, Toni, we'd just gotten divorced, I was feeling very bitter...." His voice trailed away miserably.

Toni understood at once. "You considered the possibility of a little blackmail yourself."

"Not for long," Dennis said quickly. "And never seriously. In fact, as soon as I got settled in Shreveport, I almost mailed the files back to your father, anonymously. But that would have sparked a whole investigation as to who had stolen them, and I would have become the prime suspect. Since your father never seemed to have noticed anything was missing, I decided it was smarter just to let the whole episode sink quietly into oblivion. Which it did. To be honest, after a couple of years, my life moved on and I genuinely forgot I had the darn things."

"What about the money my uncle Philip paid you? Did you ever return it?"

"No, I figured it would be just as difficult to return the money as to return the files." Dennis couldn't quite meet her gaze. "Look, I know I behaved badly, but it was a long time ago, and I'm a lot smarter now than I was then. I'm not going to add forgery and falsifying Shoreline Exploration's records to the mistakes I made fourteen years ago. And that's why I've brought Hamilton's files back, and why I'm telling you exactly how I got them."

Toni didn't feel in any position to be making moral judgments about the way Dennis had behaved during the breakup of their marriage. "I'm glad you told me what happened," she said. "And I can understand the sort of mind-set you were in when my uncle persuaded you to steal Hamilton's files. Toward the end of our marriage we both behaved like prize idiots.''

"That's for sure." Dennis spoke quickly. "So you'll put the files back in your father's office for me?"

She nodded. "If I can get in there without drawing attention to what I'm doing. Although, despite Philip's odd desire to have them, I can't imagine they're of real interest to anyone. Maybe it would be best just to toss them out. It isn't as if our family's short of memorabilia. My aunt Mary's whole house is full of sentimental knick-knacks and family doodads.''

Dennis stopped pacing and stacked the papers he'd spread out over the coffee table. "It's entirely up to you what you do with them, Toni, but I suggest you read them before you decide to destroy them. Your grandfather was a great litigator, and the insight into the way his mind worked is fascinating. In the last case he tried, the one I'm sure your uncle is interested in, Hamilton was defending an accused murderer called Rafael Perdido, who'd actually worked for the Delacroix family on their sugar plantation. Rafael was accused of murdering a young woman named Camille Gravier, who also had links to your family.''

"Camille Gravier and Rafael who?" Toni said.

"Rafael Perdido."

She shook her head. "I've never heard either name mentioned, as far as I can remember. But that doesn't mean too much. I tend to tune out when my father and Justin started talking about the law.''

"This would be a hard case to forget. In your grandfather's opinion, the rulings from the presiding judge were often flagrantly biased against his client.''

"So what happened to Rafael in the end?" Toni asked. "Did my grandfather get him off?''

"No. His case is the only murder case your grandfather ever defended and lost."

Toni winced. "That's bad for my grandfather, but a lot worse for Rafael. Did my grandfather appeal the verdict?"

"No, he had a heart attack and died before the appeal process was started. In those days, there were no automatic appeals. Rafael was sent to Angola prison and killed by an inmate there."

Toni shivered. "Then I definitely don't want to read those files."

"You might want to reconsider that decision. I'm fairly sure that the trial of Rafael Perdido is the root cause of the feud between your father and your uncle. Your grandfather makes a lot of references to Charles and Philip and their growing hostility toward each other."

Right now, investigating an old murder and finding out why her father and her uncle didn't speak to each other was low down on Toni's list of priorities. She was far more interested in making sure that Justin wasn't unfairly deprived of his appointment to the federal bench. "Well, when I can scrounge some spare time, I'll take a look at my grandfather's files. But right now I need to concentrate on the threat to Justin's nomination and the blackmail threats against you, Dennis. I'll call my brother this afternoon and tell him he needs to drive into the city and meet with me as soon as he possibly can."

"Be careful what you disclose over the phone," Dennis said. "These days, you never know who might be listening in. At Shoreline, it's company policy never to discuss major business deals unless we're on a secure line."

Toni resisted the temptation to suggest that Shoreline sounded like a corporation with a bad case of paranoia. "Don't worry," she said. "I'll make sure that I don't say anything too explicit until I meet Justin face-to-face."

Having completed his confession about past misdeeds,

Dennis was reverting to a more typical state of repressive caution. "I'd appreciate it if you'd keep my name out of any discussion that you have with your brother."

It would be difficult to persuade Justin to take the threat to his nomination seriously if she couldn't explain how she'd come by her information, but Toni sighed and promised to do her best. "I do appreciate the fact that you told me all this, Dennis. As I see it, once I've warned my brother what's going on, you're off the hook. You can tell the blackmailer to go take a flying leap from a high building."

Dennis's smile was strained, but at least it was a smile. "Yeah, if the blackmailer is your uncle, I'm sure it never occurred to him that I'd come and talk to you. And to be honest, I wouldn't have, except for Cheryl's advice."

"Three cheers for Cheryl." Toni walked over to the coffee table and opened her briefcase. "Try not to worry, Dennis. You've done the right thing, and Justin will know how to take care of this from now on. I'll be in touch with you as soon as I've spoken with him."

"I'd prefer to be involved as little as possible. This isn't the sort of situation likely to make Shoreline happy." Dennis took off his glasses and polished them on a crisply ironed handkerchief, then handed her his business card. "My home phone number is on there if you should feel compelled to reach me. It would be better if you didn't call me at the office."

Toni felt he was being overly cautious, but she didn't want to put his job at risk when he had a family to support. "With any luck, I won't have to contact you. Justin knows his way around the state's corridors of power, so he should have a good idea how to neutralize the opposition."

She tucked the files into her briefcase and held out her

hand to say goodbye. "Take care, Dennis. I'm really glad we had this chance to meet, despite the circumstances."

Dennis took her hand. He hesitated for a moment, his gaze resting on her face, then skittering away from her lips as he turned quickly and reached for his jacket. He pulled his wallet out of the inner pocket and removed a photo. "My kids," he said breathlessly. "You can't leave before I show you a picture of my kids."

Toni stared down at two children dressed up for a birthday celebration and wearing the fake grins of children told to smile for the camera. The boy wore glasses, and the little girl had a huge, old-fashioned bow in her brown hair. They were cute, although nothing out of the ordinary, but Toni was suddenly aware of such a heart-stopping sense of emptiness that she couldn't speak.

"That was Michelle's fifth birthday," Dennis said when the silence had continued rather too long.

"They're beautiful," Toni said, finding her voice. "What's your son's name?"

"Paul," he said. "Paul Dennis. My daughter is Michelle Cheryl."

"They look adorable, and you must be very proud of them. I'm downright envious, Dennis, if you want to know the truth."

He laughed, putting the photo back in his wallet, obviously not believing her for a minute. "They're good kids. Cheryl and I are fortunate."

"Yes, you are," Toni said, knowing that Dennis had no idea how sincerely she meant it.

CHAPTER TWO

TONI CALLED JUSTIN twice a day from Tuesday through Thursday without ever getting past the barrier of his secretary. On Friday, she was informed he was out of town. But on Saturday, when she rushed home from the club to get changed for her aunt's eightieth birthday party, she finally found a message from him waiting on the answering machine. Justin apologized for the delay in acknowledging her calls and suggested that they should get together on Monday afternoon at Chanson Triste, before the evening rush of customers started. It said everything about her relationship with her brother that Justin didn't know the club was closed on Mondays—as it had been every Monday since the day she bought it.

Toni spent her professional life dressing to impress her audience, so it didn't take her long to get ready for Aunt Mary's party. Satisfied that her aunt would approve of the understated elegance of the green silk dress she'd chosen, Toni gave a final quick whirl in front of her mirror, spritzed herself with perfume and took the elevator from her condo down to the underground garage.

Driving through the familiar crush of city traffic toward the highway, she found herself growing more annoyed at Justin's neglect. To help her relax, she practiced the techniques that kept her from falling to pieces with stage fright before a big concert. Every time she started to get uptight about Justin's workaholic habits, she drew in a deep breath and switched to a more positive train of thought.

She reminded herself that she was going to her favorite aunt's birthday party, and that she'd sworn she was going to be polite to every one of her relatives. Even to Justin, who was "too busy" to return a phone call that might salvage his career.

Joining the stream of highway traffic, she slipped a Billie Holiday CD into her player. The music worked its inevitable magic, simultaneously soothing and thrilling her. Toni drew in another deep breath and resolved not to think about Justin for a while. She'd think about her aunt, instead.

Mary Delacroix was far and away Toni's favorite relative. Even in her heyday Mary probably hadn't been beautiful, so it wasn't altogether surprising, given the times, that she'd never married. Nevertheless, Toni considered that the men of her aunt's generation had missed out on a great opportunity for happiness. Blinded by the superficial, they apparently hadn't noticed that in addition to being tall and gangly, with a too-big nose, Mary was kind, competent and so sweet-natured that she would have made the perfect wife and mother.

Some foolish man's loss had been the Delacroix family's gain. Mary had remained single, living quietly in the family residence in Bayou Beltane, never pursuing any career except that of homemaker. For the past few years she'd made her home in a remodeled planter's cottage less than a mile from Riverwood, keeping house for her youngest brother, William, and dispensing the balm of her kindness on the wounds the Delacroix family regularly inflicted on one another.

And today, July 26, Aunt Mary was celebrating eighty years of kind and generous living. In her honor, the Delacroix were putting aside their differences and gathering at Mary's house for a grand party and a sumptuous catered buffet. For a few hours, they would drink imported champagne, eat Aunt Mary's favorite shrimp Creole and pretend they were all one big happy family instead of two feuding clans with a half-dozen lesser feuds in active operation at any given moment. Soap operas, Toni thought wryly, couldn't begin to compare with a Delacroix family gathering for simmering tensions and potentially dramatic confrontations.

Toni switched lanes to avoid a pothole and found herself sandwiched between two giant delivery trucks conducting a drag race on the interstate. Accelerating briefly, she extricated her new Pontiac Firebird from the danger zone and crossed into the slow lane. Her exit was coming up soon, and she started to watch for the signs indicating Slidell and the north shore of the lake.

As a teenager, Toni had considered her aunt's life a tragedy, a living example of how a rigid society could crush individual freedom. Recently, she'd found herself questioning this view, along with many others. She wondered if Mary's choices had always been as limited as they seemed today. Had her aunt never rebelled? Never felt passion? Aunt Mary loved Louisiana and cherished the state's unique history and exotic blend of cultures. But Toni wondered if there hadn't been a moment when she had tried to spread her wings and fly to freedom in some distant city. For all Aunt Mary's sweetness, Toni had never felt able to pose these questions directly to her. Like her brothers, Mary made it clear that she considered the past forbidden territory, a country to which younger generations of Delacroix would definitely not be issued passports.

It had been some years since Toni devoted any time to puzzling over the dark roots of her family history, but the visit from her ex-husband had set her to thinking about the strange reticence of her father's generation. Her curiosity had intensified over the past few days, ever since she started reading Hamilton Delacroix's files.

Toni was really glad that her ex-husband had encouraged her to read these files before attempting to return them to their rightful home in Riverwood. Much of the material was either boring or illegible, but the murder case her grandfather had been working on at the time of his death was fascinating. It wasn't so much the details Hamilton provided about his client that sparked her interest, but the intriguing glimpses he gave into the lives and personalities of his four children.

At the time of Rafael's trial in 1939, Mary had been almost twenty-two, William, eighteen, and the twins, Charles and Philip, almost twenty-one. At first, when she started reading Hamilton's notes on the case, Toni had been amused to see her father's generation portrayed in a whole new light. It was fun to visualize these four dignified and elderly relatives as troublesome postadolescents causing their father heartburn and gray hairs. In some ways, her grandfather's scribbled notes were more interesting than pictures in a family album. His comments were obviously not meant to be read by anyone except himself, which gave an unexpected intimacy in his writing.

But Toni soon decided that her grandfather's notes were too intimate and too revealing for comfort, and by the time she got to the end of the file on Rafael Perdido's trial, she was no longer amused. There was an increasing note of panic in Hamilton's jottings, along with an increasing number of questions. Exclamation points and words heavily underscored littered the yellowed pages. The fact that Rafael Perdido had been found up to his waist in muddy water, holding the body of Camille Gravier, the murdered woman, was repeated frequently. The fact that Rafael was a drifter and that he'd been sex-

ually involved with the victim was written in block capital
letters.

It was almost as if Hamilton Delacroix was desperate
to convince himself that Rafael Perdido had committed
the murder of which he stood accused. An odd reaction,
Toni reflected, for a defense attorney with a reputation for
fighting tooth and nail to win acquittal for his clients. But
perhaps not so odd if you took into account the fact that
all four of Hamilton's children had known the woman
who died and the accused murderer—and all except William had been in the vicinity at the time the murder occurred.

Had the murder of Camille Gravier been such a trau-
matic experience for her father and his siblings that they
couldn't bear to talk about it? Toni wondered. Was this
sixty-year-old murder somehow at the root of all the di-
visions in the Delacroix family?

The easiest way to find out was simply to walk up to
her father, or her aunt, and ask. It was symptomatic of the
tangled relationships in her family that Toni hesitated to
do something so straightforward. She had her grandfather's files with her in the trunk of her car, but she still
hadn't decided exactly what she was going to do with
them. It was absurd to be in such a quandary about sixty-
year-old documents that had no real importance in today's
world, but unfortunately, in the Delacroix family, the obvious and simple solution to a problem rarely turned out
to be either obvious or simple.

Toni took the Slidell exit and started the long drive
northeast across Lake Pontchartrain to St. Tammany Parish and Bayou Beltane. It was a fine evening, unusually
cool and clear for late July, with none of the fog that
sometimes made driving across the lake hazardous. Toni
glanced at her watch. Barely six o'clock. She would be

at Mary's house in less than an hour, in perfect time for the start of her aunt's party.

The last time she'd visited Bayou Beltane had been two years ago, to celebrate the fiftieth anniversary of her uncle William's ordination into the priesthood. That had been a relatively tame get-together by Delacroix standards. Perhaps the presence of the bishop, not to mention at least a dozen elderly priests and nuns, had exerted a salutary effect on them all. Not a single new feud had started, no marriage had broken up, nobody had even got drunk. Her father and her uncle Philip hadn't exchanged any direct words of greeting, but at least they'd both managed to propose toasts to William without sniping at each other.

Toni herself had been remarkably well behaved, all things considered. Aunt Mary nourished the typical spinster's belief that everyone else in the world ought to be married, and she'd tried to set Toni up with a lawyer visiting from France. The lawyer was a self-important bore, convinced he was the most perfect example of Gallic charm since Maurice Chevalier. As far as Toni could detect, his major talent seemed to be that he had perfected the art of juggling a drink and a canapé in such a way that he still had a spare hand for groping.

Out of deference to Uncle William and the bishop, Toni had refrained from yelling that if he pinched her butt one more time, she'd chop off his fingers. Virtuously, she limited her retaliation to spilling a cup of hot coffee down the front of his trousers. She didn't even protest when Aunt Mary insisted that she should drive the horrible man back into town. After years of raging at her family's matchmaking efforts—why did they always pick lawyers, hadn't they noticed she *loathed* the company of lawyers?—she had finally learned that it was easier to agree to meet the men they found for her. Then, as soon as the family left, she got rid of her would-be swains with ruthless efficiency. The French lawyer had been dumped so smoothly at a bar in the Quarter that he never realized what had happened.

Toni had reached the halfway mark on the lake crossing, and there was nothing much to see but miles of blue gray water, stretching in all directions. She rolled down the car window and let the wind off the lake blow across her face, whipping her hair out of the combs she'd used to restrain it and sending it into her eyes. She pushed the heavy honey-colored strands away, thinking how strange it was that a mere two years ago she'd been entirely content with her life.

At William's anniversary party, she'd wandered through the pleasant rooms of her aunt's home, happy that she wasn't tied down, confident that the central focus of her life would always be New Orleans and the world of music, secure in the choices she'd made since she left Bayou Beltane.

She wished that she still felt the same way. She wished that thirty-five didn't seem like such a gigantic milestone. She wished she hadn't been reading so many books recently that cited thirty-five as the age at which a woman's body, however fit and healthy, began its inexorable slide into middle age.

Uncertainty about the course her life had taken wasn't something that had crept up on Toni gradually. It had been a lightning bolt that struck out of a deceptively sunny sky. She could recall every detail of the day, almost sixteen months ago, when she'd first realized that her glamorous career was no longer totally fulfilling, and that she was locked into a life-style that, deep down, was as rigid and confining as anything her aunt had confronted six decades earlier. In fact, Toni could not only remember the day, she could put an exact time to the moment of revelation. It had been 3:45 p.m. on Friday, April 12, of last year.

The day had started out pleasantly enough, a day like many others. She and Maya Johnson, the wife of her partner at Chanson Triste, had driven fifty miles out of New Orleans to visit the home of an artist whose work they had both admired in a gallery on Magazine Street. Pudge Johnson's birthday was coming up, and Maya had decided that a painting would be the perfect gift for her husband.

Maya was eight months pregnant at the time, and she spent a great deal of the journey to Dorian Cree's home complaining that if she were in charge of the universe, she would have invented a better way of bringing babies into the world than making women pregnant.

"Like making men pregnant?" Toni suggested.

Maya grinned. "Now you're talking sense, girl." She winced as the car went over a bump, and used a tissue to wipe a couple of beads of sweat from her top lip.

"Are you okay?" Toni asked, trying to be sympathetic but secretly wondering why a sensible woman like Maya, one of the most successful real estate agents in New Orleans, would interrupt her career to put herself through nine months of self-inflicted misery. Not to mention tying herself and Pudge to years of caring for the resulting child.

Maya grimaced. "Am I okay? Sure, I'm terrific. If you don't count the fact that my ankles are almost as big as my thighs, my back aches, I haven't seen my toes in two months, and I have hair growing in a line down my belly. When they write all those glowing articles in women's magazines about the joys of motherhood, they never mention things like hair growing on your belly."

Maya was the only one of her close friends who'd ever gotten pregnant, and her pregnancy had confirmed every one of Toni's prejudices about the subject. Concealing a small shudder of distaste, Toni peered ahead at a featureless road that wandered alongside a bayou and looked very much like half the other roads in this part of the state.

"Could you take another look at those directions?" she asked. "I thought the assistant at the gallery said Cree's studio was eight miles from the turnoff, and we've done more than eight miles already."

Maya referred to the sheet of paper resting on her non-existent lap. "I don't know. This says we were supposed to turn north off the highway—"

"North wasn't an option," Toni pointed out. "We had to go east or west."

"I know, so I sent you east. Maybe we should have gone west." Maya turned the scribbled map sideways and squinted at it balefully.

Toni hung on to her temper. Nonpregnant Maya was smart as a whip, witty and funny, altogether a joy to be around. It was impossible to imagine the nonpregnant Maya telling somebody to turn east without mentioning the inconvenient fact that the directions required them to drive north.

Maya didn't speak for quite a while, and since Toni realized there was no point in driving any farther down a road that might be the wrong one, she slowed the car to a stop. "Here, let me take a look at those directions...."

She broke off in midsentence, alarmed to see the sweat breaking out on Maya's forehead and the gray tinge beneath her friend's coffee-colored skin. "Hey, Maya, are you okay? If you've been sitting too long, we can get out and stretch our legs."

"It's not a walk I need, it's a doctor. Don't panic, girl, but I think you'd better take us back to civilization as soon as you can." Maya drew in a shaky breath. "I've been having contractions since five minutes after I got into the car, and they're getting closer and closer together."

"My God! Why didn't you say something?" Toni tried

not to recall too many scenes from bad TV movies in which the heroine gave birth by the side of the road. She put the car into reverse and headed back toward the highway at a speed that should have attracted every cop in a twenty mile radius. Naturally, not a single flashing red light approached.

Toni told herself to keep calm and drive with care. "Maya, swear to me that you're not going to have this baby until we get to the hospital."

"I swear." Maya managed a smile. "I think I swear." She bit her lip as Toni swerved to avoid a turtle that had wandered onto the road. "Could you try to avoid the bumps, Toni? It hurts real bad."

They didn't manage to make it all the way to Tulane University Hospital, where Maya was supposed to be having her baby, but they did at least make it to the emergency room of a hospital on the far northwest side of town. Because they couldn't manage to contact Pudge, Toni ended up playing the role of birthing coach, dressed in a disposable sterile gown and holding Maya's hand in the delivery room, where, at 3:45 p.m., the emergency room doctor eased seven pound, twelve ounce Josephine Chantelle into the world.

"Congratulations, she looks very healthy," the doctor said before rushing on to his next patient. He patted the dazed and ecstatic Maya on the shoulder. "But somebody sure messed up on this little lady's due date, since she's obviously full term. Congratulations again." He nodded vaguely in Toni's direction and strode out of the delivery room.

Full term she might be, but baby Josephine was not looking her best when she greeted the world. She was bright red and wrinkled, with a flattened face topped by a thatch of thick, straight black hair. Her nose was squashed to one side, her head molded to a point by the speed of her passage into the world, and after a quick look at her surroundings, she promptly closed her eyes and showed scant interest in opening them for the next twenty-four hours.

Toni thought she was the most beautiful human being she'd ever seen.

Her arms aching and her stomach cramping with a curious sense of longing, she watched the neonatal nurses clean the baby and wrap her in a sterile blanket. When Maya asked sleepily if Toni wanted to hold the baby, Toni couldn't speak, only nod. The nurse put Josephine into her arms. Toni looked down at the sleeping newborn and realized that she'd fallen seriously in love.

A distraught Pudge finally arrived at the hospital, and Toni left. Her friends barely noticed her departure. They were hugging each other, laughing and cooing over their new daughter, their faces suffused with joy.

Toni drove home, her legs still trembling, her stomach feeling curiously hollow inside. She went to the club, sang the midnight show as usual, then walked into her office and discovered that tears were streaming down her cheeks in an uncontrollable torrent.

When she finally managed to stem the flow, she told herself that seeing the beginning of a new human life was bound to be an emotional experience, and that as soon as Josephine started to get bigger, she would also become less appealing.

Toni's assessment of her own feelings couldn't have been more wrong. By the time Josie was six months old, Toni accepted that this love affair with her goddaughter was destined to be permanent. Josie held her heart in the palm of her chubby brown hand.

Even more surprising—and much harder to accept— was the growing yearning that she felt to have a child of her own. For a couple of months, she pushed her feelings aside, aware that they were impractical. She had fought and struggled to establish her identity as a singer, and it was disconcerting to realize that success in her chosen career no longer left her fully satisfied. She still couldn't imagine a life without Chanson Triste and the world of music, but Josie served as a constant reminder that she wanted—no, she *needed*—something more.

She was blessed with several good friends, Maya and Pudge coming right at the top of the list, but deep down inside she was lonely. Career success was wonderful. Having a baby greet you with a smile that made her entire body wriggle with joy would be even more wonderful. It had taken her a bit longer than most women, Toni reflected ruefully, but she'd finally reached the point in her life where she felt adult enough to take on the challenge of caring for another human being.

She started to think about getting married. If she was serious about having a child, then she couldn't afford to wait. She knew from discussions with Maya that after the age of thirty-five, a woman's fertility rate started to decline precipitously. Which meant that the sooner she found a husband, the better.

Despite the fact that her father assumed she led a life of wild sexual adventure, Toni's love life was actually rather tame. Max Epstein, her lover for the past six months, lived in New York but had business interests in New Orleans that brought him there at least once a month. Typically his visits lasted for five days, and before they had time to become bored with each other, Max was rushing to the airport to return to New York. His frequent absences meant that by the time his next visit rolled around, Toni was always looking forward to seeing him again.

Max had a small but delightful apartment in the warehouse district, not far from Toni's own condo at Graydon

Place. The skyline views were fabulous, and Toni thoroughly enjoyed the hours she spent with him. Max was forty years old, handsome and comfortably wealthy. He was considerate when they made love, didn't spew toothpaste over the bathroom counter and enjoyed the same books and music that she did. She didn't love him, but she really liked him and thought they would get on rather well together as a married couple, provided they didn't go overboard and try to live in each other's pockets. She spent three weeks seriously considering the pros and cons, then she'd invited Max to dinner at their favorite restaurant and asked him to marry her.

Max greeted her proposal with a stunned and prolonged silence. For the first time since she'd known him, it was clear that he was at a loss for words. Toni began to feel oddly uncomfortable.

"Max." She stretched her hand across the table and covered his fingers with hers. "Max, I'm sorry. I didn't mean to embarrass you. I know you got married right out of college and that things didn't work out, but I hoped you might have gotten over your aversion to the idea of marriage by now. I'm not suggesting any dramatic lifestyle changes for you. You don't need to move to New Orleans or anything like that, but I've been thinking more and more often recently that I'd like to have a baby, and we get along so well together that I decided you'd make the perfect father. But I shouldn't have tossed a marriage proposal at you with no warning. I've been considering the idea for weeks, so I forgot how startling it would seem to you. Please, take all the time you want to think about this. And if you say no, I'll quite understand. Not every man wants to take on the responsibility of a wife and a child."

He'd answered her then, his voice clipped and strained. "Toni, I thought you knew. I swear to you, I thought you knew. My marriage to Betsy didn't work out, but we never divorced, just went our separate ways. The fact is, I'm still married, Toni, and I already have two children.''

She wouldn't have been so devastated, Toni decided, if she hadn't felt so incredibly stupid. True, Max made his home in Manhattan and only visited New Orleans on business, but in hindsight, the signs of his married state had been clearly visible, and she'd simply refused to notice them. After Max dropped his bombshell, she'd pushed her chair back from the table and run outside to her waiting car, ignoring his frantic calls for her to come back.

At dawn the next morning she'd found herself out of gas, back in front of her own apartment building, with no memory of where she'd driven during the six intervening hours.

She hadn't spoken to Max since that night, nor had she taken another lover. She met plenty of eligible men, she even dated some of them, but she discovered that she was seriously gun-shy when it came to sex. Unfortunately, the longing to have a child hadn't waned along with her complete lack of interest in starting a new sexual relationship. So intense was her longing for motherhood that she had once got as far as making an appointment at a fertility clinic to talk to a specialist about the possibility of in vitro fertilization. But after weeks of tests and preparation, doubts had kept her from going forward. How would she explain to her child that her acquaintance with its father was limited to a brief encounter with a vial of frozen sperm?

The conclusion Toni reached seemed obvious. A testtube father was too impersonal for her baby. On the other hand, in the fourteen years since her divorce, she'd never really met a man she yearned to marry. What she needed was an intelligent, healthy man who would agree to impregnate her, then go away and never bother her again.

She had the money to support a child without any help from its father. As for the ethics of bringing a baby into a one-parent family... Well, it wasn't ideal, but she was sure her love would be sufficient to compensate for the absence of a father. Besides, based on her own experience, she was convinced that growing up with a physically absent father would be a much happier situation for a child than growing up with a father like hers, who'd always been emotionally absent.

The solution to her problem had been easy, in theory. In practice, it proved difficult to put into effect. Search as she might, Toni couldn't seem to find a suitable man for such an important role. After months of looking, she'd reached the conclusion that potential fathers were almost as difficult to come by as potential husbands. And while she continued to look, her biological clock was ticking. Relentlessly. Twenty-four hours a day.

The lake crossing ended, and Toni drove onto the highway, following the signs for Slidell. Twenty minutes later, she drew up in front of Aunt Mary's house and handed her keys to the valet parking attendant who'd been hired for the occasion. Skirting the thirty-foot-high live oak that graced the corner of her aunt's front yard, Toni walked down the long path to the front door, trying to keep the heels of her Bruno Magli sandals from sinking into the crushed shell. A parking attendant wasn't a good sign, she decided, since it meant that the guest list had reached epic proportions. Not only was she going to have to cope with dozens of relatives, it looked as if she would be shaking hands and making polite conversation with everyone who was anyone in Bayou Beltane.

As soon as she climbed the shallow stairs leading to the shaded veranda, she saw that the house was indeed full to overflowing, with guests spilling out of the dining room and parlor into a marquee that had been erected over the lawn at the rear of the house. A trio of musicians was playing Cajun folk songs, but so far nobody had ventured out onto the small, temporary dance floor.

She saw her cousin Drew deep in conversation with his father, and decided to get her obligatory two-minute conversation with that side of the family out of the way. She took a glass of wine from a passing waiter and made her way over to the flower-filled fireplace in the parlor, where Drew and Philip were standing.

Her uncle greeted her with a broad smile and a warm hug, as if she were someone he'd been waiting all night to see. He held her briefly at arm's length, studying her. "Antoinette, my dear, you look as lovely as ever. That shade of green is very becoming."

"Thank you. How are you, Uncle Philip?"

Philip twitched his bow tie. "My dear, you should know better than to ask a man of my age about his health. You stand in grave danger of hearing more about indigestion and blood pressure medication than you could possibly want to know."

"You're looking as fit as a fiddle," she said, laughing as she turned to her cousin. "Drew, it's nice to see you again."

"Hello, Toni." Drew didn't seem quite sure whether to shake her hand or kiss her, so Toni leaned forward and pressed her cheek briefly against his. Drew was less than a year older than she was, and had grown up in Bayou Beltane, attending the same parochial elementary school and hanging out in the same ice cream parlor when they were teens. Despite that, they barely knew each other, since the feud between her father and his had kept them wary of getting too close when they were young. Then Toni's early marriage and Drew's departure to college and law school ended any chance of developing a real friendship.

Consummate politician that he was, her uncle filled in the awkward silence with his usual flair for small talk. "I saw that delightful program you made for PBS last month, Toni." He smiled. "You gave such an eloquent account of the history of blues music in New Orleans that I felt I gained a whole new understanding of our musical heritage."

"I'm glad you enjoyed it," she said, returning his smile. "The station aired it so late at night, I'm surprised you were still up."

Philip's eyes twinkled. "We old'uns can still find the energy for the occasional piece of mischief, you know. Although, rather tame mischief these days, alas. Nothing like the grand exploits of my youth."

His reference to past exploits reminded Toni of her grandfather's files on the Camille Gravier murder and the fact that this charming, debonair man had bribed her ex-husband to steal them. She was on the brink of asking him a pointed question or two, then thought better of it. This was neither the time nor the place for introducing such a controversial subject. Determined to be on her best behavior for Aunt Mary's sake, she responded in a light vein.

"You sound positively regretful, Uncle Philip, but I'm sure you can count on my generation to stir up our own quota of mischief." She tilted her head slightly to look up at her cousin, who so far had said nothing. "So what mischief are you up to these days, Drew?"

"I try very hard to keep out of mischief," he said shortly. "If you'll excuse me for cutting and running, Toni, I've just seen a friend going out to the garden, and I'd like to catch up with him. He's going through a very messy divorce and he needs my advice." He didn't wait for her to reply, but walked away almost at a run.

Philip watched his son leave, then turned back to Toni

with a sigh. "Drew is determined to save the world at no charge," he said. "It falls to me to remind him that our firm does require the occasional paying client if we are to remain solvent."

She'd been here five minutes and had already waded straight into a Situation, Toni thought in silent amusement. The Delacroix family was living up to form.

"Drew always was a crusader on the side of the underdog," she said absently.

Philip's gaze narrowed. "What do you mean?"

She hadn't meant anything in particular. She'd intended merely to toss off some platitude that would avoid confrontation with her uncle and criticism of Drew. So she explained to Philip that she remembered that Drew had always befriended the unpopular kids in school and she'd admired him for doing so.

Philip frowned. "You're right," he muttered, sounding almost as if he disapproved of his son's compassion. "He's never had a clear understanding of where his own best interest lies."

Toni was suddenly remembering all the reasons why she didn't much like her uncle, and she was relieved when a gushing middle-aged woman came up and claimed Philip's attention, providing her with a valid excuse to make her escape. In her opinion, her uncle's charm never quite compensated for the bulldog tenacity with which he pursued his own goals.

She spotted two of her brother Justin's daughters chatting to each other, and edged through the throng toward them. "Hi, Marie. Hi, Charly. How are you?" Her relationship with her nieces had always been a lot friendlier and more intimate than her relationship with their father. She hugged them, genuinely pleased to see them. "What have you been up to for the past three months? I haven't seen either of you since you came to the club on Charly's birthday.''

And Charly was wearing the same black dress she'd worn on that occasion, along with the same ugly flat shoes and the same uninspired hairstyle. And if Toni wasn't mistaken, the dress was the same one Charly had worn to Uncle William's anniversary party two years ago, and it had been dreary even then. It was hard for a woman as attractive as Charly to make herself look plain, but she'd almost succeeded. Marie, by contrast, was wearing an outfit of floating amber chiffon, which should have looked ridiculous on her petite body, but instead appeared exotic and ultrafeminine.

"I like your perfume," Marie said, drawing Toni and her sister out onto the veranda. "It's woodsy, with an overtone of musk. It suits you."

"Thanks. Coming from you, that's a real compliment." Marie was a licensed aromatherapist with an acute sensitivity to the impact that scent and smells had on people's sense of well-being. Unfortunately, Justin and most of the rest of the family weren't interested in her skill with herbs and perfumes—they hadn't yet forgiven her for dropping out of medical school at Tulane University in her junior year, despite an almost perfect grade point average. Toni was well aware of the fact that at least some of her sympathy toward her nieces sprang from the fact that their relationship with Justin was almost as rocky as her own relationship with Charles. There was nothing like a shared sense of alienation to create a bond.

"So how's everything at the police academy?" she asked Charly.

"Busy. Crazy." Her niece grimaced. "Let's just say I have moments when I wonder why I didn't go to law school, after all. It would have been a lot easier."

Toni laughed. "That bad, huh? Never mind, it can't be too long until you graduate."

"Sixteen weeks, six days." Charly shoved her hands through her hair. "But I don't want you to get the impression I'm counting down the hours or anything."

"You should take a break after you graduate from the academy," Toni suggested, a little worried by the dark shadows under her niece's eyes. "Maybe you could fly out to Colorado and spend a week with your mother before you start work on the streets. You don't want to be so exhausted that you end up blowing your first official assignment as a cop because you're too tired to think straight."

"I can't afford to fly out to Colorado," Charly said, although Toni had a suspicion that money was the least of the reasons that Charly wasn't anxious to visit her mother, Madeline. Twenty minutes under Aunt Mary's roof and she'd already waded into another Situation. Toni wondered if there was any branch of the Delacroix family, however small, that functioned normally.

In a different setting, she might have pressed Charly for a more honest answer, but there were too many people milling about and this wasn't the right place. Glancing around, mentally searching for a new topic of conversation, she saw Justin come out onto the veranda, with a tall, elegant woman on his arm. They were smiling, clearly enjoying each other's company, and Toni watched them with genuine interest. Justin appeared almost relaxed, a minor miracle in itself. "Is that your father's latest girlfriend?" she asked her nieces. "She seems a considerable step-up from the last woman he dated."

Marie and Charly both turned to look. "Heavens, no!" Marie said. "That's Joanna."

Toni must have looked as blank as she felt. "You

know," Charly explained. "Joanna Gideon. Uncle Philip's daughter."

Toni blinked. "Good grief, I didn't realize Joanna had come back from California. I thought she'd shaken the mud of Bayou Beltane from her shoes forever. Is she working for her father?"

Marie sighed. "You are so completely out of the family loop, aren't you, Toni? You've no idea how envious that makes me. Joanna came back from California two years ago when her husband died."

"She wasn't at Uncle William's anniversary party," Toni observed.

"No, I guess she must have returned right after that," Marie said. "She was working for her father until about four months ago. Now she's switched allegiances, and she's working with Grandfather's firm. Uncle Philip has let it be known that he's not pleased."

Family Situation number three, Toni thought, not sure whether to be amused or saddened by this further evidence of family strife. "She's a whiz of a lawyer, isn't she? I seem to remember hearing Aunt Mary sing her praises."

"Aunt Mary thinks everyone in the world is wonderful," Charly said. "But Joanna really is good."

Marie nodded, her amber earrings jingling. "A topnotch lawyer, according to Dad. He's thrilled that she's joined the family firm, because they're trying to expand the client base in new directions or something." Marie looked vague, as if she didn't understand what expanding the client base meant, but Toni knew better. Marie was probably smarter than ninety percent of the people at this party.

Charly's expression brightened. "Speaking of new lawyers working with Dad and Grandfather, we have to warn you, Toni. Aunt Mary and the gang have a new husband all picked out for you."

Toni rolled her eyes. "Don't tell me, let me guess. He's a lawyer, right?" She gave an exaggerated sigh. "My very favorite kind of people."

Marie giggled, her eyes sparkling, making her appear younger and even more attractive. "How did you guess? Yes, he's a lawyer, a new partner in Grandfather's firm. His name's Brody Wagner, and his father was a bank president in New Orleans. Grandfather knew his father in college, and apparently Delacroix and Associates practically had to promise Brody the moon *and* the planets to lure him away from New York—"

Toni groaned. "No, please stop. I can't stand to hear any more. Point him out to me so that I can avoid him."

"As if that'll do any good once Aunt Mary gets on the warpath," Charly said, but she obligingly scanned the room. "He's not in here, Toni. But you might not want to avoid him, you know. I've only met him a couple of times, but he's a dynamite guy. Sexy as hell. Tall, with thick brown hair. Interesting eyes—"

"Also uptight, buttoned-down, anal retentive and a few other choice phrases," Toni said, laughing. "How old is he? Forty? Don't my father and Aunt Mary ever realize that there must be a reason why a guy that age is still single?"

"I guess not," Charly said. "Besides, you're still single and you're every bit as eligible and good-looking as Brody. What's your excuse?"

Toni stared at her niece. "Good grief, Charly! Since when did you climb on the Let's Get Toni Married bandwagon?"

"I didn't," Charly said. "I just pointed out that being single doesn't prove you're undesirable."

"I tried marriage once," Toni said. "I think it worked

like a vaccine and now I'm immune to the temptation of trying again."

She deliberately pushed aside a humiliating image of Max Epstein and his shocked expression when she'd asked him to marry her. She wasn't exactly lying, because she hadn't really wanted to marry Max, she'd simply wanted to use him as an impregnation device. Shutting out the memory, she smiled with false brightness. "Maybe you could do me a big favor and try to get that message across next time my dad and Aunt Mary start lining up would-be suitors. I don't want to be married."

"Don't you ever get lonely?" Marie asked, her voice suddenly focused and intent. "Don't you ever wish that you could find someone who really understands you? The person you really are, I mean, as opposed to the person everyone in the family wants you to be? You've had so much experience facing up to family disapproval, Toni, don't you ever get tired of feeling that you're alone in the world? Wouldn't it be wonderful to come home each night and know that the person you loved best in the whole entire universe was coming home to the same place? And that you really *liked* each other as well as being in love with each other?"

It was disconcerting to hear her own deepest yearnings put into words by her niece. "Of course I wish for that," Toni said quietly. "Isn't that what everyone longs for? But I've seen a lot of marriages come and go, Marie, and I guess I've concluded that most of us aren't lucky enough to find our soul mates. Speaking personally, I've decided it's much better to lead a full, interesting single life than it is to be married to the wrong person. Heaven knows, we have dozens of marriages in the Delacroix family that have been torture for everyone involved, not just for the husband and wife."

"Yes, you're right." Marie set down her glass of champagne, which was still almost full. "Anyway, for your information, Brody Wagner isn't forty. He's thirty-four."

"Isn't that how old you are?" Charly asked Toni. Then she gave a strangled gasp. "Oh, no! The bishop's coming! I have to get out of here before he reminds me for the twentieth time about how I tripped at graduation and nearly knocked him off the stage. Bye, Toni, see you around. Marie, are you coming?"

Charly disappeared into a crowd of people Toni didn't recognize, dragging her sister with her. Toni rather liked the bishop, so she stayed and chatted with him for a while before deciding that she needed to go and pay her respects to her aunt before she made a concerted attempt to track down Justin and arrange a time and place where they could talk.

Aunt Mary was seated in a position of honor by the parlor windows. A table placed to one side of her chair was already covered in gift-wrapped packages. "Antoinette!" Aunt Mary's plain features lighted up with a smile that old age had done nothing to dim. Her hair, a gorgeous mane of thick snowy white, had been styled in a soft, loose knot on top of her head, framing her face and making her appear almost handsome.

Toni bent and kissed the papery-soft skin of her aunt's cheek. Mary smelled faintly of lavender water, just as she had done ever since Toni could remember. The scent evoked a dozen childhood memories, all of them enriched by her aunt's presence, and Toni's arms tightened around her aunt ever so slightly.

After a few moments of silent gratitude, she straightened, surprised to feel a lump in her throat, and held out her gift, wrapped in yellow paper and tied with a gold ribbon. Inside was a collection of sentimental ballads and dance music that had been popular in the 1930s and forties, digitally reformatted onto a set of six CDs and raved about by music critics. Toni knew that her aunt liked the music of the big band era, and she hoped she would enjoy listening to these tunes.

"Happy birthday, Aunt Mary. It's great to see you looking so well. I love your new hairdo."

Mary took the gift, set it on the table with the others, then looked up at Toni, her eyes twinkling. "I'm not going to open it now, if you don't mind. I plan to be very selfish and make my guests stand around after dinner while I open all these lovely presents. It will be such fun. Everyone's been so generous and so thoughtful."

Toni smiled. "I can't imagine why, unless it's because we all love you."

A trio of guests arrived to give Mary their gifts and their good wishes, but when Toni made a move to leave, her aunt put out her hand and restrained her. "Don't go, Antoinette. I haven't seen you for months, and I would love to hear all your news."

Toni waited, feeling guilty. She phoned her aunt every ten days or so, but Mary was quite right, it had been months since they'd met in person. In the old days, Mary had traveled into New Orleans frequently, and Toni had never failed to meet with her for lunch, or at least for coffee and beignets and an hour's pleasant gossip. She should have noticed that Aunt Mary's trips into the city had gradually trickled away to nothing. Much as she disliked returning to Bayou Beltane, if her aunt was no longer up to making the drive into the city, Toni would have to start making the reverse trip. Mary looked well, but at her age, appearances might be deceiving. Toni resolved to add some inquiries about her aunt's health to the long list of things she needed to check out while she was here.

"How is everything going with Chanson Triste?" Mary asked as soon as the two of them were alone. She had always taken a genuine interest in Toni's career, at least in between her campaigns to get Toni married off to a suitable young man.

Toni explained her plans to serve brunch on Sundays during the tourist season, and her tentative plans to open a new club in Uptown, where the land values weren't so high and she would be able to keep her prices lower and give young, unknown musicians a chance to make a name for themselves.

Her aunt listened with interest and asked several insightful questions before skillfully bringing their conversation around to Bayou Beltane and the changes currently underway at the law offices of Delacroix and Associates. A steel magnolia on the subject of love and marriage, Aunt Mary didn't even bother to disguise her matchmaking attempts. On the contrary, she got straight to the point. "Justin has hired such a nice young man to take his place at the office when he goes off to be a judge. His name's Brody Wagner, and his father was a fine Southern gentleman, although he made a most unfortunate marriage to a woman from Chicago, who really didn't even try to fit in with the way of life down here—"

"Aunt Mary," Toni cut in with ruthless efficiency. "Before you give me Brody Wagner's entire genealogy, I think I should tell you that I have no desire even to meet this man, much less to marry him. So maybe we should change the subject."

Mary didn't attempt to pretend she had anything other than matrimony on her mind. Perhaps with Toni's thirty-fifth birthday approaching, she was getting desperate. "But how can you be sure that you don't want to marry him if you never meet him?" she asked plaintively.

"I'm taking a wild guess," Toni said, giving her aunt an affectionate grin. "A wild guess based on long experience with getting rid of the men you pick out for me. I have to say, dearest, that for a woman with such exquisite taste in other areas, you have simply lousy taste in men.''

For a moment, her aunt seemed to shrink inward, and Toni addressed several choice epithets to herself, of which idiot was far and away the mildest. To compensate for her tactlessness, she bent down and gave her aunt another hug. "On second thought, you're probably right, Aunt Mary. I'm sure Brody Wagner is just the man for me. Let's see. He's a lawyer. His father is a good friend of my father's. He's working in Bayou Beltane and he's the apple of Justin's eye. What more could I possibly ask for?''

Mary either didn't hear Toni's sarcasm or chose to ignore it. "Brody's also very handsome," she said. "And he has the most delightful little poodle.''

"He has a *poodle?* You mean poodle as in dog?''

Mary smiled and nodded. Toni barely managed to cut off a caustic comment to the effect that Brody Wagner sounded like a man destined to captivate the heart of any red-blooded American woman.

"It's such a dear little creature. White, and Brody always keeps a blue bow in its hair.''

If Toni hadn't known better, she'd have been convinced that Aunt Mary was teasing her, but on the subject of matrimony, her aunt never joked. Toni drew in a deep breath and flashed Mary a beaming smile. "I'll make sure I ask someone to introduce us, okay? He sounds like a...um...a fascinating man.''

Her aunt might be tenderhearted, but she was far from foolish. The gaze she turned on Toni was disconcertingly shrewd for an old lady celebrating her eightieth birthday. "Since you're so enthusiastic, I'm sure you'll be happy to know he's over there, talking to your father." Aunt Mary's blue eyes were suspiciously guileless. "Go over and talk to him now, Antoinette. I'll watch you from here."

"Oh, no," Toni said quickly. "I can't leave you alone."

"William is standing right behind you," Mary said, her voice dry. "Along with at least a dozen old friends. Don't give me another moment's thought, Antoinette. I'll be well taken care of, so you can run along and enjoy yourself."

Toni laughed and squeezed her aunt's hand. "All right, you tyrant. I'll go and meet this wretched Brody Wagner. But only because I love you, not because I have the faintest desire to make his acquaintance."

Her aunt smiled. "He's the perfect man for you, Antoinette. I feel it in my bones."

Mary's bones had experienced many similar feelings in the past, all of them one hundred percent unreliable. Without comment, Toni made her way briskly across the parlor, scarcely bothering to look at the man talking with her father. To please her aunt, she would spend ten minutes exchanging polite nothings with Brody Wagner, and then she'd escape. Time was marching on, and she hadn't yet spoken to Justin or her brother, Remy. She knew Justin's twins, Beau and Jax, were both away, but she hadn't seen Shelby, his second youngest, yet. Just then, she spotted her niece walking out into the garden. Shelby was another recent recruit to Delacroix and Associates, and it suddenly occurred to Toni that she might be the perfect person to consult about the problem of Hamilton's files....

Her father's voice interrupted her train of thought. "Antoinette, it's good to see you."

He kissed her, and she kissed him back but didn't hug him. Somehow, her father's manner warded off gestures of affection, and she could never have teased him as she'd just teased her aunt. She sighed, feeling thirty-five years of oppressive habit descend like an impenetrable wall between them. "Hello, Father, how are you?"

"I'm well, thank you. And delighted to see that you managed to make the long and arduous drive from New Orleans."

Toni bit her lip, accepting the implicit reproof. She refrained from pointing out that taking the Twin Span across Lake Pontchartrain was hardly a "long and arduous drive." So far, in the fourteen years since she'd left Bayou Beltane, her father had never found time to come and hear her sing. For years, she'd told herself she didn't care. Recently, in an effort to be more honest with herself about everything, she'd admitted that her father's lack of interest in her career and her nightclub hurt her deeply.

But she could feel her aunt's gaze resting on them anxiously, so she forced a smile. "You know I wouldn't miss Aunt Mary's eightieth birthday party."

"No, I didn't know any such thing," her father said. "You've made it abundantly clear in the past that you feel no sense of family obligation."

Toni felt a familiar mixture of anger and hurt, neither of which she intended to let her father see. "I'm not here tonight out of a sense of family obligation," she said coolly. "I'm here because I love my aunt and wouldn't miss her birthday for the world."

"I'm sure your aunt realizes how honored she is," Charles said.

Toni had no idea what she was supposed to reply, since nothing seemed both polite and appropriate. She would have sworn there was no situation that would make meeting one of Aunt Mary's designated suitors a welcome diversion, but she'd forgotten the difficulties of conversing with her father. Gritting her teeth, she turned blindly to the man standing next to her and thrust out her hand.

"Hi, I'm Toni Delacroix, and I believe you must be Brody Wagner."

Her hand was enveloped in a cool, firm clasp. "Yes, I'm Brody, and I'm happy to meet you. I believe your Aunt Mary has plans for us to marry."

His voice was deep and attractive, but it was what he said that stopped Toni cold. In fourteen years of dealing with her aunt's designated suitors, this was the first one who had ever acknowledged that the two of them were being set up. Shocked into momentary silence, she finally tilted her head back and took a good look at the man standing opposite her.

To call Brody Wagner good-looking was a major understatement. He was tall, at least six foot two, with thick brown hair, eyes the color of the finest bourbon and a body that displayed his dark business suit to maximum advantage. Trained by Marie, Toni detected the faintly musky scent of his cologne, and she noticed that his white shirt was so crisply starched that it crackled despite the humidity. Clearly, this was a man who expected to storm the corridors of power and conquer the opposition.

But it was his smile that most fully captured her attention. It was a warm smile, edged with just enough cynicism to suggest that Brody would not easily be deceived. In short, it was the sort of smile, the sort of face and body that were guaranteed to make any woman start fantasizing about beds, candlelight and long, slow seductions followed by hot, fast sex.

For the first time since the debacle with Max, Toni felt her heart beat a little faster. It was purely a physical reaction, of course, because on a long-term basis she couldn't imagine finding anything in common with a lawyer who wore starched white shirts and worked for her father. But still, the guy had a body to die for....

He was, in fact, absolutely perfect father material.

The realization exploded inside her head with the force of a nuclear reaction. Brody Wagner was smart enough to have made it through law school. He was ambitious and talented enough to have Delacroix Associates bribing him with the moon and the planets to lure him away from New York. His genealogy, checked out by Aunt Mary, was doubtless impeccable. And having sex with him for the purposes of impregnation would not exactly be a sacrifice.

Toni reached the amazing conclusion that the man she'd spent the past sixteen months searching for was standing in front of her.

The father of her baby. In the flesh.

CHAPTER THREE

OVER THE PAST FEW YEARS, Toni had smiled at, flirted with and unceremoniously dumped at least a half dozen of Aunt Mary's preapproved husbands, so it was disconcerting to find herself staring up at Brody Wagner without any idea of how to handle him.

An interesting choice of words, she thought distractedly. Why did she always feel that she had to *handle* the men in her life? Aside from that, was she really desperate enough for motherhood to consider asking one of Aunt Mary's men to become the father of her child?

It seemed that she was, and the need to create the right impression sent Toni raking frantically through her store of party chitchat for something that was both witty and charming to say. Naturally, she came up with nothing. *You look virile*, which was the main topic on her mind, lacked something as a suitable opening gambit.

It was her father who came to the rescue when her silence threatened to become embarrassing. "I should point out, Brody, that in sixty years of encouraging everyone else in the family to get married, my sister has never yet taken the plunge herself. Which might explain why Mary's idea of two people who will make a perfect match often comes close to everyone else's idea of a nightmare."

Brody seemed unfazed by Charles's remarks. "Are you speaking in general terms, sir, or are you warning me that your daughter and I aren't likely to be compatible?"

"I was speaking in general terms," Charles said. "However, on reflection, I can't imagine two people less suited to each other than you and my daughter. If my sister had stopped to think, she'd have realized that the pair of you have absolutely nothing in common. You're a lawyer, dedicated to reason and logic. Antoinette is a singer, and her success depends on her ability to touch people's deepest and most primitive emotions." He directed an impersonal gaze toward Toni. "I imagine you'd bore each other to tears within five minutes."

Normally Toni would have obsessed about her father's remarks, trying to read all sorts of hidden meaning into them, but tonight she had other things on her mind. She let her father's comment go unanswered while she made a rapid mental inventory of Brody's physical attributes. In addition to being tall, with bedroom eyes and a sexy smile, he had great skin, strong white teeth and a luxuriant head of thick, shiny hair, all likely signs of excellent health. Oh, yes! This man was much too promising to let slip away.

She sent Brody the sort of sultry, come-hither smile she normally reserved for the late-night performance at the club. "Let's find a quiet corner somewhere and prove my father wrong, shall we, Brody?" She lowered her voice to a husky murmur. "I'm sure we could find *lots* of interesting things to talk about."

His gaze rested on her smile, his expression somewhere between amused and appreciative, not at all the sort of awestruck look Aunt Mary's men usually gave her. "I'd enjoy that, Toni. I've been looking forward to meeting you for weeks."

She gave a mock groan. "Is that by any chance a polite way of saying Mary's been nagging you to call me ever since the hour you first set foot in Bayou Beltane?"

He grinned. "Well, she has mentioned your extraordinary beauty and exceptional talent a few times, but my desire to meet you has got nothing to do with your aunt. I heard you sing in New York three years ago, and I was instantly starstruck. Then I went to Chanson Triste last month and thought you sounded even better, if that's possible. Mahalia Jackson is my idol, and your voice reminds me of hers. You give a very powerful performance, Toni.''

"Thank you, I'm glad you enjoyed the show." Toni's flirtatious manner disappeared in a flash, banished by his obvious sincerity. "You couldn't have paid me a bigger compliment than comparing my voice to Mahalia Jackson's. I heard her perform live once, when I was a teenager. She was singing with Duke Ellington at the New Orleans Jazz Festival, and it was an incredible experience.''

"I'm sure it must have been. I'm really looking forward to attending next year's Jazzfest. As far as I'm concerned, the richness and variety of New Orleans' music scene is one of the major advantages of moving to this area.''

"I didn't know you were a jazz fan," Charles said.

Brody smiled easily. "We've always been too busy discussing the politics of oil leases to have time to explore each other's taste in music, I guess." He inclined his head toward Charles. "And now, if you'll excuse us, sir, I'd like to find that quiet corner your daughter mentioned and try to convince her I'm a fascinating man to know.''

Charles didn't seem to care that he'd been given the brush-off by his new junior partner, albeit with great courtesy. He snorted. "Five minutes," he said, turning on his heel. "She'll be rid of you in five minutes, Brody. And that's if she finds you unusually interesting." He strode away, his carriage erect and his steps spry for a man nearing eighty.

"He did that deliberately," Brody commented, clearing

a way through the crush of people without apparent effort. "A very astute man, your father."

"What did he do deliberately?" Toni asked, following Brody to a corner of the marquee that was cooled by a fan and miraculously uncrowded.

"Challenged me to keep you entertained for longer than five minutes." Brody didn't appear unduly weighed down by the challenge. "I'm debating whether I should turn a cartwheel, discuss this season's crop of Broadway plays or launch into a shrewd analysis of the last presidential election. How does a man set about impressing you, Toni?"

"The cartwheel would definitely do it," Toni said. "But I'm much easier to entertain than my father would have you believe." She snagged two glasses of white wine from a passing waiter and handed one to Brody. "Why don't you tell me about yourself?" she suggested, raising her glass. "I'm sure there must be an interesting story behind your decision to leave Manhattan in order to live and work in a small town like Bayou Beltane. I'd love to hear it."

This was one of her standard lines with Aunt Mary's men, and usually it worked like a charm. She asked the man to talk about himself, then sat back while he poured out his life history. Generally, she didn't bother to listen with more than half an ear, but in this case, given the role she had in mind for Brody, she really wanted to hear what he had to say. The story a man chose to tell about himself could be very revealing. She wondered if he'd mention his poodle. Having met the man, she was intrigued by the idea that he owned a poodle. He looked more the type to have a sleek black Labrador or maybe a giant Irish wolfhound. Something that could serve as a symbol of his aggressive masculine drive for power and success.

But Brody didn't launch into his life history; instead,

he looked at her thoughtfully. "You don't have to waste your time going through the motions, you know. Neither your aunt nor your father can see us here, so if you want to get rid of me, just say so."

Toni's eyes opened wide in genuine surprise. "Why ever would you think I want to get rid of you, Brody?"

He shrugged. "The fake smiles were my first clue. Your suggestion that I should tell you all about myself was the second."

"You consider a polite personal question proof that I'm trying to get rid of you?" Toni shook her head. "And my father described you as a man who was dedicated to reason and logic. Wow!"

"My conclusion was entirely logical," Brody said. "I can think of only two reasons why a sophisticated and attractive woman like you would start off a conversation by issuing an open-ended invitation to talk about myself. One is because you're interviewing me for a job. The other is because you've already decided to get rid of me and you don't want to waste your energy making conversation. Since you're not planning to hire me, it's reasonable to assume you're planning to dump me."

Feeling a spurt of irritation at having her behavior assessed so accurately, Toni was rather pleased to be able to point out that his logic might be great, but he'd drawn the wrong conclusion. "Your basic analysis may be on target, Brody, but you have your answers twisted around. I'm not planning to dump you. I'm considering hiring you."

He frowned. "You want to hire me? As your lawyer?"

"No, not as my lawyer—"

"What, then?"

"As the father of my baby."

Brody started to reply. His mouth opened, then snapped

shut without any sound emerging. He stared at her, blank-eyed and stony-faced with astonishment.

Toni had spoken without giving herself time to think twice about what she was going to say. For about three seconds, she enjoyed a smug feeling of satisfaction at having shocked the socks off him. She imagined it took a lot to leave Brody Wagner speechless, but she'd succeeded in spades. Hah! Served the man right for being so damn cocksure. If she was guilty of flashing fake smiles at him, he was guilty of patronizing her right back.

Then the enormity of what she'd done hit her. Good grief, the man would think she was crazy! And he'd be right. The trauma of her impending birthday was causing a meltdown of her brain cells. Sane women didn't go around soliciting impregnation from virtual strangers, especially when they were both guests at an elderly lady's birthday party!

Toni was sorely tempted to laugh off her remark, to pretend it had been nothing more than a joke in bad taste, but for some reason she let the crucial moments slip by without making any attempt to soften the impact of her outrageous statement. The band had taken a break, and the sound of her own heartbeat reverberated in her ears, her blood thrumming fast and loud over the surrounding murmur of voices.

She realized suddenly that she'd blurted out her request to Brody because she was afraid she would lose her courage if she waited until she knew him even a little better. She hadn't spoken without thought: she'd *wanted* him to know the truth. Still, her impetuosity had been a mistake. She wished she could go back fifteen minutes in time and start her meeting with him all over again. But it was already too late to start over, she could see that from his expression. He was looking at her searchingly, his attention focused on her with an intensity that was unnerving.

But his eyes were cool, and she discovered to her surprise that she missed their previous mellow-whiskey warmth.

He finally spoke. "This baby of yours that needs a father—does it already exist?"

"No." After years of performing in front of an audience, concealing and producing emotions on demand, she found it disconcerting to discover that she couldn't stop herself from blushing. Nevertheless, she forced herself to look straight into Brody's eyes as she explained. "In ten days' time, I'll be thirty-five years old. If I ever hope to have a baby, I need to get pregnant as soon as possible. I'm trying to find a man who'd be willing to…help me get pregnant."

Brody scanned her from head to toe in swift and explicit appraisal. Her blush expanded, following the path of his gaze until her entire body burned with heat—and a totally unexpected quiver of desire. "You're a very attractive woman," he said. "Presumably finding a sexual partner isn't the problem, so I don't understand why you need my help."

The trio had resumed playing, and the party was getting noisier. The bishop had taken to the dance floor and was doing a creditable rendition of the two-step with Justin's daughter Shelby. Out of the corner of her eye, Toni saw her brother Remy grab their cousin Joanna by the waist. Laughing, they whirled onto the dance floor, both of them looking young and carefree, almost like teenagers. Observing the signs of family celebration without really seeing them, Toni realized that it was beyond bizarre that she should be huddled in a secluded corner of the marquee, discussing her plans for motherhood with a man she had met less than half an hour earlier.

"Why do I need your help? Because I want a baby, but I don't have a husband." She tried to sound crisp and businesslike despite the awkwardness of the situation. She cleared her throat. "I don't think I'm a good candidate for marriage, so I need to find a man who's willing to impregnate me but who has no interest in becoming a live-in father."

"You want a man who'll screw you and run, in other words." Brody was visibly angry. "Do you expect me to be flattered that you picked me?"

She flinched. Expressed in those terms, her wishes seemed more than selfish, they seemed sordid. "Look, I know it sounds outrageous, Brody—"

"Not outrageous," he said. "It sounds totally irresponsible."

She felt her cheeks burn. "I may have given you the wrong impression. The fact is, I've done a lot of research on the subject of single motherhood, and I know I could make it work. Statistically speaking, I realize children do better in two-parent families, but my child won't be a statistic. He or she will be very much wanted and deeply loved, and that makes all the difference. Besides, whatever my views on marriage, my biological clock is ticking, and I don't have time to find a husband even if I wanted one."

"You don't have time to find a husband, but you're willing to pick out your child's prospective father after a ten-minute acquaintance at a cocktail party?" Brody sounded beyond incredulous.

"I've been trying to find a suitable father for months," she protested. "Would it be better for me to marry some man without telling him I'm really looking for a father?"

"No. But it might be a good idea to find a man who'd be a loving husband for you as well as a suitable father for your child."

"That's easier said than done. I don't know what sort of a man I want to marry, but it's relatively easy to define the characteristics I want in a prospective father for my child."

He gave her a disbelieving stare. "And I fit the bill? What the hell do you know about me beyond the fact that I'm a white male, six feet two inches tall, with brown hair and eyes to match?"

"I know a lot about you," she said defensively. "I know you're smart and hard-working, or my father wouldn't have hired you. I know you have a great family background, or Aunt Mary would never have chosen you as a potential husband for me. You look healthy, too. Although, of course, we'd have to talk about your health in more detail before we actually went ahead with the... arrangement."

"Let me get this straight. You've concluded that I'm an okay prospective father on the basis that my IQ may possibly be above average and none of my family has ended up in jail or a lunatic asylum. At least as far as your elderly aunt knows, which might not be the most reliable guide, by the way. Most families can bury skeletons pretty deep when they want to."

Toni gave a tight smile. "Trust me, Brody, on the subject of family genealogy, my aunt is better than an army of private detectives. If she hasn't found any lunatics or jailbirds in your family history, there aren't any."

He shrugged. "As it happens, you're right. There are no certified crazies or convicted criminals in my family's past. But that doesn't mean all my ancestors were terrific people to know."

"Who cares? I'm not planning to make the acquaintance of your ancestors, or even your parents."

"So once I've agreed to turn over my medical records, you think that covers everything you need to know about my suitability as the prospective father of your child?"

"Not everything," she said defensively. "But it covers all the essentials, wouldn't you say?"

"Sure," he said. "That is, if you have no interest in

knowing whether the father of your baby is kind or cruel, honest or deceitful, good-tempered or moody—''

"Those character issues would all be important if I wanted to find a husband, which is exactly why I'm not looking for one.''

"I think you should change your game plan. What do you have against marriage?''

"Nothing. But I'm a hundred percent convinced that it's better to be happily single than unhappily married. I have enough examples in my own family to convince me of that.'' Toni put down her wineglass when she realized that her hand was shaking. Sometimes—and now was one of those times—the longing to hold her own baby in her arms was so profound she felt it as physical pain.

"It's easy for you to take the moral high ground, Brody, because you're a man, and you're facing an entirely different set of biological pressures. If you wake up one morning and decide that you'd like to father a child, you probably can, whether you're thirty-five or fifty-five. Maybe even when you're seventy-five, if you've kept your health and you can find an obliging younger woman. But I don't have the luxury of waiting that long. Did you know that the oldest woman in the United States ever to undergo successful in vitro fertilization was forty-two? Did you know that by the time she reaches her thirty-fifth birthday, the typical woman is only half as likely to conceive as she was when she was twenty?''

For the first time, Brody's expression softened slightly. "You have a point," he conceded. "But if you're determined to become a mother, why don't you adopt a child who needs a home?''

"Have you any idea how long people keep their names on a waiting list before a healthy newborn baby becomes available for adoption? We're talking years, Brody, probably decades.'' She shook her head. "Plus, I'm single and

I'm a singer in a nightclub. Most adoption agencies wouldn't even add my name to their lists, not when they have plenty of respectable married couples longing to become parents.''

"There are older children who need homes, children with special needs. Adoption agencies are willing to consider single-parent homes for them.''

"I've thought about that often, and it might be a possibility,'' Toni agreed. "But if I'm really honest with myself, the reason I haven't worked harder to persuade some agency to put me on their special needs list is because I want to have the experience of being pregnant and giving birth.''

Ever since she'd witnessed Josie's birth, Toni had longed to go through the aches, pains and joy of actually bringing another human being into the world. Belatedly, she'd come to understand exactly why Maya had put up with elephant ankles and three months of morning sickness.

"Wanting to be pregnant and give birth may be a very selfish wish,'' she admitted after a pause. "But I believe it's one most women share.''

Brody sent her another brief look of sympathy, then his gaze became cool again. "I can see that you have a problem, Toni, and I understand your point about time running out for you. Unfortunately, I'm not the right man to help solve your problem. I guess I'm an old-fashioned kind of a guy. I want to fall in love first, then get married, then have kids. I have no interest in becoming an absentee father.''

"I'd be willing to keep you informed about the baby's progress.'' Toni conceded the point reluctantly.

He shook his head. "I don't want an annual report card to arrive in the mail. I want to be the guy holding out his arms when my children take their first few steps, and I want to be standing right next to their mother, cheering, the day they graduate from college. Not to mention being there for them during all the years in between.''

"Lots of people wish for that," Toni said quietly. "At least half the time, their dreams don't come true because they end up in the divorce courts.''

"You're right," Brody acknowledged. "But getting impregnated by a stranger doesn't seem like a real smart solution to the problem of too many divorces. I can't do what you're asking, Toni. I'm sorry.''

She hadn't really thought that she and Brody Wagner were going to come to terms, so Toni couldn't understand why his rejection left her feeling so emotionally raw. In fact, as little as a year ago, she'd have agreed with everything he said, but right now, she found his attitude unbearably smug. How easy it was for him to preach the virtues of love and marriage, she thought acidly. When he felt the approach of middle age, he'd marry some trophy wife in her twenties and set about producing his family. Toni, on the other hand, couldn't afford to wait and hope that she would bump into her soul mate. Where was she supposed to meet this paragon who would become her life partner? At Chanson Triste, between going over tax returns with her accountant and singing in the ten o'clock show? Or maybe while she was doing her morning jog around Audubon Park?

But clearly Brody Wagner was never going to be persuaded to her point of view, and belatedly she realized that her rash approach to him had produced more than one problem, not least the fact that she'd betrayed her most intimate secret to a man who had no particular reason to honor her confidences.

She hated to beg, but she couldn't avoid sending him a look of desperate appeal. "I'd appreciate it if you wouldn't mention to anyone what we've been talking about," she said stiffly, furious that she'd put herself in this humiliating position. "Half my family already thinks I'm dangerously wild, and I'd prefer not to give them something new to cluck their tongues over."

"I won't say anything," he said. "You have my word on it, Toni."

Strangely enough she believed him, although she wasn't entirely sure why. And as Brody would no doubt point out if given the slightest opportunity, she'd had no way of knowing he could be trusted to keep a secret when she'd propositioned him. She'd really burned a considerable number of bridges during the past half hour, Toni reflected ruefully.

Having discussed something as intimate as her desire for motherhood, she realized there was no way they could backtrack and start making polite conversation about trivialities. Brody was as aware of that as she was, and the silence between them became strained. Toni could see that he was right on the brink of saying goodbye and moving on, when Remy spotted them and came over, smiling broadly.

"What are you two doing hiding in the corner?" he asked, giving Toni a quick hug and Brody a friendly handshake. "I guess you've been talking about the music business, right?"

"Er...not exactly," Toni murmured.

Her brother looked surprised. "You do know that Brody plays the clarinet, don't you? He has a degree in music education and was offered a job with the Milwaukee Symphony before he decided to go on to law school."

Brody played the clarinet? Toni was still absorbing this piece of information when Brody spoke. His years as a lawyer had obviously trained him to think fast on his feet. "We weren't talking about my brief and totally inglorious musical career," he said. "Actually, your sister was telling me about some of her plans for the immediate future. They're...bold, to say the least."

"Did she fill you in on her ideas for opening another club in Uptown?" Remy asked, putting his arm around Toni's waist and giving her an affectionate squeeze. "It's great to know that Chanson Triste is so successfully established that she can think about starting another club. We're all real proud of what she's achieved."

"Yes, she's obviously a woman who goes straight for what she wants," Brody agreed. "And I'm sure the new club will be every bit as successful as the original."

Toni could feel tension mounting inside her. Another sly dig like that from Brody and she might not be able to contain herself. "Remy, I really need to have a private word with you." She looped her hand through her brother's arm and directed a look of appeal toward him that she hoped wasn't too openly frantic. "I know you'll excuse us, Brody."

"Of course. I need to find Justin, myself. It was...interesting...to meet you, Toni."

He held out his hand, and she forced herself to shake it, keeping her smile pasted in place. "Goodbye, Brody. I hope you enjoy settling into Bayou Beltane."

"Thanks. And good luck with your plans." Brody strode through the crowds, stopping to shake hands with four or five people before he left the marquee. He was certainly making himself intimate with the bigwigs of Bayou Beltane, Toni thought. Then she pulled herself out of her sour mood. It wasn't Brody's fault that she'd just made a monumental idiot of herself, and she shouldn't blame him for reacting to her request the way any sensible man would have done.

Remy directed a couple of searching looks in her direction, but to Toni's relief, he refrained from making any comments until they were in the dining room, safely out of Brody's sight and hearing.

"What was that all about?" Remy asked, helping himself to a serving of stuffed oysters. "About halfway into our conversation, I got the distinct impression that I'd just paddled into the middle of a bayou filled with hungry alligators and, if I didn't navigate very carefully, we were all going to get our arms snapped off."

"You're exaggerating," Toni said dryly. She served herself some shrimp Creole. "I doubt if we'd have lost more than the odd finger or two."

Remy laughed, then cocked his head quizzically. "You and Brody didn't get on? Funny, I don't know him very well, of course, but I'd have expected you to find each other good company."

"We just got off on the wrong foot, that's all. Anyway, let's change the subject. How's the swamp tour business these days?"

"Erratic. I'm making a profit—just. But I'm willing to live frugally while the business develops."

"Still no regrets for the life you left behind?"

"None. Never. Trust me, swamp critters and tourists are a hell of a lot nicer to hang out with than pimps and murderers."

Remy had spent most of his life working as a cop, but he'd walked away from a brilliant career in law enforcement four years ago, and he now made his living by guiding tourists through the swamp that stretched along the eastern boundary of Bayou Beltane.

Their father had never really approved of Remy's career choice even when he'd worked as a cop, but at least Charles considered law enforcement a "real job." Remy's current life-style was even more incomprehensible to him than Toni's. He couldn't understand how any Delacroix could give up the majesty of the law in order to stand at the front of a motorized, flat-bottomed boat, lecturing about natural conservation while forty tourists searched eagerly for a glimpse of an alligator sunning itself in the mud.

Truth to tell, Toni didn't understand her brother's sudden fascination with the bayou any more than their father, but if Remy wanted to get bitten by mosquitoes, she was happy to support his decision. After struggling all her life for acceptance of her chosen career, Toni wasn't about to pass judgment on her brother's choice.

The two of them were discussing the astonishing rate of suburban development in the North Shore area, when Toni spotted Justin coming into the dining room, accompanied by Brody Wagner. Justin saw her and waved, obviously planning to come across and talk to her.

It was frustrating that when Justin finally saw her he should be in Brody's company. Much as she wanted to talk to Justin, she wasn't about to subject herself to another dose of Brody Wagner. Catching sight of her niece Shelby leaving the dining room, she put down her half-finished plate of food and edged toward the door, planning to flee.

"Remy, I've got to run. I've been trying to speak to Shelby all evening, and I've just spotted her. I have something I really need to ask her."

"Sure," he said. "I need to talk to Uncle Philip, anyway. I found some people tramping over his land last week, and they said they were surveyors. I'd like to know exactly what it is they were surveying for, since the land they were on backs right up onto the bayou."

Out of the corner of her eye, Toni saw that Justin was making his way around the buffet table toward her. Astonishingly, Brody Wagner was still with him. Toni didn't hang around to find out why Brody would choose to put himself at risk of having to speak to her again. She simply fled to the safety of the crowded parlor and the company of her niece.

Shelby smiled as she caught sight of Toni, her gray eyes sparkling with such liveliness that her wholesome, girl-next-door looks became something much more interesting than merely pretty.

She greeted Toni with a shake of her dark hair and an exaggerated sigh of envy. "Toni, you're looking especially fabulous tonight. I wouldn't care so much about your great body if I thought you actually had to work hard to keep yourself in shape. What drives me totally crazy is the fact that I know you've never seen the inside of a health club, let alone spent thirty excruciating minutes sweating on a StairMaster."

Toni laughed. "And I'd be more sympathetic toward you if it weren't for the fact that you have so much excess energy I believe you secretly *like* working out. And I'm not totally anti-exercise, you know. I do jog. But how are things, Shel? It's been a while since we last got together."

Shelby moved as if to shove her hands into her pockets. When she realized she was wearing a cocktail dress without pockets, she seemed at a loss to know where to put them. "I don't know," she said finally. "When I was in law school, I worked so hard that I didn't have time to think. Now I'm out of school and all those annoying questions I didn't have time for have started to rear up and demand answers."

"What sort of questions?" Toni asked.

"The inevitable ones, I guess." Shelby tried to sound casual but didn't quite succeed. "Like, what am I going to do with the rest of my life? Like, why am I working for the family law firm in Bayou Beltane? Is this really what I want to do, or am I just here because everyone expects me to be?"

"Have you come up with any answers?"

"Not yet." Shelby stirred the ice in her glass without noticing what she was doing. "Grandfather is so pleased that there's finally a fourth-generation Delacroix working in the firm, but I'm wondering if that's enough of a reason. I mean, ten years—thirty years from now, am I still going to be here?"

Toni spoke quietly. "Make sure that if you are, it's because you want to be and not because some misguided sense of loyalty kept you from spreading your wings. You're not responsible for the fact that your brother and sisters chose not to become lawyers. You don't have to be so perfect that you make up to Charles and Justin for all the ways the rest of us have goofed."

Shelby stared at Toni for a moment or two, as if startled by what she'd just said. "I'd never quite thought of what I was doing in those terms," she replied honestly. "But you're right. Charly and Marie both got better grades in high school than I did, and law school would have been much easier for them, academically speaking. Part of what motivated me to slog away and make good grades all the way through law school was the feeling that I owed it to everyone."

"Not to everyone," Toni said. "Not to anyone except yourself, in fact."

Shelby's expression held a mixture of affection and admiration for her aunt. "I don't know what it is about you, Toni, but somehow I always end up telling you the stuff I can't bring myself to discuss with anyone else."

Toni pulled a wry face. "I messed up my life so badly in my teens and early twenties that you know you're talking to a sympathetic listener. You're so amazingly together, Shelby, at least in comparison to most people. It's embarrassing for me to think back and remember what a total flake I was."

And if her recent conversation with Brody was anything

to go by, Toni thought, then she hadn't changed very much since the time she was a teenager.

"You weren't flaky, you were incredibly talented." Shelby grinned. "Although I guess sometimes it might have been hard for an outsider to tell the difference."

"Hard for an insider, too." Toni laughed. "Have lunch with me next week, Shel?" she suggested. "I've heard of a wonderful new restaurant that's supposed to make the best jambalaya in New Orleans. We could give it a try."

"Sounds great. I'll call you to set up a date." Shelby tilted her head to one side inquisitively. "Was there something special you needed to say to me, Toni? You had a purposeful look on your face when you came over here."

Her purpose had been to escape from Brody Wagner, but it occurred to Toni that this might be a good moment to ask her niece for help in returning Hamilton Delacroix's files to their rightful resting place. Shelby was obviously uncertain about the precise direction she wanted her career to take. Reading the personal work notes of her great-grandfather—the man who'd been the founding partner of Delacroix Associates—might give her a better idea of where, or even if, she wanted to fit into the eighty-year legal traditions of the Delacroix family.

"Yes, as a matter of fact, I do have something to ask you. It so happens that I've acquired some papers that really belong in the firm's archives." Toni stepped back to avoid a waiter hurrying through the parlor with a tray of empty glasses and almost bumped into Aunt Mary's table of birthday gifts.

"Are they legal documents?" Shelby asked.

Toni shook her head. "Actually, what I have are four thick files of notes that Hamilton Delacroix accumulated during the course of his last few criminal cases. I have the impression that some of the comments and notations he made were a lot more personal than most lawyers would include in a work file nowadays."

"How intriguing! But why do you have them and not my grandfather?"

"Don't ask," Toni said, rolling her eyes. "In fact, that's why I've approached you, Shelby. I can't tell you exactly how I acquired these files, but I'd sure appreciate it if you could return them to the appropriate place in my father's office. Preferably without pointing out to anyone that they've been missing for several years. Of course, if Justin or my father notices that the files have reappeared, don't hesitate to tell the truth about where you got them. I'm not asking you to lie for me."

"Well, of course I'll put them back for you, Toni—"

"They belong in Dad's office at home, in Riverwood. Not in the law offices."

"Okay. But are you sure we shouldn't say anything about them to Grandfather? After all, Hamilton Delacroix was his father, and he might find it really interesting to read his notes—"

"To be honest, I'd prefer you to return the files without mentioning them to anyone." Toni pulled a wry face. "There's a long and complicated story attached to how I acquired these files, Shelby. I assure you that nobody currently employed at Delacroix and Associates had anything to do with removing them, and I'd like to avoid drawing my father's attention to the fact that they were ever missing, if that's possible."

"Well, of course, if you say so." Shelby sounded a little doubtful. "Hamilton's been dead for a gazillion years, so presumably the files don't contain any important information."

"I'm sure they don't. But there's some interesting stuff in there, even though it's not relevant to anything the firm's working on today. There's an entire folder containing notes Hamilton made during the last case he handled before he died.''

"You have Hamilton's notes on his last case?" Shelby exclaimed. "The Rafael Perdido murder trial? That's *really* interesting. I was looking through the firm archives only a couple of weeks ago, and I noticed there's almost nothing there about that case.''

Toni frowned. "That's odd, because the papers I have are strictly personal notes. I'd have expected there to be another entire set of documents that were the official records of the case.''

Shelby grimaced. "It's not as strange as it sounds. You can't begin to imagine how haphazard the record keeping was in the early days of the firm. Our archives are something of a joke until about 1960. In fact, the only reason I know anything about Hamilton's last case is because I happened to come across some old newspaper clippings from the *Beltane Bugle*, which ceased publication during World War II.''

Toni was intrigued. She wondered if the newspaper accounts included pictures of the people that Hamilton's notes had brought to life for her. "I'd like to see those clippings sometime," she said. "When I read Hamilton's notes, I was surprised at how caught up I became in the story of the trial, at least as far as I could follow it. Did you know that Rafael Perdido was the only accused murderer Hamilton Delacroix ever defended who was found guilty?''

Shelby nodded. "Yes, those newspaper clippings mentioned that several times. And this was a bad case for Hamilton to lose because he died before the verdict could be appealed. And then poor Rafael Perdido was killed while he was in prison—''

The noise of crashing furniture interrupted Shelby's final words. She and Toni both swung around, to be greeted by the horrifying sight of Aunt Mary, crumpled on the floor, half covered by brightly wrapped birthday gifts that she'd knocked off the table as she keeled over. She was blue-lipped, groaning and barely conscious.

"I'll get Dr. Hummel," Shelby said, and took off at a run.

Toni knelt beside her aunt and held her hand, stroking it gently. She had no idea what else to do. For a moment, Mary seemed to regain awareness, and she struggled to speak. "Rrr...Rrr..."

Toni smoothed back her aunt's hair and spoke softly, forcing herself to keep her voice calm. "Relax, Aunt Mary, you're going to be fine. Don't worry about anything." It was agonizing to watch her aunt gasping for breath, trying to speak. "Please, dearest, don't try to talk. You'll feel better soon."

Shelby ran back into the room with a thin, gray-haired man at her heels. Thank God, Toni thought, recognizing Edward Hummel, Bayou Beltane's resident family practitioner. With profound relief, she yielded her place at Mary's side to the doctor.

"What's the matter?" William asked, coming into the parlor. "Dear God, Mary!" His words were a prayer, not an oath. "How did she fall? What's happened?"

The doctor looked up from his examination, his face grim. "She's had a heart attack. William, call an ambulance immediately. I must get her to the hospital right away."

CHAPTER FOUR

MARY WAS RUSHED to St. Tammany Parish Hospital in Covington, where the emergency room doctors concurred with Dr. Hummel's diagnosis that she'd suffered a minor heart attack. Fortunately, Mary had been in good health for a woman of her age, and the doctors didn't consider the attack life-threatening, although they wanted to keep her in the hospital for a few days while they ran a series of tests.

Despite this promising assessment, it was one in the morning before Mary's condition was finally upgraded to stable and Toni felt able to leave the hospital. She offered her father and William a ride back to Bayou Beltane, but they both refused to leave Mary's side, although Toni tried her best to persuade them that they needed a good night's rest in a comfortable bed.

"Mary needs me far more than I need my bed," William said, his gentle voice taking on a note of unusual firmness. "And she needs my prayers."

From long experience dealing with her uncle, Toni knew that it would be useless to point out that God could hear his prayers just as well from home as from the hospital. If sweet-natured Mary could become a tyrant on the subject of marriage and families, affable William could turn into an iron man where spiritual issues were concerned.

"Do you have a spare pair of glasses, Uncle William?" In the confusion of getting Mary out to the ambulance,

William's glasses had fallen off and been trodden on, and Toni noticed that he kept rubbing his eyes as if the strain of trying to see without them was causing a headache. "I'd be happy to bring them into the hospital for you, if you'll tell me where I can find them."

William patted her on the arm. "You're a sweet child, Antoinette, but that won't be necessary, thank you. It's all taken care of. Now, I must get back to my sister. Drive safely, my dear, and God bless." He walked back to Mary's bedside, his neck craning forward as he peered shortsightedly ahead.

"I'll make sure Uncle William doesn't overdo things," Remy said, moving out into the corridor with Toni. "Maybe it's just as well he can't see clearly enough to tackle anything very demanding. He looks exhausted, and we don't want to have another invalid on our hands."

"No, we sure don't. Uncle Philip's reaction was scary enough. When he realized what had happened to Mary, I thought he was going to faint."

"Mmm, but our uncle Philip is a bit of a hypochondriac, so I don't know if the palpitations he complained about were real, or just the result of a vivid imagination."

"He's seventy-nine years old," Toni said dryly. "I'd tend to go with the belief that his health problems are genuine."

"Well, real or imagined, the palpitations kept him at home, which is a blessing. It means one less elderly gentleman hanging around Mary's bedside, and to be honest, I'm glad Philip and Dad aren't glaring at each other from opposite corners. The two of them drain all the energy out of a room when they get together, and we don't want Mary to have to start playing the peacemaker the moment she wakes up."

"What are we going to do about Dad?" Toni asked, pushing the call button for the elevator. "You know he's the exact opposite of Philip where his health is concerned. Dad could be at the end of his tether, but he'd never admit it. He'll just stand ramrod straight at Mary's bedside, not admitting how tired he is, until he passes out. Did you see how he simply ignored me when I offered to drive him home?''

"Stop worrying, Toni, I promise to take care of Dad. I'll give him another half hour to reassure himself that Mary's doing fine, and then I'll insist on taking him home.''

Despite her weariness, Toni chuckled. "Mmm, that's a scene I'd like to see. You ordering Dad to do something he doesn't want to do.''

"Yeah, that'll be the day, I guess.'' Remy shrugged. "Justin should soon finish conferring with the doctors, and you know he finds it easier to handle Dad than either of us. For once, I'm more than willing to step back and let him take charge.''

The mention of her oldest brother's name reminded Toni that she still hadn't managed to get Justin alone so that she could warn him about the campaign being organized to block his nomination to the federal bench. Obviously, the emergency room hadn't been a suitable place to start explaining something so complex, but it was worrying to think that five days had gone by since Dennis had contacted her, and yet Justin remained blithely unaware of the blackmail scheme being mounted against him. She would have to call Justin tomorrow at Riverwood and keep calling until he spoke to her, Toni decided. They couldn't afford to spend another week playing telephone tag, or the FBI would have started their investigation and her brother's appointment as a judge would be in serious jeopardy.

The elevator arrived, and she touched her hand lightly

to Remy's cheek. "Take care, big brother. Don't let any alligators eat you out in the swamp tomorrow."

"Bayou alligators don't worry me," he said with a wry smile. "It's the human variety I can't handle. Now, are you sure you don't want me to escort you to your car? The cop in me is screaming that I should."

She shook her head. "Ignore your cop instincts. I'm parked right in front of the hospital, there's a security guard downstairs, and the parking lot's brightly lit. I'll be fine. It's more important for you to get back to Aunt Mary and try to persuade Dad to go home. As for Uncle William, I realize he's a lost cause, but see if you can at least get him to sit down every now and then."

"I'll do that. And don't worry, Toni. Dad and Uncle William may be elderly, but they're both stronger than they look. You need to get some rest yourself. We've all run you ragged tonight, just because you happened to be the person standing right next to Aunt Mary when she collapsed."

The elevator buzzed, indicating somebody else was waiting. "You'd better go," Remy said, removing his hand from the door. "We shouldn't hold up the elevator." He waved goodbye, and walked with agile steps back down the corridor toward their aunt's room.

Toni leaned against the utilitarian gray walls of the elevator, letting the fatigue flow over her. She was exhausted. A reaction, she realized, to the stresses of the night, since she was accustomed to being up at this hour and shouldn't have been tired. The elevator creaked and cranked downward, stopping on the second floor to admit a nurse who looked as if she was even more exhausted than Toni.

They yawned in unison, and the nurse gave a wry chuckle. "I have another six hours to go, but at least you look like you're going home."

"I am," Toni said. "And I only just realized how tired I am."

"Have you seen what the weather's doin' out there?" the nurse said, smothering another yawn. "I surely do hope it's stopped rainin' by the time I have to drive home."

"I didn't know it was raining," Toni said. "It was a fine night when we brought my aunt into the hospital."

The nurse rolled her eyes. "Well, honey, you should see it now. I do believe this is the most rain we've had since that last hurricane hit town."

The nurse hadn't been exaggerating, Toni realized when she reached the lobby and looked outside. A storm had blown up and moved inland from the Gulf, bringing a torrential downpour of rain with it. The trees in front of the entrance were tossing wildly, scattering twigs and leaves, but so far no big limbs had been downed, at least not close to the hospital. The downpour was so heavy she couldn't even see out into the parking lot, which was almost obliterated by a slashing screen of rain.

Toni sighed. The prospect of driving home to New Orleans in this sort of storm was anything but appealing, especially since she'd promised to come back and visit Aunt Mary tomorrow, which meant that she'd have to turn around and do the whole trip in reverse. Perhaps she should find a motel and spend the night on this side of the lake? She had no change of clothes with her, but she could always make a quick run to the mall tomorrow morning and buy a pair of shorts and a T-shirt. Not to mention sneakers and clean underwear, and toothpaste and deodorant....

It was better to go home to New Orleans, she decided, despite the storm and the difficult driving conditions. That way, she and Pudge could have their regular Sunday meeting at midday and resolve all the minor crises that would inevitably have cropped up. If Aunt Mary's health didn't improve, Toni would want to take some time off. Fortunately, Pudge knew everyone who was anyone in the New Orleans music business and should be able to perform the miracle of lining up a replacement entertainer at a day or two's notice. On Monday, thank goodness, Chanson Triste was closed, so once the Sunday-night shows were over, she had a little wiggle room in her schedule.

"You want a plastic bag to hold over your head?" the night guard asked her as she hurried through the lobby. "You goin' to get real soaked, miss. It sure is pourin' down out there."

"Mmm, that would be great. Thanks for the offer." Accepting the plastic bag with a grateful smile, she held the flimsy pink shield over her head and made a dash for her car. Unfortunately, once she got outside, her Firebird was all too easy to spot in the almost-deserted parking lot. Not because it stood alone, or even because it was bright red, but because its headlights were on—and looking very dim.

Alternating prayers and curses, Toni jumped puddles and ran the last few yards toward her car. She forgot about holding the plastic bag over her and the rain pounded down on her head in a soaking sheet, leaving her drenched within seconds. She scarcely noticed the water streaming down her face, just kept wiping it away so she could see.

Damn! How could she have been so careless as to leave the lights on? Not careless, she thought, pushing strands of sopping wet hair out of her eyes and fumbling for her keys. It was worry that had made her forgetful. Aunt Mary had still been unconscious when they arrived at the hospital, and Toni had been too panicked to remember mundane things like car lights.

At least she hadn't been so distracted that she'd locked her keys inside the car. She opened the door and slid behind the wheel, greatly relieved when the interior lights came on, albeit a bit dim and flickering. The car was new, she reassured herself, and batteries were much more powerful these days. Maybe the car would start, after all.

And then again, maybe it wouldn't. Five minutes later, with nothing to show for her efforts except a flooded engine, Toni gave up. Sighing, she searched through her purse for her Triple A card. She was obviously going nowhere, home or motel, until somebody with cables came out to jump-start her battery.

To call for help, she'd have to go back into the lobby of the hospital. Switching off the lights—about three hours too late—she got out of the car and returned to the hospital at a run.

She was so wet that her dress was clinging to her body, and streams of rain dripped off the hem and ran between her legs. Quite apart from the fact that her favorite green silk evening dress was now ruined, she was shivering with cold and wretchedly uncomfortable.

The security guard eyed her in disbelief. "What happened to you?" he asked.

"My car battery died," she said. "My car won't start. I need to call Triple A."

The guard grunted in sympathy. "Phone's around the corner, ma'am." He pointed helpfully.

Toni waited a long time for someone to answer her call, but when she got through at last, a chirpy operator told her that she was in luck. A tow truck had been called out an hour ago to fix a flat tire for a motorist whose car had run over broken glass on the interstate, and that truck should be passing near Covington right about now. The operator called the truck driver on his mobile phone, and then assured Toni that the rescue truck would be at the hospital within ten minutes.

She hadn't expected to be so lucky, if lucky was the

right word to use about anything that had happened so far tonight. She hung up the phone, then tried without success to squeeze some of the excess water from her dress. The silk clung stubbornly to her skin, turning from cold to icy as the wet cloth chilled in the hospital's fierce air-conditioning. Covered in goose bumps, teeth chattering, she decided to step out of the lobby into the relative warmth of the covered portico.

She exited the hospital doorway just in time to bump into Brody Wagner.

Toni wouldn't have thought it was possible for her situation to get any worse than it already was. The arrival of Brody Wagner suggested that she hadn't even begun to plumb the depths of misery this night had in store for her. Why him? she thought miserably. Why here? Why now?

In contrast to her own bedraggled state, Brody looked infuriatingly gorgeous. And *together*. He carried an oversize black umbrella so that his khaki pants and his sweatshirt embossed with the logo of the University of Chicago were bone dry. Toni wondered why it was that in the movies, rain-soaked women always appeared dewy-fresh and sexy, whereas she felt like a cross between a drowned squirrel and an overused floor mop.

She shrank into the shadows, sending up frantic prayers that he would walk on without recognizing who had bumped into him. But of course that was a vain hope. Brody stared into the corner where she was cowering— why was there never a convenient hole in the ground when you needed one?—and did a visible double-take.

"Toni!" He walked over to her, closing his umbrella as he approached. The spillover of light from the hospital revealed the stubble of a night's growth of beard and a faint scar above his left eyebrow that she hadn't noticed earlier. "My God, what happened? Did you have an accident? Here, let me help you inside." He extended his hand.

"Thanks, but I'm fine," she muttered, ignoring his outstretched hand. No way on God's green earth was she going to admit to Brody Wagner that she had left her car lights on and drained her battery. He already thought she was irresponsible and borderline crazy. She wasn't about to add *stupid* and *inefficient* to his list. She wondered why he'd come to the hospital at this unlikely hour, but she didn't ask. To ask a question, she would have had to look at him, and that was something she didn't plan to do. She concentrated hard on making herself invisible.

With the impeccable timing that she might have expected on this generally disastrous night, the rescue truck chose this moment to roll into the parking lot, at least five minutes earlier than promised.

"Excuse me," she said to Brody. "I have to go." With what scraps of dignity she could muster, she emerged from her shadowy corner and walked toward the truck without even glancing in his direction.

"Yeah, sure." There wasn't a trace of comforting Southern drawl in Brody's crisp response; it was all brisk, Yankee disdain. "Good night, Toni."

She pretended not to hear, a ploy that she hadn't used since she was a sophomore in high school. Head erect, she crossed the parking lot, indifferent to the rain, which now seemed to be cascading with a force roughly equivalent to a hydroelectric dam opened to full throttle. She never once turned to look, but she knew the exact moment that Brody stopped staring at her back and walked into the hospital. Her shoulders slumped as if all the air had suddenly whooshed out of her. Thank goodness he'd gone.

She trudged the final few yards to her car, her feet squelching in her ruined evening sandals—so much for splurging on Bruno Magli—and her dress feeling as if it was coming apart at the seams. She greeted the mechanic, who proved to be friendly, helpful and efficient. Despite all those admirable qualities, however, he was unable to get her car to start.

"It's not just your battery, miss. You have a problem with your alternator."

"But I can't have!" Toni protested. "It's a new car!"

The mechanic gave her a pitying look from beneath the shelter of his bright yellow rain hat. "Yes, ma'am, I see that. You have a problem all the same. I can tell you, this car ain't goin' to be driven no place tonight, no, ma'am. Your battery won't hold the charge."

Toni was shocked to feel herself poised right on the edge of tears. Fortunately, even if she cried, her tears would be invisible in the rain dripping off her hair, her forehead, her nose and every other section of her anatomy. She swallowed over the lump in her throat and finally managed to speak. "What do you suggest I do?" she asked.

"I can tow your car to any repair shop of your choice. Or I can take it back to my garage and work on it to-morrow. I have a mechanic who'll be coming in around noon. We should be able to fix you up before five o'clock. Always providin' we don't find nothin' real serious."

Resigned, she asked the driver to tow the car to his repair shop and when he requested a local phone number, she shook her head. "I need to find a motel," she said. "I'd be very grateful if you could drop me off somewhere on the way back to your garage. Anywhere that you think is clean and safe."

The mechanic eyed her with genuine sympathy. "Wish I could, miss, but that's against every regulation in the book. We ain't allowed to take passengers into the tow truck, no, ma'am. You'll have to go back into the hospital

and call for a taxi.'' He reached under his slicker, fumbled
for a few seconds, then pulled out two cards. "Here's my
number at the garage. You call there tomorrow afternoon
and I'll let you know what's goin' on with your car. The
other card is for a taxi service. You tell my friend Joe that
I've got your car in my garage and he'll take real good
care of you. He always has a driver on call. Shouldn't
take more than a half hour to get a cab out here for you,
no, ma'am.''

"Thank you." She took the cards and made her way
back to the hospital, so wet that there seemed no point in
hurrying. Shivering as the icy blast of air-conditioning hit
her once again, she was beyond the point of humiliation
when she looked across the lobby and saw Brody Wagner
stepping off the elevator.

Of course, she thought in numb resignation, what else
had she expected? No doubt Brody's presence at the hospital was some form of cosmic punishment for having
been such a fool as to ask him to become the father of
her baby. The fates obviously didn't approve of her unconventional plans for motherhood and were driving
home their disapproval.

She didn't attempt to scurry away and hide. What was
the point? He'd already seen her. She pushed a few of the
most sodden strands of hair out of her eyes and stared
straight ahead, putting on the most dignified expression
she could manage, given that her dress was plastered to
her body and she was standing in a puddle of water she
herself had created.

Brody strode across the lobby at a fast pace. When he
came near her, he nodded briefly to acknowledge her presence, said good-night to the security guard and walked
outside.

He hadn't spoken to her! If he hadn't paused under the
portico to open his umbrella, he'd probably have been in

his car before Toni gathered her wits sufficiently to realize that, in her bereft state, pride was a luxury she could ill afford. She ran outside and tugged his arm to attract his attention.

Brody turned and looked at her from beneath the shelter of his umbrella. "Yes?"

The only minor blessing to the rain dripping down her face was that it probably disguised the fact that she was blushing. It had to be ten years—at least—since she'd felt so gauche and embarrassed in a man's presence. She drew in a ragged breath. Ragged, because her lungs wouldn't allow anything deeper. "My car wouldn't start and I had to have it towed. I wondered…"

Her voice trailed off and he waited in polite silence, refusing to help her out by interjecting a comment of his own. Remembering the teasing, friendly way in which he'd introduced himself, making light of the awkwardness of Aunt Mary's matchmaking efforts, Toni felt an unexpected pang of regret. It was quite an achievement to have screwed up her relationship with this man so totally and within such a short space of time, she reflected.

She licked her lips, the only part of her entire body that felt dry. "I…um…wondered if you would be kind enough to give me a ride to a motel on your way home."

He continued to look at her, his expression impossible to read. On the whole, Toni was quite glad not to know what he was thinking. "Remy should be coming down in a few minutes," Brody said finally. "I'm sure he'd be happy to give you a ride back to Bayou Beltane, and then you wouldn't need to find a motel."

It was a measure of how mentally exhausted she was that she'd forgotten about her brother. Good grief, what was the matter with her? She'd humbled herself in front of Brody for no reason.

"I'm sorry to have troubled you," she said stiffly. "Of

course I'll wait for Remy.'' She turned to go back into the hospital lobby, but Brody caught her arm and swung her around to face him.

''I gave you the wrong impression,'' he said. ''I'm more than willing to drive you to a motel, Toni, but I thought you might prefer to wait for Remy. He and your father should be coming down in ten minutes or so.''

''Is that why you're here at the hospital? You came to see my aunt?''

''In a way. Since I live in Covington, I volunteered to bring Father William his spare pair of glasses. The driving's so bad tonight, it seemed crazy for anyone to make the round-trip between here and Bayou Beltane.''

''Oh, I see.'' No wonder her uncle had seemed so unconcerned about his glasses; he'd already made arrangements for Brody to bring him a spare pair. A trickle of rain rolled off the tip of her nose and she rubbed it away. ''Well, good night, Brody. I'll go back inside the hospital and wait for Remy and my father.''

''Toni...'' She could sense Brody's hesitation, even though she wasn't looking at him. ''Where did the Triple A people take your car? To a repair shop here in Covington?''

She nodded. ''It was towed to Main Street Auto Repair.''

''If you don't want to go back to Riverwood for the night, I can drive you to a motel here in Covington. That way, you'd be right on the spot when your car's ready to be picked up tomorrow morning.''

In normal circumstances, Toni would have said that spending the night at Riverwood was right at the top of her list of least favorite things to do. But when the alternative was driving around Covington with Brody Wagner, Riverwood began to look like a great choice. The wind blew a cold gust of rain inside the portico, and she shivered, her reserves of body heat all used up. What to do? Riverwood—or Brody Wagner? Which was the lesser evil?

Brody saw her shiver. He made a small, impatient sound and took the decision out of her hands. "Come on, you can't hang around here any longer. You need to get somewhere warm and dry or you'll be sharing a hospital room with your aunt." He put his arm around her waist, held the umbrella over both their heads and strode into the parking lot at a pace that had her running to keep up with him.

He kept her clamped to his side, under the protection of the umbrella. In contrast to her damp chilliness, his body blazed with heat, but Toni knew perfectly well that the shivers rippling across her skin had very little to do with her sudden proximity to a source of warmth.

She splashed across the lot to his car, trying to maintain a few inches of space between them. All she succeeded in doing was making herself even more aware of the fact that his arm felt wonderfully comforting around her waist, that his body was hard and muscled, and that he moved with an athletic grace that felt as good as it looked.

He stopped by a black BMW and opened the door on the passenger side to reveal an interior with polished walnut dashboards, velvet pile carpeting and gray glove-leather seats. "This is a very expensive interior for me to drip water on," she said.

Brody shrugged. "The seats will dry. You'd better get in so that I can shut the door before any more rain blows in."

She slid into the front passenger seat without further protest, welcoming the slightly stuffy warmth of the interior. "Nice car," she said as Brody fastened his seat belt and turned the key in the ignition.

"It drives well. I like the way it holds the road, especially on a night like this one."

"Is it new?"

"Yes. I rewarded myself when I left Manhattan. This is the first car I've owned since I had a fourth-hand Mustang in college."

Toni tried to think of something more to say and realized that she was fresh out of small talk. Usually, she found it easy to make casual conversation. As the owner of a nightclub, she'd trained herself to be pleasant to patrons from many different walks of life. She could listen to right-wing Republicans and left-wing Democrats and be equally polite to both. She enjoyed chatting with suburbanites from the Midwest every bit as much as she enjoyed hearing gossip from patrons who were part of the inner circle in Hollywood, or the White House, or Wall Street, or some other self-anointed power center. But tonight, her mind seemed wiped clean of chitchat. There were a hundred different questions she'd have liked to ask Brody, but the humiliating memory of their earlier conversation kept her silent.

Unfortunately, in the absence of conversation, all she could hear was the echo of her own voice, making the same outrageous request over and over again. *Hello, Brody. I want you to be the father of my baby.*

For a second, the words were so clear inside her head that she was afraid she might have spoken them aloud for a second disastrous time. She sneaked a quick glance at Brody and was relieved to see that he was staring straight ahead, wearing his inscrutable expression again. She shifted on the seat, where she was sticking wetly to the leather, and turned to look out of the window, resolving to let him worry about finding something to talk about. It took two people to create a silence filled with this much tension.

The drive already seemed to have lasted for about three-and-a-half lifetimes, but since they'd only progressed two blocks from the hospital, she was willing to acknowledge that her sense of time might be a little off. Taking refuge in the pretense that she was falling asleep, she leaned back against the seat and closed her eyes, only to find her mind flooded by larger-than-life images of herself and Brody. Erotic, sensual images that shocked her with their explicitness and intensity. Now that she had propositioned Brody and been rejected, it was as if her subconscious was determined to weave fantasies about everything she was missing.

Since pretending to sleep was only making her more edgy, she sat up again and resumed her inspection of the darkness. She couldn't see much except rain and wet roads, but anything was better than staring at Brody's profile and letting herself drift off into a new set of fantasies. She was grateful when he slipped a CD into his player and filled the silence with a recording of baroque chamber music, obscure compositions that she didn't recognize. Toni let the unfamiliar melodies wash over her as they drove through the town, concentrating on them so determinedly that she was genuinely caught up in the wonder of the music when Brody slowed the car to a stop.

She looked up and saw that they were parked outside a small motel. A large sign stating No Vacancies glowed with neon brightness through the rain. A smaller printed card in the office window repeated the same message. Toni didn't even feel surprise. Of course the motel was full. What else had she expected on this night from hell?

"Is there another motel nearby?" she asked, trying not to let her weariness show in her voice.

He shook his head. "No, this is the only one I know about. I'll see if I can use the phone in their office." Brody started to open the car door and the rain gushed in.

"This is crazy," he said, shutting the door again. "We're both too tired to drive around in this kind of a downpour. I suggest you come back to my place. I only moved in a few weeks ago, and I'm still fixing things up, but the guest room has a bed, which is the main thing we need."

He meant that the bed was important because they were tired and would want to get to sleep as soon as possible, but they both seemed to realize the possible double meaning at the same moment. He stared at her, his gaze faintly predatory. His hands tightened on the steering wheel, but he didn't attempt to explain away what he'd said.

Toni registered the surprising fact that Brody was as aware of the sexual tension swirling around in the car as she was. Belatedly, it occurred to her that the CD might have been as much of a defense against the silence for him as it had been for her.

For a moment the atmosphere was explosive with possibilities that neither of them wanted to explore. Then Brody put the car into gear and reversed out of the parking lot at a speed that set his wheels spinning on the loose gravel. He drove swiftly, almost recklessly, through the deserted streets of Covington, coming to a halt at a turn-of-the-century home built on the outskirts of the town. In the dark and rain, Toni could see nothing much about the exterior of the house except that it was painted white and was separated from the street by a walled courtyard more typical of New Orleans than the old towns of the North Shore.

Brody opened the garage with a remote and drove in. "I apologize for bringing you in through the side entrance. But if we use the kitchen door, we won't get so wet."

Toni refrained from pointing out that it was hard to imagine any possible combination of circumstances that would make her wetter than she already was. She was glad, finally, to be able to say something, even if it was utterly trivial. "Of course I don't mind going in through the garage."

The sound of the garage door opening was the signal for an outbreak of excited, high-pitched yapping that reached a crescendo as the two of them walked into the kitchen and switched on the lights. A bundle of exuberant white fluff hurtled down the tiled hallway and launched itself at Brody's feet, nipping at his shoes and generally displaying the most advanced stages of canine ecstasy.

Brody bent down and scooped up the tiny poodle. She quieted instantly. "Her name's Fifi," he said. He smiled—increasing his sexiness quotient by several devastating degrees. "Not very original, I guess, but she was already named when I got her."

"She's cute." Toni scratched a spot just behind Fifi's topknot and narrowly avoided having her face slathered with kisses. She laughed. "And *very* free with her favors. Have you had her long?"

"About five years. She was two when I got her." He didn't explain who'd owned Fifi for the first two years of her life. A former wife? Toni wondered. A girlfriend who'd been the love of his life and Fifi was all that was left to remind him of her? It was shocking to realize that she didn't even know something as basic as whether or not Brody had ever been married.

He put down the dog and gestured toward the refrigerator. "Would you like something to eat or drink? Some cola or a glass of juice? Cheese and crackers? Ice water?"

She shook her head. "No, thank you, not even water." She'd consumed so much vending machine coffee while they waited for news about her aunt that her stomach felt as if it was lined with acid. "What I want more than anything else right now is to get out of these wet clothes and take a hot shower. If that wouldn't be too much trouble."

"No trouble at all. I can loan you a T-shirt, and there's a bathroom right opposite the guest room. If you don't want anything to drink, why don't we go upstairs?"

"You go first, Brody, since you know where you're going."

He walked into the hall, flicking on the lights as he went. He snapped his fingers in Fifi's direction and she yapped happily before scampering ahead of them.

"Your house is terrific," Toni said as they walked through the downstairs hallway. "I love these high arches, and the floors have aged so beautifully."

"The floors were the first thing I had repaired after I took possession of the house. They were covered in wall-to-wall shag carpeting when I bought the place, a different color in every room." He grinned. "Still, that carpeting made the place look so bad it must have saved me several thousand dollars on the purchase price, so I'm not complaining."

Toni shook her head. "Covering these floors is almost vandalism," she said. "I know people used to do it all the time, but I've never understood why."

"Tastes change," Brody said. "This house was last remodeled in the early seventies, and the owners did some very strange things by today's standards. The carpeting wasn't even the worst of it. They also painted over all the original woodwork and covered the ceilings in silver foil wallpaper. Must have cost 'em a fortune to make it look so ugly."

"And now you've spent another fortune getting the foil off and stripping the paint from the woodwork."

"Of course. But who knows? Maybe in twenty years' time, silver foil will be back in fashion."

"Never," she said with fervent conviction.

He laughed. "You sound so fierce, but it could happen. Bet you never thought lime green bell-bottom pants would come back and be a hot fashion item."

Toni pulled a face. "I'm pretending that fashion fad never happened," she said. "Once was more than enough."

They arrived at the top of the stairs, Fifi prancing confidently ahead. Brody pushed open a door on the left side of the hallway. "This is the guest bathroom. The good news is that it exists, and it's all yours. The bad news is that the fixtures are chocolate brown and the tile is bright orange. You might need sunglasses tomorrow morning."

"If the shower dispenses hot water, I won't even notice the color of the tile," Toni said with heartfelt sincerity. "And if you can loan me a bottle of shampoo, I'll consider myself surrounded by total luxury."

"There's shampoo in the shower. There's even a new toothbrush in the medicine cabinet. Also toothpaste."

"Wow! That's more than luxury, you've brought me to a veritable palace." Caught up in their exchange, she moved right with him into the cramped bathroom. Brody opened the cupboard under the sink and found her a big white towel.

"And here's the toothbrush," he said, handing her a cellophane-wrapped package. "Soap's already on the counter next to the sink. Ditto toothpaste."

Toni hugged the towel to her chest, smiling. "You have to be as wet as I am to know how wonderful this towel feels. Thanks, Brody."

"You're welcome." He looked at her, his eyes narrowed. Then he turned abruptly, just as she stepped forward into the corridor. Their shoulders brushed and they pulled apart, only to end up wedged in the small bathroom doorway, facing each other across less than two inches of space.

Their gazes locked, and they both stood absolutely still. For a moment, Toni even forgot to breathe. She would have walked away if she could, but it was like the drive from the hospital, only worse. Now, in addition to paralyzed vocal chords, it seemed that the rest of her body was paralyzed, as well. Her brain sent out clear instructions to move. Her muscles had forgotten how to obey.

Temptation shimmered between them, made all the more potent because reason warned them both to resist. Their silence was so intense that the air around them vibrated with the force of it. Slowly, very slowly, Brody reached out and traced the contours of her face with his hand.

That one light touch was all that was needed to break their trance. Toni felt a soft thud at her feet and realized she'd dropped the towel. Without ever taking his gaze from hers, Brody picked the towel up and tossed it behind them.

"I should...go," Toni said.

"Yes, you should." Brody backed her up against the doorjamb, his body thrust full length against hers. His head was a dark shadow, blocking out the light, and then his mouth came down on hers, hot, hard and demanding.

Lightning didn't strike, the heavens didn't open, but Toni was pretty sure that the earth moved. His tongue thrust against hers, and his hands twined in the wet strands of her hair, holding her still. She closed her eyes and dizziness roared in her ears, a sound as well as a sensation. Brody's heartbeat thudded against the palm of her hand, where it rested on his back, and she felt the tingle of her nipples as they pressed against his chest. It was strange to be so intensely aware of the texture and shape of his body when she'd already lost all sense of where her own body ended and his began.

It was a long time before the kiss ended. Brody finally

drew back, breathing hard. Once again, they stared at each other from opposite sides of the doorway in a silence thick enough to make the air feel heavy.

Brody spoke first. "That was a mistake," he said, his voice flat.

"Was it?" Toni picked up the towel and held it to her chest like a security blanket. "Don't worry, Brody. Last I heard, you can't get a woman pregnant just by kissing her."

Brody's eyes darkened. "I wasn't thinking about pregnancy," he said, moving out into the corridor. "That's your obsession, Toni, not mine."

"Then, I don't understand what's bothering you."

"I know you don't," he said. "And that's the problem."

CHAPTER FIVE

DESPITE THE FACT that Brody had walked Fifi last thing before he went to bed, the dog woke him at eight-thirty on Sunday morning with an urgent demand to be taken outside. Grumbling as he pulled on shorts and scuffed his feet into a pair of battered loafers, Brody obliged.

The storm had passed over without leaving any major damage, and the sun was climbing into a high, cloudless sky. Summer heat had returned with a vengeance, and the shiny leaves of an old magnolia tree in the corner of his paved front courtyard were steaming. The humidity was oppressive, the air thick with so much moisture that even Fifi was willing to forgo a morning run and escape back into the coolness of the air-conditioned house.

Yawning and stretching, Brody made his way to the kitchen. He shook kibble into Fifi's bowl and poured himself a glass of orange juice, sipping slowly. Usually on a Sunday morning he spent a couple of hours reading the newspaper and drinking his favorite dark-roasted coffee while he fooled around with the crossword. This morning, the clues all seemed either stupid or impenetrable, and he finally tossed aside his pencil and scooped Fifi into his lap. The poodle gave him a couple of consoling licks on the back of his hand.

Brody stroked her fluffy ears and stared broodingly at the coffeemaker. "She's driving me crazy, but you already know that, don't you? She looks at me with those big blue eyes of hers, and I'm damn near willing to say that of course I'll be the father of her baby. Why not? Hell, she knew me for at least three minutes before she propositioned me. Obviously, she's the sort of thoughtful woman I always planned to select as the mother of my children. And the sex sure would be great."

Fifi yapped twice, and Brody scratched the dog under her pointed chin. "Yeah, you're right. However great the sex would be, it's not worth it." He gave a short laugh. "Would you like me to try saying that one more time? Maybe that way we'll both believe it."

A light tap on the kitchen door interrupted his one-sided conversation, and he looked up to see Toni standing in the entrance. She was barefoot and wore the T-shirt he'd loaned her last night. It was black, with the slogan Eschew Obfuscation emblazoned across the front in neon pink letters. The T-shirt had been a gift from Jill right before they broke up and he came to Bayou Beltane, and he wondered what subliminal impulses had been at work to make him select that particular shirt for Toni. She, of all people, didn't seem to have the slightest problem stating her wishes with razor-sharp clarity. The shirt was a man's size extra large, and it hung off Toni's shoulders, ending at the top of her thighs and allowing him the dubious pleasure of confirming with his own eyes that her legs were every bit as long and shapely as he'd dreamed about.

"Come on in," he said, putting Fifi down and scrambling to his feet, hoping like hell that Toni hadn't overheard what he'd been saying to the dog. He sometimes thought Fifi was one of the more understanding females he talked to these days, but he'd have preferred not to be caught by Toni Delacroix discussing his sexual fantasies with his poodle. "Did you manage to sleep okay?"

"Very well, thank you." Toni's singing voice was crystal clear, but her speaking voice had a slight trace of huskiness that Brody found erotic in the extreme. She walked into the kitchen, and he followed her progress with the same fascination as a high school freshman peeking into the girls' locker room. Toni was one of those women whose bone structure was so perfect that she looked beautiful all the time, whether she was dressed up for a party or half drowned in a rainstorm, but this morning she had a drowsy, rumpled look that wasn't only beautiful, it was also irresistibly sexy.

She stopped at his coffeemaker and held up the pot. "May I?" she asked.

"Yes, of course. Do you take milk or sugar?"

"No thanks, I drink it black."

He tugged open the door of the fridge. "I have fresh orange juice, too, but there isn't much to eat unless you like cereal."

"Cereal would be fine." She took a sip of coffee and let out a small sigh of pleasure. "This is great, Brody, exactly what I needed. You've made it strong, the way I like it."

"I'm just starting to get used to the chicory blends everyone here seems to prefer." Brody took two boxes of cereal from the pantry and put them on the kitchen table along with bowls, spoons and a carton of milk. "Such as it is, breakfast is served. Take your choice, muesli or cornflakes."

She poured cornflakes into one of the bowls and added lots of milk. "Actually, your menu is perfect. Cereal is my favorite breakfast."

"Is it? With all the great bakeries in New Orleans, I'd have expected you to go for croissants and beignets."

She shook her head. "Only when I'm eating out, or when I have visitors. Usually, I stay away from fancy meals when I'm at home. Our chef at the club tries out all his new recipes on me, and he serves up some pretty exotic meals, so when I'm eating alone, I live on cereal and yogurt, with the occasional piece of fruit thrown in. That way, I manage to convince myself I'm eating a healthy, well-balanced diet."

"Same for me," Brody said. "These days, I seem to be entertaining clients all the time, and I've discovered that the citizens of New Orleans take their food very seriously."

"Here in New Orleans we take a very French view of food. What's life about if not eating?"

He laughed. "Well, that philosophy sure makes for some terrific restaurants. I don't think I've eaten a bad meal since I arrived here, which is great in some ways. But after a while, you come home and discover that you're craving peanut butter and jelly, or a grilled cheese sandwich made with the sort of processed cheese that sticks to your teeth and tasted so great when you were a kid."

"Or a po'boy." Toni looked dreamy eyed. "That's my favorite comfort food. If you grew up here, you can't go too long without craving a po'boy." Smiling, she scraped up her final spoonful of cornflakes. "So, how come you're spending so much time with clients in New Orleans, Brody? I'm not up-to-date on what's going on with Delacroix and Associates, but Dad and Justin always seemed determined to keep the firm's client base centered firmly on this side of the lake."

"That was true in the past, but not anymore," he said. "Where the practice of law is concerned, Justin is more conservative in his choice of clients than your father, and with his imminent departure—"

"Justin's more conservative than Dad?" Toni rolled her eyes. "I didn't know anyone could be more conservative than my father about anything, especially the law."

Brody looked at her in surprise. "Don't confuse your father's liking for three-piece suits and sober striped ties with his attitude toward Delacroix and Associates,'' he said. ''Where the practice of the law is concerned, I'd say that Charles has a well-deserved reputation as an innovator.''

''You astonish me,'' Toni said after a moment's silence. ''But I don't believe I was basing my opinion of my father on anything as superficial as his taste in clothes.''

''What, then?''

She hesitated. ''General experiences when I was growing up,'' she said finally. ''My father always seemed the quintessential conservative to me. He acted as if every step I took toward independence was going to lead to disaster. Like my choice of career. He was overwhelmingly opposed to the idea of me becoming a professional singer, and for reasons that would barely have made sense in the social climate of the 1950s, let alone in the eighties.''

''Singing's a tough career in which to make a living,'' Brody pointed out. ''Although, your talent is so unmistakable, Charles should have known he didn't have to worry.''

Toni's smile was tinged with bitterness. ''My father told me I could find a perfectly satisfactory outlet for my musical ambitions by singing in the church choir.''

Brody was startled. The Charles Delacroix he knew sounded like a different person from the man Toni was describing. ''I guess it's hard to see a person objectively when you love them as much as Charles loves you. His desire to protect you probably overcame his common sense. Which must have been frustrating for you, of course, but those are natural feelings for a father, I should think.''

Once again, she stared at him as if he'd said something utterly astonishing. Finally, she shook her head and cradled her hands around her mug of coffee. "It's fascinating to see my father through your eyes. For my part, I have to say I'm still having a hard time visualizing him as a man working on the cutting edge of the legal profession."

"Well, let's not go overboard." Brody grinned. "Cutting edge might be pushing it a bit. Charles is almost eighty and semiretired, after all. But let's say that where the firm is concerned, your father is more willing to take risks than your brother. Your father can wax quite passionate about the fact that in the past, Delacroix and Associates has spent too much time defining itself simply as being different from your uncle's firm. Justin has always been so involved in the criminal side of the practice that he comes at things from a different perspective. He can't work up any enthusiasm for commercial law, so he assumes anyone working in that area must be doing it strictly for the money, not because he enjoys it."

Toni pushed her coffee mug away, her brows drawing together in a tiny frown. "It's...interesting...that you should mention Justin's boredom with the commercial side of the firm's practice. That's the second time I've heard something similar in the space of a week."

"Don't get me wrong," Brody said quickly. "Justin is a brilliant litigator, and he's going to be an excellent judge. I honestly believe that one day the Supreme Court might not be out of the question for him. But for all his brilliance, he isn't cut out to be the managing partner of Delacroix and Associates, whereas your father has done a truly impressive job in that position. It's Charles who has a clear vision for the future of the firm, and it's Charles who's the driving force behind the firm's expansion into commercial law."

"Commercial law has always been Uncle Philip's specialty, and he's never made any bones about the fact that he won't tolerate competition from my father and Delacroix and Associates," Toni said. "What does he think about Dad's sudden invasion of his territory?"

"Naturally Philip doesn't confide in me, but gossip around the bayou suggests that he's extremely unhappy. I have reason to believe that he'd like me to pack my bags and take the next available flight back to New York."

Toni looked up, her expression unexpectedly serious. "Watch your back, Brody. My father may be the man Uncle Philip really dislikes, but you're a highly visible target since you're the point man for the firm's expansion, and Philip doesn't always play fair. In my opinion, he could be a dangerous man to cross."

"So I've been warned by several people." Brody got up to prepare a fresh pot of coffee. "But Philip Delacroix would be smart not to aim any of his knives in the direction of my back. I survived eight years in a major New York law firm and made it to partner. You don't do that without learning to play hardball when you have to."

"You looked very aggressive and masculine when you said that, Brody." Toni's mouth curved into a faintly mocking smile that sent an unexpected flash of desire arrowing through him. "I bet you'd have made a great prosecuting attorney."

"You're wrong. I'd have made a lousy prosecuting attorney."

"Why?"

He shrugged. "I've never gotten over the view that the law should have something to do with truth and justice. Efficient prosecuting attorneys can't afford the luxury of being so naive."

Toni massaged Fifi's belly with her bare foot, and Brody tried not to feel jealous as the dog squirmed with sensual pleasure. "I guess you know this already," she said, "but it's not just Uncle Philip who'll be opposing your efforts to expand the client base for Delacroix and Associates. You're going to have a hard time competing with the law firms already established in New Orleans. A couple of the biggest partnerships have been going strong for a hundred years, and they don't take kindly to having their turf invaded. New Orleans can be a very closed and unfriendly society to outsiders when it chooses."

"Maybe. But I'm damn good at what I do, and word will get around. I'm going to double the client base of Delacroix and Associates before this time next year, and that's a promise you can take to the bank."

She seemed amused. "I'm glad to see that you don't have a problem with self-confidence, Brody."

"Not where my work is concerned. False modesty gets you nowhere." He held her gaze. "Are you a good singer, Toni?"

"Yes."

No hesitations and no qualifications. He liked that. He grinned. "You see?"

She laughed, acknowledging the hit. "Okay, I get your point. So, to change the subject slightly, are you commuting across the lake each day? That must be tiring after a while."

"Right now I'm commuting two or three days a week, and spending far too many nights sleeping in hotels, but I plan to rent an apartment in the city sometime soon. I don't think the firm can ever make effective inroads into the New Orleans market unless we have a presence right there in the city. In fact, I'm in the process of negotiating a lease for office space in the central business district, and I'm starting to recruit the support staff next week."

She looked at him, half amused, half genuinely admiring. "Good grief, Brody, you *are* a man who likes to challenge the opposition on their home ground."

"Yeah," he said. "I guess I've learned over the years that attack is often the best form of defense."

She drew her legs up onto the chair beneath her, pulling the T-shirt over her knees and resting her chin on her folded arms. "My brother mentioned at Aunt Mary's party that you started out as a music major in college, and that the Milwaukee Symphony offered you a job, which means you must be a really talented clarinet player. How come you ended up as a lawyer?"

"Lawyers make more money," he said with a smile. It was his standard response, so automatic that he no longer needed to think before offering it.

She looked at him thoughtfully. "I don't believe you care all that much about money."

"You're wrong," he said. "I grew up poor, and I'm here to tell you that there's nothing character building or fun about not having enough money to pay your heating bills in winter."

She might have asked him why, with a father who had been one of the richest bankers in New Orleans, he'd grown up in such a state of deprivation. Instead, she tipped her head to one side and gave him another long, considering look. Then she grinned. "I always want to be the best, too," she said.

His eyes narrowed in surprise. Then he gave her a reluctant, answering grin. "Okay," he admitted. "You've found me out. The fact that young musicians barely earn a living wage didn't have much to do with my decision to turn down the Milwaukee Symphony. The truth is, a few weeks working with the pros showed me I wasn't all that good. I was better than the average kid in the high school band, but I didn't have a huge supply of natural talent, not like you do. I was never going to be sought after by the recording companies, and the Berlin Philharmonic wasn't going to come knocking at the door, trying to recruit me. So you're right. I chose to be a first-rate lawyer rather than a second-rate musician.''

She didn't question his judgment, didn't protest that she was sure he'd been better than he thought. "How did you know you could be a first-rate lawyer?" she asked.

"Instinct, maybe. Or arrogance and a bit of luck. Before I started law school, I assumed hard work and hitting the books was all it would take to make me the best in the business. I soon realized that the law is like music, or teaching, or any other profession. You can get to be adequate, maybe even good, just by working hard. But the really great lawyers are born, not made.''

"Are you a really great lawyer, Brody?"

"Not yet. Not even close, right now. But one day, with enough experience, I believe I can be. My field of expertise is commercial law, and most of my career, so far, I've been dealing with international contract negotiations. On the surface, that may seem dry as dust, but I've discovered that there's no contract, however technical, that doesn't come down in the last resort to brokering a deal among people. Often people with diametrically opposed goals and needs. And that I'm good at.''

Laughing, she uncurled herself from the chair and helped herself to more coffee. "Now I've got you categorized, Brody. You're a masochist. You must be if you enjoy the torment of positioning yourself in the middle while the people all around you scream and yell at one another.''

"No," he said. "I enjoy being the person who stands in the middle and explains why there's no need for anyone to scream or yell.''

She quirked an eyebrow. "Is that what it's all about for you, then? A power trip?''

He'd asked himself that question a couple of times recently, especially during the last few months of his career in New York, when he'd been brokering deals that affected the oil supply of millions of people and carried investments of hundreds of millions of dollars in their wake. He had enjoyed the power rush, no denying it. But he'd enjoyed even more the certainty that his skills as a legal negotiator meant that the deals he brokered would withstand the test of time and enable all parties to the agreement to make long-term plans without fear that the deal would fall apart at any moment. People who had great creative ideas sometimes changed the world, but Brody had learned that without talented administrators and lawyers to come along and take care of the details, even the greatest and most visionary innovations could get hopelessly bogged down.

"I like to make changes in people's lives," he said finally. "If that makes me power hungry, I guess I accept the trade-off."

She cradled her coffee mug. "Is there going to be enough scope for you here in Louisiana?" she asked him. "The North Shore is developing fast, but in many ways, Bayou Beltane is still a bit of a backwater."

"That's why I'm expanding Delacroix and Associates into new areas," he said. "I believe that there's a lot of potential for the firm to be on the cutting edge of the changes that will take New Orleans into the twenty-first century."

Toni pulled a face. "You're going to have your work cut out for you, that's for sure. This house is so great, but it doesn't sound as if you're going to have much chance to enjoy it. Will you have to sell it before you even have the chance to get it fixed up the way you want?"

"I hope not." He shook his head. "I'll need to spend at least one day a week on the North Shore, and I want to spend weekends here, too. Living in a small town is a new experience for me, but I've discovered that I like it."

"Where did you grow up, Brody? Not in a small town, obviously."

"In Chicago." He usually didn't elaborate when people asked him about his childhood, but for some reason, he found himself expanding on his answer, although he still skirted around the edges of the truth. "Your aunt probably told you that my father was a banker, New Orleans born and bred, with roots in the city that go back five generations. But my mother was from Illinois—her parents had moved there from Puerto Rico—and since she had custody of me after their divorce, that's where I was raised."

She made a sympathetic noise. "It's rough for a kid to be shuttled back and forth between parents who live thousands of miles apart, especially when the cities are as different in character and climate as New Orleans and Chicago."

"I didn't do too much shuttling." Once again, Brody was surprised to hear himself acknowledge the truth. "My father was a widower who had two children from his first marriage, and he only married my mother because she was pregnant with me. Once the sexual attraction faded away, they realized they had nothing in common. As far as I can tell, the only thing about their divorce that seems to have surprised anyone is that they managed to live together for three years before they split up."

"I'm sorry..."

"Don't be." He spoke dismissively, although his father's rejection was a wound that had ached all his life. A wound that could never be healed, since his father had died four years ago, after having made it plain that he was no more interested in the grown-up Brody than he had been in the skinny, brown-eyed child. The Puerto Rican cuckoo had never found a home in the blond, blue-eyed Wagner nest.

"No wonder you reacted so strongly yesterday when I

asked if you'd be the father of my baby," Toni said. She drew in a shaky breath, visibly gathering courage to speak. "We have to talk about what I asked you at Aunt Mary's party, Brody, and this is as good an opening as I'm likely to get. I want you to know that I'm sorry for approaching you so carelessly. I should never have propositioned you without knowing anything about you or your family background. It was crass, it was stupid, and I deserved exactly the response I got from you."

She'd finally broached the subject that had been lodged precariously between them, too big to ignore, but too threatening to discuss. Her apology was generous, but Brody found that he couldn't react with equal generosity, or even with conventional politeness. She'd exposed the emotional scars left by his father's contempt and his mother's neglect, and he'd discovered that they were still painfully tender.

"The problem is that you *didn't* ask me to be the father of your child," he said, his voice clipped. "You asked me to become a sperm donor, and then get the hell out of your life. And since I grew up with an absentee father who basically gave me nothing more than his genes, I'm aware of exactly how much a kid in that situation is missing."

She didn't attempt to defend herself, just looked at him out of huge blue eyes that suddenly seemed haunted by sadness. "Is there any way for us to start over?" she asked, her hands stretching across the table in a silent gesture of appeal. "I wish we could, Brody. I have the feeling we might be really good friends if we gave ourselves a chance."

A sheen of unshed tears glittered in her eyes. She looked so vulnerable—so desirable—as she leaned toward him that Brody felt a flash of anger at his own susceptibility. He spoke coolly. "Are you sure it's a friend you're looking for, Toni?"

She drew back. "What do you mean?"

He shrugged. "You're a beautiful and sexy woman. It occurred to me that you might be planning to seduce me into fatherhood if you couldn't get me to agree willingly to impregnate you."

She recoiled, jumping up from the table so fast that her chair toppled over. "You have no right to suggest I'd do something so contemptible," she said, her voice low and furious. "I would never—*never*—deceive a man about something that important."

"God, Toni, I didn't mean—"

She didn't stop to listen to him. She ran out of the kitchen, and he rushed after her, catching up with her at the foot of the stairs. He quickly moved in front of her, standing on the first step so that he blocked her passage upstairs. "Now it's my turn to apologize. I'm sorry, Toni. What I said was way out of line."

Her gaze connected briefly with his, then dropped. "That's okay. Apology accepted."

"No, I want you to understand what was going on with me just now." He ran his hand through his hair while he searched for words. "Ever since I heard you sing in New York three years ago, you've stayed in my mind as one of the most desirable women I've ever seen. But the woman I was attracted to was *Antoinette,* the famous blues singer. She was my fantasy, a woman made out of the music, the lights, the stage and your performance. It never occurred to me that I'd find you every bit as desirable once we met in person—but I do."

She didn't say anything, and Brody put his hand under her chin, tilting her face upward so that she was forced to look at him. "I want to have sex with you, Toni, and you want to have a baby. Put those two wants together for long enough and it scares the hell out of me to think what could happen.''

"Nothing," she said huskily, her gaze locked with his. "Nothing is going to happen between us, Brody, because I realized, when you were talking about your father and how he'd never played any part in your life, that I couldn't go through with my plans. I've been justifying my urge to get pregnant by saying to myself that lots of kids end up living with a single parent, and they usually turn out fine."

She made a small, deprecating gesture. "Well, you know exactly how I've been justifying my plans because you heard all my excuses last night, at Aunt Mary's party. But listening to you talk about your absentee father in the kitchen just now, I was forced to admit that I have no right to bring a child into a family situation where I'm deliberately depriving him of half the love he's entitled to. I would love him, but that might not be enough, and I can't take the risk just because I desperately want a baby and my biological clock has moved into fast-forward."

Her voice became less and less steady as she spoke. Looking at her, Brody felt a twist of emotion in his gut, something hot and sharp that wasn't quite lust, although he was aching to take her to bed. "You don't have to give up your dream of having a baby," he said quietly. "Toni, don't look so sad. You still have plenty of time to fall in love and have a family the old-fashioned way."

"Yes, sure, I know you're right. I've allowed myself to obsess about the fact that my thirty-fifth birthday is right around the corner, and I'm acting as if it's now or never as far as having a baby's concerned. Obviously that's not true. I know there are plenty of women in their forties giving birth to healthy babies."

He found her resolute cheerfulness heartbreaking. Her eyes were bright with the tears she was determined not to shed, and her lips were soft and full, trembling slightly with the effort of keeping a smile in place. Brody knew he was watching the death of a dream, and he hated every moment of it. He traced the outline of her smile with his finger, unable to resist touching her. Her lips parted and he bent his head slowly toward her, surrendering to the inexorable pull like a magnet to its counterpart.

Last night their kiss had been hot and explosive, sexy as hell, and seriously arousing. This kiss was every bit as arousing, yet it was slower and sweeter, with a subtle new hint of intimacy. Brody slid his hands over her hips and drew her up high and tight against his chest. As their bodies fused, the sweetness of the kiss sharpened rapidly into something fiercer and more darkly passionate.

They both heard the sounds of a car pulling into his driveway at the same moment. Toni drew back, breathing heavily, her cheeks flushed and her mouth swollen from his kiss. "Brody, listen. There's a car outside, and it's stopping here."

He realized she was right. He muttered a curse as the engine cut out and he heard the sound of a car door slamming. Seconds later the front doorbell rang.

"I'll wait upstairs," Toni said, turning to go.

"Whoever it is, I'll get rid of them."

"Yes, we need to talk some more—"

The doorbell rang again and Toni fled upstairs. Muttering a fresh string of curses, Brody strode across the narrow hallway and opened the front door.

"Hi, Brody!" Foot tapping with excess energy, Shelby waited outside on his porch, a copy of the *New York Times* tucked under her arm. She looked crisp and fresh despite the soggy heat, a trick that native-born Louisianians seemed to have perfected and that Brody could only envy.

"Shelby!" He managed a smile—but only just. "It's...um...great to see you."

She laughed. "Well, aren't you going to invite me in?"

"Maybe." He gave her an exaggerated inspection. "I'm checking first to see if you're carrying a briefcase."

Chuckling, she held up her hands. "I'm innocent. Not a file or a document anywhere in sight. This visit hasn't got anything to do with work."

"Okay, in that case it seems safe to let you in." He unfastened the chain and opened the door wide. "So, how come I get the pleasure of a visit from you on a Sunday morning?"

"The nurses threw me out of Aunt Mary's room and told me not to come back to the hospital until after lunch." She gave him a sunny smile as she strolled into the hallway. "They said she's had so many visitors this morning that she's going to have a relapse if she doesn't get a few minutes of peace and quiet. Joanna and Marie have gone off to do some shopping, but I'm not in the mood to search for antiques, so I came to beg a comfortable chair and your help with the crossword."

Brody liked Shelby a lot, and appreciated the way she'd welcomed him into the tightly knit inner circle of Bayou Beltane residents. At this precise moment, however, he wished that she was in Alaska or on a remote Pacific island. Anywhere, in fact, except inside his house.

He ushered her into the living room, wondering how the hell he was going to get rid of her. Should he mention the fact that Toni was upstairs? Why was he even hesitating? How hard could it be to explain that Toni got caught in the storm without a car and that he'd offered her a bed for the night?

"How was Aunt Mary this morning?" he heard himself ask. "Doing fine, I hope."

"She's doing great." Shelby frowned. "Great, that is, apart from the stress of having Uncle Philip pat her hand and remind her at two-minute intervals that Hamilton—

that's their father—died of a heart attack when he was only in his forties. You know, Brody, I've decided that even if my grandfather hadn't been feuding with Uncle Philip since the dawn of time, I still wouldn't want to talk to Philip. He's so self-centered, it's physically uncomfortable to be in the same room with him.''

Brody perched on the arm of the sofa, listening for sounds of Toni moving around upstairs. He didn't hear any. Did that mean she didn't want Shelby to know she was here?

"How is your grandfather doing, and Father William?'' he asked, postponing any mention of Toni once again. "To be honest, I was a little worried about them last night. They looked so tired and stressed. Did somebody finally persuade them to go home?''

"My father did in the end, thank goodness, but not until about 3:00 a.m. They're all exhausted this morning, of course. Dad was just getting up when I left Riverwood an hour ago, and Grandfather was still sleeping. Uncle William, too.''

Shelby sat down in the old-fashioned wing chair by the French doors and searched in her purse for something. "Hah, found it!'' She held out a ballpoint pen with a flourish. "Okay, whiz kid, now I'm ready to take you on. I have this great feeling that today's the day I'm finally going to finish the crossword puzzle before you do.''

He should have mentioned Toni the moment Shelby walked into the house, Brody realized. But having kept silent for several crucial minutes, he couldn't find a casual way to slip the fact of her presence into the conversation.

"Brody?'' Shelby said, pen poised in midair. "Is something wrong? I'm getting the weirdest vibes from you this morning. What's up?''

There was something almost comic about the fact that he was having such a hard time explaining the simple truth that Toni was upstairs. He cleared his throat. "Your aunt's here."

"My aunt?" Shelby wrinkled her forehead in confusion. "Which aunt?"

"He means me." Toni strolled into the living room, Fifi prancing along beside her. Her bare feet made no sound on the wooden floors, and since she had nothing else to put on, she was still wearing the same black T-shirt he'd loaned her last night, and her bare legs still seemed to stretch to infinity. She looked so damn sexy that, despite Shelby's presence, Brody had to quell a strong desire to walk over to her and clamp his arm around her waist in a primitive male gesture of possession.

Toni, on the other hand, didn't so much as glance at him. "Hi, Shel," she said, curling gracefully onto the sofa and sending a casual wave in her niece's direction. "Nice to see you again. I didn't know you and Brody were such good friends."

"Toni!" Shelby sprang to her feet, grabbing for her purse, pen and puzzle and missing all three. "What in the world are you doing here?" she asked, scrabbling around on the floor, collecting sections of newspaper and ramming spilled objects back into her purse. "No, forget I asked that. It's none of my business what you're doing here. I'll get out and leave you two alone. I'm sorry to have butted in. I didn't think—"

Brody finally got his sense of humor back. Laughing, he knelt down to help retrieve her scattered belongings. "Shelby, sit down and shut up for two seconds, will you, please? There's no reason for you to rush out of here like Road Runner. Toni spent the night at my house because her car broke down and she had nowhere else to stay, that's all."

"Oh." Shelby's gaze switched doubtfully from Brody to Toni and back again. She didn't seem entirely convinced that her presence was welcome. "Well, if you're sure I'm not interrupting anything...?"

Toni continued to avoid Brody's eyes. "Yes, of course you interrupted something," she said, giving Shelby a teasing smile. "The truth is, Brody and I were wrapped in each other's arms, exchanging madly passionate kisses, when you rang the doorbell. And the fact that you arrived when you did is the only reason we aren't curled up in his bed, right this minute, having wild, red-hot sex."

Shelby laughed, but there was still a trace of uncertainty in her expression. "You're kidding me, right?"

Toni's eyes opened very wide. "No, Shelby, I'm telling you the absolute truth. Brody and I can't seem to keep our hands off each other."

Brody felt a chill ripple up and down his spine. By God, she'd told the exact truth, word for word, and managed to make it sound like a complete lie. A frightening talent, he thought grimly. Another thought immediately rushed in. How much of what she'd told him earlier had been the same sort of truthful lie?

Shelby, however, seemed totally persuaded by Toni's performance. She sat down again, embarrassment fading. "Okay, I get the picture. This was strictly a sleepover of convenience."

"*Convenience* is the last word I'd use to describe what happened to me last night," Toni said, and once again, Brody was aware of the subtle double meaning. "In fact, you're a lifesaver, Shel. I got soaked in the rainstorm last night, and my clothes are ruined. Brody's found me this T-shirt to wear, but my shoes are coming apart in three different places, and he can't help me there, so I'm trapped. Without shoes, I can't even go out to buy new stuff. Could you do me a big favor and make a run to the nearest discount store on my behalf? I need you to buy me a pair of shorts and some sort of a top and a pair of sneakers. Almost anything will do that's in my size. It doesn't have to make a fashion statement, I just need something respectable to put on so that I can go and pick up my car from the repair shop and visit with Aunt Mary before I go back to New Orleans.''

"I can go shopping for you if you want," Shelby said. "But if you don't mind wearing castoffs, I happen to have an entire plastic bag full of clothes in my trunk. I've been meaning to donate it to Goodwill for the past three weeks and never got around to dropping it off. We're close enough to the same size that there must be something you could find to wear. And you don't have to worry that it's grungy or anything. Everything was laundered before it went in the bag.''

"That's great!" Toni exclaimed. "Exactly what I need. Except for shoes, which might be a problem.''

"There are a couple of pairs of shoes in the bag. What size do you wear?''

Toni extended her foot. "Seven medium.''

"And I wear seven-and-a-half," Shelby said. "But that shouldn't be too much of a problem. I know for sure I put in a pair of sandals that pinched my toes, so they should be just right for you. I'll go fetch the bag and you can go through it in here. Pick out whatever you want.''

"Let me bring the bag in," Brody said, standing up. "It might be heavy.''

Shelby shook her head. "Thanks, but it's not that heavy, and there's a sack of Marie's clothes in the trunk, too, and you won't recognize which is which.''

"Would it matter?''

"Yes, because Marie's so petite, none of her stuff would fit Toni. It won't take me a minute and I'll be right back." She laughed as she walked toward the door. "And don't start any of that mad, passionate kissing stuff again while I'm gone.''

The front door closed behind her, and Toni turned quickly to Brody. "I know what you're thinking," she said.

"I doubt it."

"Shelby was embarrassed and uncomfortable. She felt that she was butting in, so I did what needed to be done to make her feel more at ease." Toni paced the room, long legs flashing. "I'm a performer, Brody. I've been trained not just to project my singing voice but to create illusions, and that's what I did for Shelby. I created an illusion so that she wouldn't feel she'd intruded where she wasn't welcome."

"And is that what you did for me, Toni? Created an illusion when you kissed me so that I wouldn't feel threatened, wouldn't feel that I was being set up as a living, breathing sperm-producing factory?"

She swung around, outrage in every tense line of her body. "No," she said. "I didn't perform for you, Brody, not once. Everything that happened between us was from the heart. Believe me, if I'd been turning in a performance, I'd have done a much more convincing job than—" She broke off. "We can't talk now. Shelby's coming back."

Brody wasn't sure whether he ought to feel relieved or sorry. He did know that Toni had been absolutely right about one thing: if Shelby hadn't arrived when she did, he and Toni would have spent the morning in his bed, making love.

Who was he kidding, Brody reflected wryly. There was no ambivalence to his feelings, none at all. Despite the many reasons why it was a terrible idea for him to get involved with Toni Delacroix, he wished like hell that his good friend Shelby hadn't chosen this particular Sunday morning to pay him a visit.

CHAPTER SIX

DECKED OUT IN SANDALS, a pair of faded cotton shorts and a bright yellow shirt rescued from Shelby's sack of Goodwill donations, Toni slipped quietly into her aunt's hospital room, Shelby following in her wake. The blinds had been adjusted to stop the sun shining directly on Mary's face, and in the dim light, the room looked stark and dreary. The hospital bed dominated the small room, and the only sounds were the ominous beeping of electronic monitors and the faint rumble of Mary's breath.

Their aunt was a woman of sturdy build, but the IVs, monitors and other medical paraphernalia reduced her to a frightening appearance of fragility. Shelby and Toni exchanged unhappy glances across the bed. There was a long, shallow gash on Mary's cheek, surrounded by a multihued bruise, which she must have gotten when she tumbled off her chair at her birthday party. Toni found the violent-looking cut almost more disturbing than the tubes going into her aunt's nose and the electronic recording devices taped to her arms and fingers. The bruises seemed a violation of her aunt's gentle spirit.

She and Shelby stood at Mary's bedside for no more than a minute before their aunt's eyes fluttered open. Her head happened to be turned toward Toni, and she gave a weak smile. "Antoinette..." Her voice faded, then gathered strength. "It's nice to see you."

"Shelby's here, too," Toni said, reaching around the IV stands so that she could hold her aunt's hand. "We brought you some flowers, but I can see a few other people already had the same idea.''

Mary managed another faint smile as her gaze flickered along the shelf crammed with colorful floral arrangements. "Everyone knows I love...flowers." She turned her head slowly, encumbered by the tubes inserted into her nose. "Shelby...so glad you're here. And you brought freesias and columbines, my favorites. Thank you." She reached out to take the flowers, but her hand fell before she grasped them. Her voice drifted off, and her eyes closed.

"She looks worse than she did this morning," Shelby whispered. "She didn't keep dozing off when I was here earlier."

"She's probably woozy from the drugs they're giving her." Toni spoke with a lot more confidence than she felt.

Biting her lower lip, Shelby stared at the equipment monitors. "Do you know what they're recording? Are those green lines supposed to jiggle up and down as much as that?"

"I guess so, or else a nurse would have come in to check." Toni stared with equal lack of comprehension at the screens. "These machines are all hooked up to the nurses' station, aren't they?"

"They must be."

"Don't worry." The intrusion of Mary's soft voice startled them both. "I'm fine," she said. "Just tired, and very sleepy."

"Then we'll leave you to rest," Toni said, bending over to kiss her aunt's forehead. "We only stopped by to let you know that we're thinking about you—"

"And we're looking forward to having you home again real soon," Shelby added. "I'll come back and visit tomorrow, when you're feeling stronger."

"No, don't go," Mary said, her head shifting on the

pillow as her gaze darted from Shelby to Toni and then back again. "I have to talk to you...something I need to say."

As Mary spoke, the blips on one of the monitors started to sound with increasing frequency. Shelby shot an alarmed look at Toni before taking her aunt's hand and leaning closer to the bed. "We're listening, Aunt Mary, but maybe you should wait until you're feeling better."

"No, this is important." A line of sweat had started to bead across Mary's forehead.

As unobtrusively as she could, Toni maneuvered herself to the head of the bed and pressed the call button to summon a nurse. She smoothed a limp white strand of hair off her aunt's forehead. "Look, you mustn't worry about anything, Aunt Mary. What do you want to talk to us about? Are you worried about Uncle William? Don't be. You know we'll make sure he's being looked after properly and getting enough rest—"

"Not William..." Mary started to cough and gasp.

It was horrible to watch her aunt's pain. Where the hell was the nurse? Toni wondered, giving the call button another push. "If there's something you want me or Shelby to do, just tell us what it is and consider it done."

"My father's files," Mary said hoarsely. "I want you to destroy them."

Toni stared at her aunt, so surprised by the nature of the request that for a moment she didn't quite grasp what Mary was asking. Then she realized that Mary was talking about Hamilton's old files, the ones Dennis had just returned. How bizarre, Toni thought. Why in the world was Mary worrying about Hamilton's old papers at a time when so many other things ought to have seemed more important?

Disturbed by Toni's silence, Mary reached out and clutched her wrist. "You and Shelby are young, so you think the past doesn't matter. But you're wrong, Toni. The past sometimes holds the power to cause terrible damage to innocent people. Promise me you won't start digging around, uncovering things that would be better left buried. Promise me, Toni. You, too, Shelby.''

If Mary had wanted to inspire intense curiosity about exactly what Hamilton's scribbled notes actually meant, she couldn't have chosen a more effective way of doing it, Toni reflected wryly. But looking at her aunt's ravaged face and trembling hands, she knew there was only one possible response to her aunt's plea. ''Of course we won't do anything at all that would make you unhappy, Aunt Mary. We wouldn't try to uncover information that would hurt or embarrass anyone in the family.''

Mary's breath came out on a frazzled sigh. ''And you'll destroy Hamilton's files?'' she persisted.

''Of course we will,'' Shelby said gently, smoothing the pillow and helping her aunt to lie down again. ''Nobody's looked in those files for almost sixty years, so I guess we can be fairly confident there's nothing there that we're likely to need in the near future.'' She smiled reassuringly. ''Now, you have to promise us that you're going to stop worrying about something so unimportant and concentrate on getting better.''

A nurse hurried into the room, carrying a tray of medications. ''Now, what's goin' on with you, Miz Mary? Why are you lettin' these young ladies get you all excited?'' She reached for the blood pressure cuff and wrapped it expertly around Mary's arm. ''We just got you all nice an' relaxed, and now you're overexcited again.''

''We'll go,'' Toni said to the nurse. She closed her hand around her aunt's fingers and squeezed gently. ''Now, remember, Aunt Mary, you've promised Shelby and me that you're not going to worry about anything except getting better. And in exchange, we're not going to make any inquiries into the subject you were talking about. Do we have a deal?''

Mary smiled feebly, her eyes closing. "Deal."

"Goodbye, Aunt Mary." Shelby rested her hand lightly against her aunt's bruised cheek.

"Could we have a word with you when you're finished taking my aunt's blood pressure?" Toni asked the nurse.

"Sure thing, I'll be right with you. Miz Mary and I just have a couple more things we need to take care of to help her feel better."

Toni and Shelby stopped at the nurses' station and exchanged puzzled glances. "What a strange conversation," Shelby said. "What in the world do you think that was all about?"

"I haven't the first clue."

"How did Aunt Mary even know about the files?"

Toni frowned, thinking. "We were standing in the parlor quite close to her when I was telling you about them," she said. "Aunt Mary must have overheard what I was saying to you. There's no other way she could have known that I had her father's files, or that I was planning to hand them over to you."

"It doesn't seem rational for her to be obsessing about something so...irrelevant when she's so ill. Maybe the medication is doing strange things, like distorting her sense of time."

"She didn't seem disoriented," Toni pointed out. "Tired, and in pain, but she seemed quite lucid when she was talking about the consequences of letting the past intrude into the present."

Shelby glared at a painting of an overblown iris on the wall. "Do you remember exactly what you and I were talking about right before she fainted?"

"No," Toni said. "Not the precise details. Mary's heart

attack scared me so much it's wiped everything else clean out of my mind.''

"We were talking about Rafael Perdido's trial, and the fact that he was killed while in prison," Shelby said. She was obviously struck by a sudden thought, and she stared at Toni, appalled. "Aunt Mary must have known before now that Perdido was killed, right? I mean, what I said couldn't have come as a shock to her, could it? A big enough shock to cause a heart attack?''

Toni thought for a minute, then shook her head. "No, that's not possible. The trial was reported at length in the local newspaper, and it must have been a daily topic of conversation at Riverwood. In fact, knowing what family dinners are like at Riverwood, I'm guessing Mary and William were bored witless each night listening to Hamilton go over the details of the case with Charles and Philip.''

"That's true." Shelby visibly relaxed.

"Besides, although Aunt Mary's incurably tender-hearted, I can't imagine that she's going to have a heart attack because you said something to remind her that sixty years ago a man who did odd jobs around Bayou Beltane was convicted of murder.''

"You're right. Even if she did overhear what I was saying, her heart attack must have been coincidence." Shelby went back to staring at the iris, her foot tapping as she spoke. "But don't you think it's weird that the very first time she sees us after her heart attack, she asks us to destroy Hamilton's files?''

"Sure I find it weird. But we don't know why she asked that, or what it is in the files that she doesn't want revealed. We're assuming that the murder trial of Rafael Perdido is the piece of the past she doesn't want us to explore just because we happen to find it an intriguing case. But Aunt Mary probably has no interest in that at all. When you think of it, why would she? On the other hand, there could be a dozen scandals buried in those files that don't mean a thing to me but might be important to people of Aunt Mary's generation—if the material ever came to light.''

"Which I guess it won't, since the files will all be destroyed." Shelby sighed. "The lawyer in me hates to think of so many important papers getting shredded, even if they are sixty years old.''

Toni didn't say anything, and Shelby looked up. "You *are* going to destroy those papers, aren't you, Toni? I mean, you promised Aunt Mary you would.''

"I didn't promise to destroy the files," Toni said, acutely aware that her exchange with Aunt Mary was the second time in the space of a few hours that she'd deliberately set out to create an impression that amounted to a lie. "And don't look so horrified, Shel. As far as you're concerned, you're off the hook, ethically speaking. You've never laid eyes on the files, and you don't have possession of them, so you can't destroy them.''

"But you're not off the hook," Shelby said. "You have the files.''

"Yes, I do. But what I promised Aunt Mary was that I wouldn't start digging around, trying to uncover the past. And I won't. I don't intend to open Hamilton's files again as long as Mary is alive, much less discuss the contents with anyone. But I can't just go home and shred those files because they *may* contain details of some scandal that Mary is too kindhearted to want revealed. You know how sweet and naive she and William are. Her definition of a horrible, earth-shattering family scandal is probably that Uncle William once kissed a girl before he went into the seminary. Heck, Shelby, those files need to be preserved. Even I found some of the stuff Hamilton wrote fascinating, and you know I'm the last person to get caught up in family history."

"Well, I guess you have a point." Shelby still sounded doubtful.

"I know it isn't a perfect solution," Toni said quietly. "But you know what, Shel? I've discovered that life rarely presents us with clear-cut choices. Sometimes we just have to muddle along, trying to decide what's the lesser of two evils. And I've decided that keeping those files locked away, unread, is the best way to honor Aunt Mary's request without vandalizing a piece of family history."

"Here comes the nurse," Shelby said, sounding relieved to have an excuse to change the subject. Toni sighed. She knew that she'd slipped a little bit off the pedestal where Shelby liked to keep her, and she wondered if maybe she should have taken the easy way out and agreed to destroy Hamilton's files. After all, a week ago she hadn't even known they existed.

She stood back and let Shelby check with the nurse concerning their aunt's progress. Shelby was asking question after question, her features animated and her eyes lively with intelligence. No way her niece was going to leave the hospital without understanding what every blip on every machine meant. She was still so idealistic and enthusiastic and...young, Toni thought, torn between envy and a touch of cynicism. Shelby still believed in right and wrong, good and evil, love and hate, a world full of black-and-white choices. It had been a long time since Toni had managed to fit her world—or her emotions—into such neat, clearly defined compartments.

The doors of the elevator parted to reveal her brother Justin and her uncle Philip. Now, there were a couple of relatives for whom she felt entirely mixed emotions, Toni reflected. And yet, although her feelings toward each of them were confused, she knew that she loved and admired Justin, despite the fact that he often provoked her, whereas she felt neither love nor admiration for her uncle.

Despite the heat, Philip was dressed in an old-fashioned linen suit, complete with his trademark bow tie. Justin looked as close to informal as he ever got in a white cotton knit shirt and immaculately pressed khaki slacks. He and Shelby exchanged greetings before he turned to Toni with a friendly smile. "Hey, little sister, what a nice surprise. It has to have been years since I've had the pleasure of seeing you two days in a row."

"Dare we hope that next time she won't wait for someone in the family to have a heart attack before she condescends to spend a night on this side of the lake?" Philip delivered his comment with a beaming smile that did nothing to remove its sting.

"You can hope," Toni said, smiling just as broadly. "There's no charge for hoping."

Philip blinked, then acknowledged Shelby's presence with a courtly inclination of his head. He saved his warmest smile for the nurse. Consummate politician that he was, Philip never forgot that every vote counted. As a senator, he'd been wooing his constituents for so long that it was second nature to him by now.

He automatically noticed the nurse's name tag and made a point of speaking to her directly. "Lucille, Ah want you to know we're all real grateful to you and the fine staff of this hospital for takin' such good care of my sister. How's she doin' today?" Philip's speech slipped into good ole Southern country boy without a moment's hesitation. Political campaigns weren't won in Louisiana by people who sounded as if they'd had all the juice frozen out of them by spending too long mingling with the Yankees up in the cold wastes of the north.

"She's comin' along real well," the nurse said. "We're all real pleased with how she's doin'."

Toni left Philip to earn campaign points with the nurse and tapped her brother's arm, delighted that she was at last going to get a chance to speak with him alone. "Justin, we need to talk," she said, keeping her voice low and very aware that Philip was the last person she wanted to overhear this conversation with her brother.

"Of course," he said, catching the note of seriousness in her voice at once. "Let's find a quiet corner."

"Shelby, can you give me five minutes with your father?" Toni asked, drawing her niece away from Philip, who was now exerting campaign charm on a trio of nurses' aides and a janitorial assistant, as well as Lucille. "It's kind of important."

"Sure. I'll wait for you downstairs in the gift shop. I noticed they had some cute baby clothes and I need to stock up on gifts." Shelby's expression hovered between bewilderment and wistfulness. "It seems like half my friends from law school got married the day after they graduated and now they're all having babies or planning to get pregnant. What happened to all those career women from the eighties who were held up to us as role models, that's what I want to know?"

"They're taking family leave," Toni said lightly, suppressing a now familiar pang of longing. Over the past few months she'd got used to the fact that when you wanted to get pregnant, the entire world suddenly seemed full of references to birth and babies. "Coming, Justin?" she asked, casting a wary eye toward Philip, anxious to get away before her uncle turned his attention away from politicking and back to them.

"Sure. Let's try the lounge, shall we? It'll be easier to talk there."

They had the visitors lounge to themselves. Finally!

Toni thought. At times over the past week, she'd begun to wonder if she'd have to camp outside her brother's office door in order to get a word alone with him.

"What's up?" Justin asked, pulling out a chair for her. "Is there a problem with Aunt Mary? Something the nurse wasn't telling us?"

"No, this isn't about Mary. When Shelby and I saw her just now, she seemed tired and frail, but nothing worse, fortunately. Justin, I need to be quick, because I don't want Uncle Philip to come in and interrupt us. I don't want him to hear what I'm about to tell you. I received some information at the beginning of this week that came to me from a source I'd prefer not to disclose, and it basically concerns—"

"Philip just came into the lounge," Justin said quietly.

Toni swallowed a scream of frustration and lowered her voice to a murmur. "Justin, pay attention, because this is important. I need to talk with you. I don't care if you have to blow off the governor of the State of Louisiana and his entire cabinet. Meet with me tomorrow at Chanson Triste. Three o'clock. Be there."

"Yes, of course, but what's this—"

She interrupted him with a swift kick under the table. She hadn't turned to look at her uncle, but an odd sensation of uneasiness prickled at the nape of her neck, and somehow she felt quite sure that Philip was straining to hear what she was saying. Acting on gut instinct rather than logic, she leaned toward her brother, deliberately raising her voice just enough to be sure that Philip would hear.

"Look, Justin, I need your help. I've never asked for legal advice from anyone in Dad's office, but the IRS has been hounding me for weeks, and I can't get them off my back. I need you to meet with me. Is that too much to ask?"

Justin's eyes narrowed. "I'll help if I can, but Brody Wagner would be much more likely to know something about a tax matter—"

"No," she said, getting to her feet. "I'm not taking this outside the family. I need to talk to you, Justin." She hoped like hell Justin had got the message she was trying to convey about the need both for urgency and secrecy, and that his mention of Brody's name had just been his way of playing along.

A visit from Brody Wagner would be all she needed to ruin her week, Toni thought. Her feelings toward Brody were so confused that she didn't plan to meet with him again until she had at least some handle on how she actually felt about him. Right now, she was so darn conflicted that she turned hot with embarrassment at the mere mention of his name. The knowledge that she was drawn to him physically in a way that was very different from the mild attraction she usually felt toward the men in her life didn't make her ambivalence any easier to sort out. Brody had blown away her assumption that she was past the age when a man could induce a storm of desire just by standing near her or giving her a faint, crooked smile, Toni reflected with rueful self-mockery.

"Well, if you really think it's necessary for us to meet, I guess I can spare half an hour or so," Justin said.

"Thanks. I'll count on seeing you at three." She repeated the meeting time and turned toward the door, pretending to be slightly miffed at Justin's obvious reluctance to meet with her.

She gave what she hoped was a convincing start when she saw Philip standing only a couple of feet away from her. "Uncle Philip! I hadn't realized you were here."

He smiled with the sort of insincere charm she would have expected, making it impossible for her to guess whether or not he believed her hastily improvised ploy about needing to consult with Justin concerning a tax battle with the IRS.

"I'm sorry to interrupt your tête-à-tête with your brother," Philip said smoothly, "but it seems that Dr. Hummel is expected at any moment and I felt sure Justin would want to consult with him concerning Mary's progress. Alas, I become so overwrought when I see my poor sister looking so frail and helpless that I neglect to ask the most obvious questions."

"Yes, of course I want to speak with the doctor." Justin walked briskly toward the door. "I'll see you tomorrow afternoon, then, Toni. Make sure that you have all the relevant paperwork ready and waiting. Bye for now."

"Goodbye," Toni said. "See you." She headed for the elevator before Philip could subject her to any more of his fake smiles and false charm. Her uncle was best taken in very small doses, she decided. Too much contact with Philip Delacroix could leave you with a very nasty taste in your mouth.

CHAPTER SEVEN

AFTER A FIFTY-YEAR acquaintance, Justin Delacroix was still trying to make up his mind how he felt about the city of New Orleans. The organized, workaholic side of him despised the potholed streets, the decaying splendor of its old buildings and the general air of indolence that hung in the air as luxuriantly as the scent of withered magnolia blossoms. Another side of him, repressed for most of his life, responded to the brilliant colors, the tropical lushness, and the chaotic pulse of life marching to an erotic, sensual drummer.

This afternoon, after he had interrupted a particularly busy schedule in response to Toni's urgent summons, the workaholic side of him was in charge. He failed to find anything amusing in the congested traffic and the chronic inability of the city to cope with its parking problems. Compelled to leave his car a good six blocks away from Chanson Triste, he strode along the crowded sidewalks toward the club, swearing beneath his breath.

He dodged tourists and hustlers, the sights and sounds of the Quarter familiar enough that he scarcely registered them, although he spared a quick smile and a couple of dollars for the young boy—no more than nine or ten—tap-dancing on the sidewalk. The child's presence summed up his conflicted feelings about the city in a nutshell. The kid was talented, and obviously enjoying himself. As another plus, he was probably raking in a nice supplement to his family's income. But when school started next month, Justin had an uneasy suspicion that if he came back to this same street corner, the boy would still be there, dancing his heart out for the passing tourists.

Increasing his pace despite the afternoon heat, Justin lifted his impeccably starched white shirt cuff and checked the time. Two-forty-five, and he really needed to be back in Bayou Beltane by five. He had a brief to go over with his father, followed by a dinner date with some woman whose name he now couldn't remember. Deanna? Debbie? Dolores? The fact that he couldn't remember her name was indicative of how little he wanted to spend time with her.

He scowled at the prospect of another evening wasted on a pointless date. Sometime in the past year his two middle daughters had realized how pathetically empty his social life was, and they'd launched a full-scale campaign to find him a new wife. He appreciated the kindness of their intentions; it was the endless parade of boring women he couldn't stand. He knew he should have refused to go out on this dinner date with Deanna-Debbie-Dolores, but Marie and Shelby had gone to so much trouble to set him up for the "accidental" meeting at the country club last week that he didn't have the heart to disappoint them.

Hot and frazzled, he arrived at the intersection of Giramond and Royal. The facade of Chanson Triste was narrow, but the door was elegantly painted in black, highlighted with fresh gold trim, and the windows were so clean they sparkled in the sun. Well-tended window boxes cascaded ivy toward the sidewalk. Since his last visit— more than three years ago, Justin was ashamed to realize—waist-high pedestals had been placed on the sidewalk, supporting pewter urns overflowing with tropical vines and cleverly creating the illusion of a more spacious entrance to the club. The effect was both attractive and decidedly upscale. If appearances were anything to go by, after its struggle to get launched five years ago, Chanson Triste was starting to enjoy real financial success. Ignoring the sign on the door that read Closed, Justin pushed on the panel and walked in.

In the dim light of the dining room, he heard Toni before he saw her. She was singing "Amazing Grace," her voice soaring with rich, full-bodied perfection from one familiar note to the next. Justin turned toward the small stage, keeping quiet so that she wouldn't notice him. He realized that his spine was tingling as she reached the final bars of the hymn, and he swallowed over a sudden tightening in his throat. When his sister sang secular music, her style was sultry and her voice took on the deep, throbbing sensuality that was the hallmark of a great blues singer. When she sang gospel music, it seemed that the whole quality of her voice changed into something more lyrical yet even more powerful. Justin had almost forgotten the startling range of his sister's voice and the purity of sound she was capable of producing.

The last note died away, and Toni turned to her accompanist, putting down the mike on top of the piano. "What do you think, Pudge? Did we finally get it right?"

"It took a few tries, but I do believe the Lord his own self would like how you sang that time, girl."

Toni smiled. "But the Lord's a lot easier to please than you are, Pudge. What do *you* think?"

"You done fine, girl. Real fine."

Her smile widened with relief. "Well, now I know it's okay. Thanks, Pudge." She bent and kissed the pianist's angular black cheek, then turned, tossing her long, honey-colored hair back from her face in an impatient gesture that was familiar to Justin from her childhood. He stepped forward, out of the shadows, suddenly anxious to talk with her.

She finally noticed that he'd arrived. "Justin, you're here! I should have known you'd be early!" She walked toward him, her body as supple and fluid as her voice. She was tall, but wearing sneakers, as she was now, she barely reached his nose. Justin felt a sudden sharp longing to put his arms around his sister and hug her tight. He did nothing so out of character, of course. Instead, he smiled and said politely how much he'd enjoyed listening to her sing.

"Thank you. I'm glad you liked it. We're thinking about serving a brunch on Sundays once tourist season starts, and Pudge's trying to convince me that it wouldn't be hokey to throw in a set of gospel songs. I'm still mulling the idea over."

"Pudge has my vote. You gave me goose bumps just now, and I'm a hard sell."

She pulled a face, but he sensed that she was pleased by the compliment. "Come into my office, Justin. Mondays we're officially closed, but the wait staff are about to set up for a private party, a wedding reception, actually, and we'll never get a moment's peace and quiet out here." She grinned. "The bride's daddy has got big bucks and her momma's got no taste, so you can imagine what a production this reception is turning out to be."

She was already moving away, too full of energy to stand still. From the time she was a teenager, the prospect of an upcoming performance had always electrified her, leaving her edgy, restless—and sheer dynamite once she got out on stage. Along with the rest of the family, Justin had always tried to calm Toni down instead of accepting her tension for the creative force it was. Looking back, he wondered how they could all have been such fools. How was it possible that they'd had somebody so talented in their midst without recognizing it? Instead of nurturing her, they'd tried to quash her gifts, gloss over her talent, ignore the way she stood out from the crowd. In retrospect, he couldn't understand why they hadn't been bustin' their buttons with pride.

Justin reached out and grabbed his sister's wrist, halting her in her tracks. "Toni, wait a minute!"

"Yes?"

"I just wanted to tell you how proud I am of all you've achieved, Toni." He stumbled to a halt, searching for words. In court, his skill as an impassioned, eloquent speaker was one of his greatest strengths. When it came to expressing his feelings to people he cared about, he was a rank amateur. "It must have been tough for you, growing up surrounded by family members who are all basically tone deaf. We gave you...I gave you...no support. I want you to know how much I regret that."

She looked at him thoughtfully, her eyes more gray than blue in the muted light. "Thanks, Justin, but I wasn't nearly as isolated as you seem to think. You forget that your ex, Madeline, loves music, and she always took an active interest in my career. And my mother—your stepmother—was an excellent pianist, almost professional standard, in fact."

"I never realized that."

She gave a quizzical smile. "Dad never paid any attention to my mother's talent, so why would you? That's the interesting thing about the Delacroix family. Dad has laid down the law about how we're all supposed to view ourselves, and anyone who doesn't fit in just gets ignored. Or squeezed and pressured and twisted until we conform to what Dad has decreed is the acceptable Delacroix image."

"You're always too hard on Dad," Justin said. "You've allowed your teenage quarrels with him to cloud your judgment. He was in his forties when you were born, and that made for a bigger generation gap than usual."

"No, you're wrong, Justin. My differences with Dad aren't just generational, they're much more than that. I admire Dad, but I see him for what he really is—a proud, honorable, stubborn man who can't bear his family to do anything that's in the least unconventional. A man who's frightened of deep emotion, afraid to let his children get too close—"

Toni broke off in midsentence. "That's odd," she said, more quietly. "I never realized I knew that about Dad until this minute, but it's true all the same. Dad has never let *any* of us get close to him emotionally. Not me, of course, and not Remy, either. But he's even held you at arm's length to a certain extent."

Justin shook his head, smiling faintly. "You think all emotional bonds require fireworks, Toni. Sometimes the deepest and most important feelings can't be easily expressed."

"Maybe." She shrugged. "But if you can't express them, what use are they except to give you ulcers?"

He laughed at that, and Toni joined in. "Okay," she conceded. "So I tend to be a bit more expressive than other people.... But that's a reaction to the way I grew up, surrounded by relatives who've made an art form out of hiding what they're feeling. I know I couldn't stand living the way my father and mother did, or the way you and Madeline—"

She broke off, then quickly resumed speaking. "My father's relationship with my mother was polite and dignified, but so cool I often wondered how they managed to produce me. The truth is that when I'm around Dad for any length of time, I always find myself wondering why love and intimacy scare him so much."

Justin wanted to defend their father, but he had no idea what to say. Toni already understood that Charles wasn't cold or passionless, he simply refused to let his feelings show. The worst of it was, Justin had begun to see himself repeating his father's mistakes. His five children respected him, even loved him, but they didn't confide in him or treat him as a friend. And his relationship with his former wife, Madeline, had been such a disastrous desert of unexpressed feelings and miscommunication that it made his father's two marriages appear successful by comparison.

Pudge provided a welcome diversion to Justin's gloomy thoughts by strolling toward the exit, tipping his hand to Toni and Justin as he passed. "I'll be back at six, Toni, when the rest of the band gets here. Gotta be home to give my baby girl her bath or her momma will get real mad."

"And nobody wants to make Maya mad if they can help it." Toni chuckled. "Give Josie a big kiss from me, Pudge. Tell her I have a new toy for her."

"You're spoilin' her, girl." Turning to Justin, Pudge rolled his eyes. "That child of ours thinks *Toni* is another word for present. Anyway, it's good seein' you again, Mr. Delacroix, but it's been too long since you came to hear your sister sing. You need to come hear her again real soon." He grinned, sending Toni a look of mingled respect and friendship. "Now that she's been hangin' with me for a coupla years, she's gettin' to be a halfway decent singer."

"You're right," Justin said. "It's been much too long since I heard Toni sing. But from the look of things around here, you and the club seem to be doing just fine without my patronage."

Pudge held up crossed fingers. "We're surviving, and in this economy, that ain't bad." He gave another casual salute, then left, humming cheerfully beneath his breath.

Toni turned and headed once more toward her office. "Justin, we have a lot to talk about, so let's get started. But first things first, what would you like to drink?"

"Iced tea would be great."

Toni nodded to the man polishing glasses behind the bar. "Bring us a couple of iced teas, would you, Miguel?"

Justin had never been in his sister's office before, and he sat down across the desk from her, surprised at how neat and organized everything was. She caught him eyeing her computer, and she laughed. "What did you think, big brother? That I kept my accounts and tax records on the back of old menus? I employ thirty-three people, not counting contract cleaners, which is probably almost as big a payroll as Delacroix Associates."

"Almost. Although the office Brody's opening in New Orleans will take us up to forty full-time employees as soon as he completes his hiring." Justin sighed. "I should know more about your career than this, Toni. You're my sister and I…care…about you. Where did we go wrong? How come we've done such a lousy job of keeping up with each other's lives?"

"You're eighteen years older than I am," she suggested. "I think that must have a lot to do with it. When I was learning to walk, you were trying to decide which girl to date for the Cotillion. You and Madeline were married, with Beau and Jax on the way, before I was in first grade. When I was a little kid, you were more like an uncle than an older brother."

"True, but once we both got older, the gap in our ages should have closed."

"How could it? Your life was wrapped up in the law. I was wrapped up in my music, and we're both obsessive-compulsive by nature. It was real easy for us to develop acute cases of tunnel vision."

"But we lived in the same house!" Justin protested. "Riverwood's big, but not that big. Looking back, it's downright strange that we allowed our lives to run on such separate tracks. How did we do that for so many years?"

Toni looked at him with an emotion that hovered between disbelief and sympathy. "Living in the same house doesn't guarantee intimacy," she said quietly. "You should know that better than most people."

Her response hit him not with the force of a blow, but with the precision of a scalpel inserted straight into the heart of a wound. Given that he had successfully ignored a talented and loving wife, Justin reflected bitterly, it was not in the least surprising that he'd also failed to pay attention to the needs and interests of his young half sister. He wondered if there was any way to make Toni understand the demons that had driven him, or if it was already too late to start building a deeper relationship with his sister, just as it was a decade too late to save his marriage.

"Work is like any other addiction," he said at last. "To begin with, it merely adds spice and interest to your life. Then you start to plan your life so that you can accommodate the addiction. Eventually, it takes over until there's nothing left except the addiction."

"Is that how you plan to spend the rest of your life, Justin? Addicted to work?"

"I hope not," he said with quiet passion. "After Madeline divorced me, I had nothing left but my work, so I just carried on even more obsessively than before. Then, sometime during the past year, it dawned on me that it's never too late to kick a bad habit, and that the stronger the addiction, maybe the more you need to cut it out of your life." He shrugged in rueful self-awareness. "These days, I'm working hard at not working so hard."

Toni was silent for a moment, then she looked up at him, smiling with a warmth that illuminated her whole face. "Don't beat up on yourself too much, Justin. If we could live our lives in retrospect, I guess we'd all do a lot better. Speaking for myself, it isn't the mistakes and the major screwups in my past that bother me so much.

What bugs me are the careful plans I've made that worked out just the way they should have done—and now I find I hate the results!''

He chuckled ruefully. "Yeah, I guess I have a few of those, too."

A knock at the door interrupted them. The bartender came in with two tall glasses of iced tea and set down the tray on Toni's desk. "Anything else I can get for you, Miz Toni? A sandwich, maybe, before the rush starts?"

Toni glanced at Justin and he shook his head. She smiled at the bartender. "No thanks, Miguel, this will be all we need."

"Sure thing, Miz Toni. You think of anything you want, you let me know. By the way, Robert said to tell you the wedding cake, it arrived from the bakery. Very big cake." His hands drew an enormous circle in the air. "It have sugar angels playing plastic harps and frosted roses that are so big, they look like cabbages. An' a fountain sendin' out jets of golden water. Very pretty, no?"

He rolled his eyes in disgust, and Toni laughed. "Real pretty, Miguel."

All the staff at Chanson Triste were appalled by the current fashion for wedding cakes that practically required a civil engineer to set them up. "I'll look forward to seeing this one," she said. "Tell Chef I'll be ready to confer with him in fifteen minutes, okay?"

"Yes, Miz Toni." Miguel left, and she glanced at her watch, reminding Justin that time was a commodity in short supply for both of them.

"We'd better get down to business," he said. "Why did you need to see me so urgently, Toni? I concluded from that odd scene at the hospital yesterday that you didn't want Philip to know what we were discussing. Which means, I guess, that whatever else this meeting is about, it's got nothing to do with your tax problems or the IRS.''

"No, I threw in that idea strictly for Uncle Philip's benefit. This conversation is supposed to be about you, Justin, not about me." Toni leaned across the desk. "Tell me how badly you want to get your appointment to the federal bench confirmed.''

"It's important to me," he admitted. "Very important, in fact.''

She stirred her tea with her straw, dragging melted ice to the surface. "Is it important because of the prestige?''

"Not just because of that." He shrugged, self-conscious at revealing his dream. "I want to put my knowledge of the law to good use, and—without being corny—I'd like to raise the integrity of legal proceedings in this state. There are a lot of people who think justice in this state is a hit-and-miss kind of thing. We need to change that perception, and I'd like to be a part of that change.''

Toni's fingers drummed on the desktop. "I'm searching for a way to break bad news tactfully, and I'm wasting time," she said finally. "So I'll get to the point, which is this. I've been told your appointment to the federal judiciary is heading for big trouble. As I heard it, you have opponents who are determined to see that your nomination isn't confirmed.''

For a moment, Justin felt as if someone had closed their hands into tight fists around his lungs and squeezed out all the air. With his personal life in a shambles, his nomination to the federal bench was the most important and exciting thing that had happened to him in years. He'd been working toward a federal judgeship for the past five years. Until this moment, however, he hadn't recognized just how much he was looking forward to changing the scope and direction of his career.

"I've got some powerful supporters, here and in Washington," he said when breathing was a bit easier. "I realize I have opponents, too, but I doubt if they have the clout to cause real trouble. What makes you think differently?"

Toni shifted in her chair, clearly uncomfortable. "Look, Justin, I'm going to give you this information as it came to me, with no explanations as to how I acquired it, and I'd appreciate you not pressing for more details, okay?"

He nodded. "Yes, of course—"

"From what I've been told, it doesn't much matter how many political supporters you have in Washington, because your opponents plan to derail your appointment before it ever reaches the Senate."

"How the hell can they do that?"

"They're going to make sure that the FBI presents an unfavorable background report on you to the Judiciary Committee."

Justin's stomach plummeted. His appointment would be killed stone dead if the FBI background report wasn't favorable. "How do they expect to do that?" he demanded tersely. "FBI agents can't be bought."

"Your opponents aren't planning to bribe anyone. They're going to lead the FBI to an incident in your professional career that will make you ineligible for a judgeship."

"However much some of my political opponents may dislike me, they're going to have a tough time finding anything in my career they can use to disqualify me," Justin said, relaxing slightly. "Don't get me wrong—it's not that I'm such a perfect human being, far from it. But the ways in which I've messed up aren't the ways that leave a black mark on your professional résumé."

Just black marks on your soul, he reflected bleakly,

thinking of Madeline and the disastrous end to their marriage.

"You're underestimating the opposition, Justin." Toni flicked her hair out of her eyes and got to her feet, too tense to stay seated. "They've already uncovered the incident they're going to use to nail you."

He went cold. "What incident is that?"

"You might have a hard time remembering the details. About five years ago you sold a hundred acres of land to a company called Louisiana Properties. You were acting on behalf of clients of yours, an elderly couple—"

"The Hendersons?" Justin asked, vaguely recalling a transaction along the lines Toni was describing. "The land was near the river, swampy, but no endangered species lived in the area. The land had been in the Henderson family for years, and they'd never had the capital to develop it. Or the energy they'd have needed to get permission to drain marshland."

"Yes, that's the transaction I mean. You sold your clients' land for half a million dollars because you assumed Louisiana Properties was buying the land in order to build houses. They had no such intention. In fact, Louisiana Properties is a subsidiary of Shoreline Exploration—"

"My God!" Justin jumped to his feet, leaning across Toni's desk. Shoreline Exploration was one of the most aggressive companies in the brutally competitive oil business. "How much would Shoreline have been willing to pay for the land?"

"Five million."

Justin slumped back in his seat, feeling sick to his stomach. He'd thrown away four-and-a-half million dollars of his clients' money. He'd held a power of attorney for the Hendersons, who were both in their eighties at the time of the deal, and in frail health. They were dead now, and probably couldn't have spent the extra money during their lifetime, anyway. But that wasn't the point. They'd trusted him, and he'd failed them because he'd been bored by the negotiation. Bored—and more than a little arrogant.

He let the guilt wash over him for a full minute before turning to Toni, his expression grim. "I suppose there's some attorney at Shoreline willing to come forward and give chapter and verse in order to make the case against me for dereliction of duty?"

"I'm sorry, Justin, but it's much worse than that. Your opponents have found a way to put the squeeze on someone inside Shoreline Exploration, and they're planning to cook the books so that it looks like you sold your clients out in exchange for taking a kickback."

Justin's hands balled into fists at the enormity of what his sister was saying. "How big a kickback?" he asked, clenching his teeth.

"Two hundred thousand dollars."

He smiled without mirth. "Well, it's good to know that my enemies don't think I can be bought cheap."

Toni didn't crack even a small answering smile. "Who *are* your enemies, Justin?"

"Do you have a couple of spare hours?" he asked wryly. "There's quite a list. I'm considered a judicial conservative and a social liberal, which means that there are plenty of days when I offend everybody."

"But you have friends, too, otherwise you'd never have been nominated. You need to call in some favors, Justin, and find a way to kill this story. Otherwise, trust me, more people than you are going to be hurt in the fallout."

"There's no way to kill this by trying to cover things up," he muttered, thinking rapidly. "If there's one thing people in public life ought to have learned over the past few years, it's that the harder you try to suppress a story, the more virulent and powerful the story becomes. I'm not going to make the mistake of mounting a massive cover-up operation to hide something that was careless but in no way criminal.''

Toni sent him a dubious glance. "I understand the principle of what you're saying, Justin, but I don't think you can sit back and count on the truth to save you. By the time your opponents have finished blackening your character, you're not going to look careless, you're going to look as if you take bribes. And the opposition is going to have the documents to prove everything they're saying. I've told you, they're putting the squeeze on someone inside Shoreline to falsify the record.''

She was right, damn it. His feet seemed set on a greasy slide that could end up costing him everything he'd spent a lifetime working to build. Justin's frustration hardened into cold, hard resolve. With Madeline gone, his reputation for professional integrity was all he had left, and he would damn well fight tooth and claw to save it.

"Maybe I should do the exact opposite of what these opponents of mine expect," he said. "Instead of calling in favors and running around as if I have something to hide, I should tell the truth about the Henderson deal to the FBI before somebody else feeds them a pack of lies.''

"You mean you would deliberately bring the Henderson case to the FBI's attention?''

"Yes." He nodded, gaining confidence in his proposed solution. "Yes, I'll tell them I've been warned that someone's trying to set me up, and that people inside Shoreline are being pressured to cook the books in regard to my role in this transaction. I'll suggest that the FBI should go into Shoreline now—immediately—and check the records of the deal before anyone can alter them." He shot his sister a quick glance. "As far as you know, the records haven't been falsified yet, have they?''

"Not as far as I know, no. Although I've been trying

to tell you about this situation for the past week, and I'm not sure what might have transpired by now."

He winced, hearing the justifiable reproach in his sister's voice. "I'm sorry I didn't get back to you earlier, Toni, but I'm trying a really tough case right now, and by the time I was through each night, I knew you'd be here at the club, starting your performance...."

His words faded into silence as he remembered the dozens of other occasions when he'd provided similar excuses to Madeline. All of them equally true, all of them equally irrelevant. He drew in a deep breath. "I should have called you," he said tersely. "If I'd set my mind to it, I could have found some way to call you."

"It doesn't matter," Toni said. "At least I've told you now, and, with luck, it won't be too late. Once the FBI is alerted to the truth, there'll be nowhere for the opposition to go with this story."

"Not even to the press," Justin said, feeling marginally more cheerful. "Nobody can create much of a scandal out of the fact that I once sold land for less than it's worth to a company that was deliberately hiding its true intentions behind a screen of dummy corporations."

"With everything that goes on in this city, that shouldn't make more than a footnote at the bottom of a local newspaper column," Toni agreed. "So I guess the only significant question left now is who is doing this to you, Justin. Who *is* the opposition?"

He grimaced. "The possibilities are so many and varied that I doubt if we'll ever know the answer to that. I've won a lot of cases that important people wanted me to lose, and lobbied for a lot of legislation that special interest groups would have preferred not to see passed. That makes for powerful enemies as well as grateful friends."

"Speaking of powerful enemies, how do you and Uncle Philip get along, Justin?"

He shot her a quick, amused glance. "That wasn't exactly subtle, Toni."

"It wasn't meant to be." His sister looked anything but amused.

"Philip and I stay out of each other's way as much as possible, and rub along quite well when we can't avoid each other."

"Would he say the same?" Toni asked. "I'm not talking about how you interact at functions like Aunt Mary's birthday party. I mean in the real world—the dirty, scruffy world that exists outside the peaceful fantasy land Aunt Mary and Uncle William have created for Delacroix family gatherings. Uncle Philip's been actively involved in state politics for longer than I've been alive. He's a state senator. He must have fingers in dozens of political pies all over the state. How does he feel about your appointment? Does he oppose it?"

His uncle associated with some people and factions Justin considered less than honorable, but he couldn't begin to visualize Philip resorting to the sort of dirty tricks and blackmail that Toni had outlined.

"Philip and I have been on opposing sides on a couple of political battles," he said. "But that wouldn't be grounds for him to pull a stunt like this. In fact, Philip's never shown much interest in issues of criminal law and criminal justice. He's much more involved in legislation that affects business, finance and commerce. He's been at the forefront of the state's campaign to attract new business, and I'm all in favor of that."

"Aren't we all?" Toni commented dryly. "Justin, just for a moment, shake loose from your conviction that all members of the Delacroix family are saints-in-waiting. Try to see Philip not as your uncle, but as a major political powerhouse with turf to defend that maybe you're threatening."

Justin frowned. "You can't tell me why you suspect him of being involved?"

"No, not without betraying a confidence. But because of the way this scam was set up, I do have valid reasons to suspect Uncle Philip of being involved. Please, Justin, go away and think long and hard about any reasons our least favorite uncle might have to be opposed to your nomination." She gave her hair an impatient shake, tossing it out of her eyes. "And stop giving me that pitying look, big brother."

"What look?"

"The one that says Toni is off on one of her wild kicks again. You need to take my warning about Uncle Philip seriously."

"I do. Believe me, I'm taking everything you've told me today very seriously." Justin walked around the desk and took his sister's hands into his. "You're misreading my expression, Toni. I was actually thinking that right now, this minute, it doesn't matter so much who's opposing me. What matters is that we neutralize their plans, and thanks to your information, I hope I'll be able to do that."

Toni's eyes met his, her gaze skeptical. They might not be as close as brothers and sisters ought to be, but she understood him well enough to know that he fully intended to find out who was behind this attempt at dirty tricks. She decided to take his words at face value and not press him for answers. "All right, Justin, if that's the way you want to handle things. Let me know when you've spoken to the FBI, will you? I'd like to be able to pass on the word to my informants that you've taken care of the situation."

"I sure will," he said. "And thank you, Toni. I really appreciate the fact that you warned me what was going on."

"You're welcome." She came out from behind her desk and hooked her arm through his. "I know you're dying to get back to Bayou Beltane, Justin, and I have to go check on the status of the wedding preparations. I'll walk you to the door."

"I wish I could stay and visit for a while," he said. "But unfortunately, you're right. I do have to get back." He surprised himself by adding, "My kids have decided that it's time for me to get married again, and they keep setting me up with all these appalling women. I'm supposed to be taking one of them out to dinner tonight, and I'm dreading it."

Toni laughed. "Poor you. What's so appalling about them?"

"Well, where should I start? Maybe with the fact that my kids seem to feel that I need a combination sex kitten and earth mother. God knows where they manage to find all these perky forty-year-olds with an overwhelming desire to hop into bed and hop out again to darn my socks."

Toni laughed again. "*Appalling* sounds like the right word." She squeezed his arm. "Anytime you want to escape, come and stay with me, big brother. I guarantee that the women I fix you up with won't want to mother you, because I don't know any women like that. Maternal instincts are in short supply in the crowd I run with."

"Lucky you." Overcoming his inhibitions, he swept her into a bear hug. "I'll look forward to seeing you next week when Aunt Mary comes home from the hospital," he said, brushing his knuckles across her cheek. "You are coming to see her again, aren't you?"

"Yes, of course."

"Good. Stop by Riverwood when you come, Toni, and stay for dinner. Dad would be thrilled. He misses you more than he'll ever admit."

She raised an incredulous eyebrow.

"Take one step toward Dad, Toni, and he'll take two steps toward you, I guarantee it."

"Maybe." She hunched her shoulders, shoving her hands into the pockets of the gauze dress she was wearing. "It's just so exhausting to be around someone who's determined to repress every darn emotion he's ever felt. He ends up making me feel guilty because I can't be as cool and controlled and repressed as he is."

Is that what his children felt around him? Justin wondered. Exhaustion and the need to repress their true feelings? God, he hoped not.

Unable to deal with that chilling possibility, he gave his sister a final smile. "Thanks again for passing on the information about my nomination being in jeopardy, Toni. I really appreciate the fact that you kept calling me, even when I didn't answer your calls."

"You're welcome." She put her hand on the small of his back to prevent him from bumping into a waiter hurrying past with a tray of wineglasses. "Go get 'em, Justin. Whoever's behind this scheme, don't let them win."

"They won't," he said. "You can count on it."

CHAPTER EIGHT

TONI WAS HALFWAY THROUGH her show on a Tuesday night in late August when she realized that Brody Wagner was sitting in the audience at a table to the right of the small stage. He was alone, nursing a tall drink, and she had no idea how long he'd been sitting there.

Her heart swooped, as if she'd suddenly developed an attack of stage fright, and for a split second she lost control of her breathing so that the showcase high A she was reaching for emerged sounding slightly thin. She quickly recovered and got to the end of the song without any more mishaps, despite the fact that her breathing still wasn't as controlled as it should have been.

Nobody in the audience seemed to have noticed her momentary lapse in concentration, but Pudge—who knew every nuance of her voice—sent her a worried glance. She smiled at him in silent reassurance, tilting her handheld mike toward him in a signal that she was fine, and ready for him and the band to segue into the introduction to her final set.

Pudge complied, and after a few words of introduction, Toni began her medley of songs from Gershwin's *Porgy and Bess.* She was too experienced a performer ever to lose total awareness of her audience, but she recognized partway through her rendition of "Summertime" that she was singing only for Brody. He was a trained musician, and she knew he would recognize any technical deficiencies in her performance, so she pulled out all the stops, giving him every ounce of her hard-won expertise along with every ounce of her natural talent. She didn't look at him, didn't acknowledge awareness of his presence in any way, but the lyrics and melodies poured out of her, liquid with intensity, flowing toward him as if the two of them were alone in the room. At the conclusion of any show, Toni always felt that she'd handed a piece of her soul to the audience. Tonight, the piece of her soul was going exclusively to Brody.

Gershwin was a perennial favorite, and the audience applauded enthusiastically when she finished, eager to hear more. As a grand finale, in tribute to the musical roots of her singing, she normally ended her performances with one of the traditional favorites that the New Orleans marching bands had made famous way back in the 1920s. At funerals for community leaders, the bands played the century-old songs, originally composed to encourage friends and neighbors of the deceased to honor his memory by dancing in the streets as the coffin was carried in procession to the cemetery.

Far from being gloomy, most of the funeral hymns were joyous songs with rousing choruses, songs that set feet hopping and provided plenty of opportunities for virtuoso jazz riffs by various players in the band. A few of the songs had such catchy melodies and rhythms that their popularity had spread far and wide across America, making them familiar to people who cared little or nothing about the rich history of New Orleans jazz and blues.

But tonight Toni knew that she wasn't going to end her show with one of the easy crowd pleasers that often brought the patrons of Chanson Triste to their feet in cheering applause. Tonight, she was going to sing her last song just for Brody.

"Thank you," she said as the applause for her Gershwin medley died down. "Tonight, for my final selection,

I'd like to sing for you one of my own particular favorites, called "All My Life." This song was made famous by Ernestine Anderson, one of the all-time jazz greats and it always gives me a special thrill to sing it."

She turned to Pudge, and then to the other members of her band, smiling, keeping up her patter for the audience, giving the band time to make the mental switch from her usual standby to this unexpected choice of a ballad. "Ready when you are, friends," she said.

Pudge gave her the nod. Toni filled her lungs and waited for her entrance, letting the soft cadences of Pudge's introduction seep through her skin and settle deep inside her. This time, she didn't bother to pretend she was singing for the audience at large.

She turned to Brody, finally letting him know that she knew he was there—that she'd known he was there all along.

She sang of loss and betrayal, hope and trust. She sang of love. Most of all, she sang with the passion and clarity of feeling that only music ever allowed her. As her voice soared from note to note, her spirits soared, too. For the brief duration of this song, she was confident of her own emotions and fully aware of her power as a woman. On the very last bar of the music, she allowed her eyes to meet with Brody's.

Perhaps it was a trick of the dimmed lights and flickering candle flames at each table, but what she read in his gaze swirled through her with the force of a whirlwind, sending her voice flying, hitting the final note of the song and then taking it on upward to an improvised high C of shattering power.

For at least ten seconds there was silence in the club, the sort of silence that almost never happened in a busy establishment serving food and alcohol to a hundred diners. Then Pudge—*Pudge!*—started to applaud, and the patrons joined in, thunderously. Flushed, exhausted and triumphant, Toni realized she'd brought her audience to its feet, after all.

She bowed in silent recognition, returned twice more to acknowledge the applause, then backed off the stage into the cramped backstage area that contained facilities for the band and her own tiny dressing room. Alone, she paced the narrow room, too wired to stand still, much less to sit down and start the mundane task of removing her makeup. For the past four weeks, she and Brody had been meeting with increasing regularity, but by mutual consent, they'd avoided invading each other's professional territory. She had never visited his new law offices, and he had never visited Chanson Triste. It was as if they both understood that they weren't ready to recognize anything more than that they enjoyed each other's company and liked to spend their free time together.

Brody's presence at the club tonight changed the whole basis of their relationship. He'd flung down a challenge, and she had to decide how she would respond to it.

A knock came at her door, interrupting her reverie, and she pulled it open without bothering to ask who was there.

Pudge walked into the dressing room. "That was some performance you turned in tonight, girl." He put a fragrant, steaming cup of chamomile tea on the dressing table. "Here's your tea, just the way you like it."

"Thanks." She stared at the cup, then resumed pacing.

"Here." Pudge picked up the cup and clasped both her hands around it. "Drink up, girl, and calm yourself down some. Man, you're really flyin' tonight."

She did as she was told, taking first a small sip and then drinking the entire cup in a ravenous gulp. The simple act of swallowing the soothing herb tea brought her down from her performance high just enough that she was able to stop pacing and focus on her partner. "I needed that," she said, putting down the cup. "Thanks for doing such a good job on that final number tonight, Pudge."

"It was my pleasure. You were something special out there tonight, girl. You want to tell me who you were singin' for? He surely does know how to set you on fire."

She avoided his gaze, slathering her face with cold cream to remove the heavy stage makeup. "I was singing for you, the audience. The usual people."

Pudge gave an inelegant snort. "You want us to try that question and answer over again?"

Another knock at the door saved Toni from having to make a more honest reply. Wiping her face with a tissue, she opened the door and found Miguel waiting on the other side. "There's a man out front wants to talk to you, Miz Toni. He says he is a friend of yours."

Occasionally fans would make a nuisance of themselves, so the rule was that the staff were never to let anyone backstage without Toni's prior permission. "Did he give his name?" She tried without success to make the question sound casual.

Miguel held out a folded piece of paper. "No, but he wrote this note for you."

Toni's heart started to beat a little faster as she unfolded the note. "You were magnificent," Brody had written. "Will you come out with me for a nightcap?"

Toni stared down at the note, rereading the simple message as if it were written in an obscure foreign language or a cipher that needed decoding. When she realized that both men were staring at her with puzzled frowns, she gathered her scattered wits. She tapped the note against her thumbnail. "It's from this guy. He...um...we... um..."

She gave up on explanations and plunked herself into the chair in front of her dressing table. "Tell him I'll meet him out front as soon as I've changed, will you, Miguel? I'll be ten minutes."

"Sure thing. I'll let him know." Miguel disappeared down the tiny hallway in the direction of the kitchens.

Toni glared at Pudge's reflection in her mirror. "Would you like to tell me what you're smiling about? You look like the Cheshire cat after a meal of prime fish heads."

"I'm not smilin'," Pudge said, a huge grin plastered all over his face. "Leastways, I'm not smilin' just like you weren't singin' for anyone special tonight. What's his name, this dude who isn't special?"

"Brody Wagner." She yanked a brush through her hair when she realized that Pudge was now openly laughing. "All right! Okay! So there was a guy out there tonight I wanted to impress. But he's a lawyer in my father's office, and that's the only reason I agreed to meet him. It's common courtesy, that's all. I have absolutely no interest in him. Not in the way you're thinking, anyway."

"I don't believe you have the least idea what I'm thinkin', girl."

Toni screwed the lid back on her jar of cold cream, a great excuse for not looking at Pudge. She walked over to the sink fitted into a corner of the room and splashed cold water on her face. "Brody's setting up an office for Delacroix and Associates here in the city. He's a new arrival in town and he doesn't have many friends, so I've been showing him a few of the good places to go. You know, stuff that isn't on the tourist maps—"

"That's real generous of you." Pudge chuckled. "Now, isn't he just this town's luckiest young man to be on the receivin' end of your fine act of Christian charity?"

"Don't you have to get home and read Josie a story?" Toni said with heavy sarcasm.

Pudge's eyes twinkled. "Josie will be asleep, as you very well know. But I could always try and interest Maya in a bedtime story, I guess. Sometimes she comes up with a real interesting line in stories.''

Toni laughed and Pudge took her hand, squeezing it briefly. ''Enjoy yourself tonight, Toni. You're a grade A singer and a great business partner, but you need more in your life than this club.'' He held up his hand. ''No, honey child, don't you waste my time tellin' me why I'm wrong and why you don't need nobody, 'cause I won't be listenin'. But you can give this Brody Wagner the message that if he makes you unhappy, he'll have me and Maya to answer to.''

Once Pudge had left, Toni took less than three minutes to get out of her glittering costume and slip into the simple, low-necked cotton dress she'd worn to work earlier that night. She twirled around in front of the mirror, wishing she'd worn something more alluring than loose-fitting green paisley, then scolded herself for thinking the word *alluring* in the same sentence as she thought of Brody. Over the past few weeks they'd become friends, that was all, and she had no plans to change the nature of their relationship, no matter what Brody might be contemplating.

The patrons had all left, and the restaurant was on the point of closing by the time she came out of her dressing room, so it was easy to spot Brody. He sat at the bar chatting with Miguel, who was busy with his nightly cleanup. Both men seemed to be laughing a lot, enjoying each other's company.

''Your friend, he speak real good Spanish,'' Miguel said as she approached.

''Does he?'' She turned to Brody. ''You're a man of many talents. What other surprise skills do you have tucked up your sleeve?''

''None that I can mention in polite company.'' Brody slid off the bar stool.

"That didn't sound like college Spanish you were speaking. How did you get to be so fluent?" After so many hours spent in each other's company, Toni was constantly amazed at how much she still had to discover about Brody.

He shrugged. "In the part of town where I lived when I was a kid, you had a real hard time of it if you didn't speak Spanish. It took me a while, because I was stubborn as hell, but I finally realized that learning Spanish was a lot easier than getting beaten up every day."

He touched the faint scar above his eyebrow in a gesture that Toni felt sure was unconscious. Had that scar come from being beaten up when he was a child who refused to conform to the dictates of his neighborhood bullies? They hadn't talked much about Brody's childhood since the first few hours of their acquaintance, but now her curiosity returned full force. Why would he have been living in such a tough neighborhood when his father belonged to one of New Orleans' wealthiest families?

"Given that your father was so successful, I'm surprised you didn't grow up in one of Chicago's fancy suburbs," she said. "Winnetka, or Lake Forest, somewhere like that."

Brody hesitated for a moment. "After my parents divorced, I went to live with my grandparents," he said. He stopped her asking any more questions by taking her arm and tipping his other hand in a farewell salute to Miguel, who was listening to their exchange without even bothering to pretend otherwise. "'Night, Miguel."

"*Buenas noches, señor.* Enjoy your evening with Miz Toni."

"I will." Brody turned and his gaze sought hers. "Are you ready?"

"Mmm, I don't know." She smiled. "Ready for what?"

"Whatever happens," he said, and he didn't laugh or even smile.

Toni felt her cheeks flame. She looked from Brody to Miguel, who was polishing wineglasses as if his life depended on it, ears almost visibly flapping. This was crazy, she decided. Having spent most of the past several weeks acting as though they were the most platonic of friends, Brody was now coming on to her in full view of her employees. "We're going to have a nightcap," she said to him. "That's all."

Brody didn't dispute her words. He brushed his knuckles across her cheekbones, just once, then let his hand drop back to his side. "I was planning to take you to the Café Natchez, unless there's somewhere else you'd prefer," he said, ushering her toward the club's exit. "It's only three blocks away from here, and it's a fine night, so we could walk, if you're up for that."

"Sounds great," she said, deciding that she was going to stop overanalyzing everything and just enjoy the pleasant finale to her evening. "I love the Café Natchez, especially their garden courtyard. And walking there would be a great way for me to unwind."

She was forced to stop on their way out of the dining room to avoid tripping over Maurice, a waiter who'd been with her ever since the opening of the club. A handsome man with flaring nostrils and passionate dark eyes, he'd grown up as plain old Morris in Fort Wayne, Indiana, but liked to pretend he was French and ultrasophisticated. Fortunately, the tourists at Chanson Triste seemed to enjoy his fake Parisian accent as much as Maurice did.

Maurice was making no bones about the fact that he was inspecting Brody Wagner. Toni was disconcerted anew by the intense interest all her employees seemed to be taking in him. Good grief, this wasn't the first time she'd left the club in the company of a man, although you'd have thought she'd spent the past five years living like a cloistered nun, judging from the way everyone was behaving. She glared at the waiter. "Yes, Maurice, is there a problem?"

"Nothing, *madame*. Here, all is very fine." Maurice stepped out of their path and pulled open the door with a grand flourish. Behind Brody's back, he gave Toni the thumbs-up sign. "Have a good evening, *madame*. Enjoy your date. Did I hear you say that you were going to the Café Natchez?"

"Er...yes."

"A fine choice."

"Thanks for the official seal of club approval." Toni cast a quick glance back over her shoulder and saw that sometime within the last few seconds, half her employees had congregated in the main dining room, where they were staring at her and Brody with open curiosity.

Exasperated, she swung around and confronted them, back to the door, hands on her hips. "It's midnight, and I'm not paying overtime. Do any of you have a reason why you haven't gone home yet?"

A chorus of shaking heads greeted her question. "Okay. Well then, I suggest you get the hell out of here before I find something for you all to do. Good night."

She stomped through the door in Brody's wake. As they emerged from the air-conditioned chill of the club into the balmy night air, Toni realized Brody was laughing. "I feel like I've been transported back to high school," he said, "with all the parents of all the girls I ever dated lined up in one accusing row."

She glared at him, feeling foolish at the overprotectiveness of her staff. Then she laughed, too, leaning her head back and holding her arms wide to the night sky. "I guess they're trying to tell me I need to get a life. My social calendar must have been pretty pathetic these past few months if they get this excited because I have a date.''

"Is this a date?" Brody asked. "A real date, I mean."

"I don't know." She struggled to put a name to what was happening between the two of them, frustrated by her inability to sort through her emotions and pin on neat identifying labels. Then she remembered that she'd decided not to overanalyze. "When we had lunch together on Sunday, you didn't say anything about seeing me again this week," she said finally.

"No, I didn't." He turned to her. "But we both know we can't continue pretending that we're just good friends. It's time for us to decide what happens next in our relationship."

"Yes," she acknowledged. She drew in a deep breath. "I'm glad you came to hear me sing, Brody."

"You were wonderful. Thrilling, in fact." He smiled at her, and she forgot about the crowded pavements, the tourists milling around them and the voice in her head telling her that she was getting too deep and too fast into something she wasn't equipped to handle. Tonight, whenever Brody smiled, it seemed that she melted. It was an automatic reflex, something beyond her conscious control, like cats purring when they were stroked.

He held out his hand, and she laced her fingers with his. His clasp tightened, and they walked along the crowded sidewalks together, hands linked. A group of swaggering teens sauntered toward them, too busy showing off for one another to pay attention to where they were walking. Brody pulled her close, his arm going around her waist in a protective gesture that felt natural—almost inevitable. But nothing about her relationship with Brody was really inevitable, Toni thought. In fact, the exact opposite would be closer to the truth. The fact that she'd propositioned him within seconds of being introduced lay between them, a giant stumbling block on their path to intimacy even after all these weeks.

They arrived at the Café Natchez, and the hostess led them out to a table in the center of the courtyard. The scent of jasmine and eucalyptus was strong in the night air, and the buzz of insect wings mingled with the louder buzz of conversation. A waitress came to take their order.

"You go first," Toni said to Brody. "I'm still deciding."

"I'll have an espresso, with a twist of lemon peel on the side, and a cognac," Brody said. "Toni? Have you decided what you'd like?"

I would like you to be the father of my baby, she thought with sudden fierce longing. Only moments earlier, she'd been regretting her impulsive proposition the first night they met, and yet here she was, with the same inappropriate longing still floating just beneath the surface of her thoughts. She forced the longing back under control and found a polite smile for the waitress. "I'd like a cappuccino, please, and a chocolate praline to go with it."

The waitress scribbled down their orders and hurried off, shoving her order pad into the rear pocket of her eye-poppingly short shorts. The only qualifications for waitresses at the Café Natchez that Toni could discern were to be under thirty and have gorgeous legs. Brody, Toni was gratified to see, didn't seem to have paid any attention to their waitress and her gorgeous legs.

He leaned across the wrought-iron table, taking the menu from her and covering her hands with his. His eyes were focused on her face with such total concentration that she felt as if there was nobody in the garden except the two of them. "I wrote it in the note, but I need to say it again. You were magnificent tonight, Toni. That was an incredible performance, and I'm in awe of your talent."

"Thank you." Compliments about her singing always

left her stumbling for a response, and she didn't know what else to say. She looked down at their joined hands. His were unusually tanned and strong for a man who worked in a law office, with blunt tips and short nails. A musician's hands. "Do you still play the clarinet?" she asked.

"For my own pleasure, when I'm alone." He leaned back in his chair, his mouth twisting in self-mockery. "Or maybe *pleasure* is the wrong word. Sometimes I think I play just to torture myself. To remind myself that there are skills in life that require more than technical mastery."

Somehow, she didn't doubt that his technical mastery of the instrument was absolute. Brody impressed her as a man who would will himself to perfection in any task he undertook. Including making love. She shut off a flood of too-vivid images. "Will you let me hear you play one day, Brody?"

With his index finger, he traced the outline of a treble clef on her palm. "If you promise not to lie about how good I am."

"I promise." Looking at him across the small table, Toni discovered that she was having difficulty catching her breath, and she was almost relieved when their order arrived.

The waitress set the cappuccino and chocolate praline in front of Toni with barely a glance, all the while directing a dazzling smile at Brody. "If you decide you'd like dessert, just let me know, okay?" She was off in a flash of tanned legs and aggressively wiggling hips.

"Now, there's a young woman whose natural assets definitely outshine her technical skills," Toni said waspishly.

Brody laughed. "Jealous, honey? Don't be. You have even better legs than she does."

"How would you know?" Toni gave a disgusted sniff

as she registered the significance of Brody's comment. "Hah! I should have known you were looking at her legs even though you pretended not to!"

"Trust me, Toni, any semiconscious male would have noticed her legs."

She wrinkled her nose. "Men are so annoyingly...basic."

"Are we?" He pressed his finger to the tip of her nose, then ran his hand down the side of her face, his touch feather light. The laughter slowly vanished from his eyes.

"I was looking at the waitress," he said, "but I wasn't thinking about her. I was thinking about you, Toni, and how I want like hell to make love to you."

Toni's stomach tightened in reaction. She looked past him into the flame of the candle flickering between them. She wanted to kiss him. She wanted a lot more than that. She wished she'd invited him back to her apartment, where they could have been alone. Her heart beating very fast, she swayed toward him, letting her eyes drift closed. A burst of laughter from the table behind them pulled her back into awareness, and she sat up quickly, removing her hand from his and reaching clumsily for her cup of coffee.

"Brody, this isn't the right time, or the right place..."

"No," he said. "It isn't. But I have a room at the King's Court Hotel, just across the street."

He didn't ask her to go there with him, just let his statement lie between the two of them. Did she want to accept his unspoken invitation? Only a moment ago she'd been yearning for privacy, and now he was offering her that possibility. Was she ready to make love to him? To accept that she could have Brody in her life, but probably never on the terms she really wanted?

Toni's cup rattled in its saucer as she put it down. "I don't know what I want to have happen between us, Brody. Everything's happened so fast. One minute you were nothing more to me than one in a long line of Aunt Mary's ridiculous candidates for bridegroom, and it seems like almost the next minute you were..." Her voice trailed away.

"The next minute I was what?" Brody asked softly.

"The man I couldn't stop thinking about," she admitted. "The man I want to have in my bed. But that doesn't mean I'm ready to run across the street to your hotel room and spend the rest of the night making wild, uninhibited love with you."

"I can't tell you how sorry I am to hear that."

She smiled as he'd intended her to. "I'm sorry, too, but I think this is one of those times when I need to know where the road will end before I decide if I want to take it."

"And sometimes, if you wait until you know exactly what's going to happen at the end of the road, it turns out that you're too late to take the crucial first step forward."

There was truth to what Brody was saying, Toni acknowledged, so why did she have this feeling that starting an affair with him would be fraught with potential hazards—hazards that might prove emotionally devastating? In the years since her marriage ended, there had been few men in her life. But when she was attracted to a man, she didn't usually expect promises and commitment and vows of eternal devotion before she went to bed with him. Witness what had happened with Max, and the mess she'd gotten herself into precisely because she hadn't required promises and insisted on commitment. The interesting question was why she felt so differently about Brody, and why it seemed almost threatening to visualize starting an affair with him. Was she afraid that what he felt for her might fizzle away into nothingness? But that had happened with all her relationships in the past, even her pitiful attempt at marriage. Was that a reason to deny the very real attraction she and Brody felt for each other?

She put down the spoon and pushed her coffee cup away. So much for enjoying the evening and not letting herself dissect what was happening between the two of them, she reflected wryly. "The bottom line, Brody, is that before we take this too far, we both have to be sure that we're not getting involved with each other for the wrong reasons."

He swirled his cognac, staring into the depths of his glass. "We're attracted to each other, and we both think the sex would be great. We're single and unattached. Why do we have to make this more complicated than it is?"

"I expected you to be more honest than that," she said quietly. "Look me straight in the eye, Brody, and tell me you're absolutely convinced that I have no ulterior motives in starting an affair with you. Tell me you're one hundred percent positive I'm not planning to seduce you simply in order to get myself pregnant."

He put down his brandy glass. "You already told me that you would never do that."

"And you believe me—totally?"

"Yes."

She smiled grimly. "That didn't exactly come out loud and clear, Brody."

"I've told you before, getting pregnant is your obsession, not mine. Trust me, Toni, I don't look at you and think about babies. I look at you and think about sex."

Tension coiled in her stomach. "You're lying," she said. She leaned across the table and grabbed either side of his head, holding it between her hands and staring straight into his eyes. "Look *at* me, damn you, not through me! Look at me and tell me you don't have this nasty, lingering doubt that I just might be so desperate to get pregnant that I'm planning to make you a father against your will.''

He exhaled a harsh breath, then took her hands and pulled them away from his face. "Okay," he said tersely. "Maybe you're right. Maybe at some level, I do have a couple of doubts about your motives—"

"Then, I don't see how our relationship has anywhere to go." Toni gripped the hard iron rim of the table, hurt by Brody's admission even though she'd pressed and poked and prodded until he made it. "You can't trust me, and I'm not willing to start a sexual relationship with a man who doesn't trust me."

"Trust seems to be an easy word for you to toss around," Brody said tersely. "But my life has been a bit low on practical demonstrations of trustworthiness. My mother seduced my father and deliberately got herself pregnant without his knowledge and against his will. I'm here to tell you that being the bouncing baby boy born into that situation didn't lead to a Norman Rockwell childhood."

Toni had to take several breaths and force herself to speak calmly, despite the emotions churning inside her. "What happened to you when your mother and father got divorced, Brody? Why did you end up living with your grandparents?"

"It doesn't matter," he said. "It's a boring story."

"I don't find anything about you boring, Brody. What happened that was so bad you don't like to talk about it? Were your grandparents cruel to you? Were you abused?"

"No, they were a great couple. Unfortunately, they were also very poor. When my mother left me with them, it was all they could do to keep me clothed and fed and supplied with schoolbooks. They'd scrimped and saved to give all five of their kids a decent education, and they never had the money to move to a better area, even when the crack epidemic hit the streets and our neighborhood started to go to hell with the influx of gangs and drug money.''

"I see," Toni said, although she really didn't. It sounded as though Brody's mother had dumped him on her elderly parents, knowing they didn't have sufficient money to support him. But even if she couldn't care for Brody herself, why hadn't she paid for his care by supplementing her parents' income with regular gifts of cash? Had Brody's father made such an inadequate divorce settlement that his ex-wife hadn't been able to support their son?

Brody gave a humorless smile. "You have a very expressive face, Toni. You're trying to decide what would be the polite way to ask how come my grandparents weren't given any money to help pay for the costs of raising me."

"Well, yes, I guess I am. The Wagners are a wealthy, established New Orleans family. I would have thought pride alone would have made your father negotiate a decent financial settlement when he divorced your mother."

"He did." Brody's shrug didn't quite manage to convey indifference. "My mother didn't use his money to support me, that's all."

"But why not?" Toni was appalled. When Brody remained silent, she said, "Did your mother take the money your father intended for you and use it for herself?"

Brody didn't answer her question directly. "That money represented a chance for my mother to lead the life she'd always dreamed of. She hated being poor, she hated the fact that her parents spoke English with a funny accent. She worked really hard to put herself through secretarial school, and landing my father was a great coup. She hoped to cut herself off from her Puerto Rican roots completely when she married my father. Unfortunately for her, the Wagners never let her forget where she came from, or the fact that my father had only married her because she'd trapped him by getting pregnant. He started asking for a divorce after less than a year of marriage. When she gave up and agreed not to fight to stay married, she considered the money from the divorce settlement was hers—something that she'd earned by living through three years of humiliation at the hands of the Wagners.''

Toni didn't trust herself to comment on the behavior of either the Wagners or his mother. "Where's your mother living now? Are you still in touch with each other?"

"Occasionally." Judging by his expression, it didn't appear as if Brody's visits with his mother brought him much joy. "My father's money allowed my mother to relocate in Phoenix, where nobody knew or cared about her past. She established herself there as a well-heeled society matron, with no ties and a comfortable income. It was the sort of life she'd always dreamed of living, and on the few occasions I've seen her, it seems as if she's living out her dream very happily."

Toni could contain herself no longer. "Damn it, you're entitled to be angry at what she did to you, Brody." She reached her hand across the table. "I'm so sorry...."

"Don't be. Living with my grandparents taught me that having a loving home is a lot more important to a child than having plenty of money. I'm probably fortunate that my parents were both anxious to get rid of me, otherwise I'd have grown up in a household with plenty of money and a zero supply of the things that really matter. As it was, I got the best of the bargain. Especially since my grandfather Wagner had put the money for my college education in a separate trust fund that my mother couldn't touch. So when I really needed financial help, it was there for me."

But no thanks to his mother, Toni reflected. And his

father seemed to have been careless of Brody's welfare to the point of outright neglect. Still, at least his grandparents had been wonderful surrogates. Plenty of kids weren't even that lucky in the wake of a bitter divorce. "Are your grandparents still alive, Brody?"

"No, unfortunately. My grandfather died when I was in law school, and my grandmother died five years ago."

"She must have been very proud of you."

"She was proud of all her grandchildren, and we all loved her." After a slight pause, Brody added, "Fifi was my grandmother's dog. As far as Nana was concerned, she couldn't imagine anything more elegant and sophisticated than taking a walk down the street accompanied by a white poodle wearing a satin ribbon and a fancy jeweled collar, but there was no way she could ever afford to own anything so frivolous. I gave her Fifi for her seventieth birthday, and it was love at first sight for both of them. I figured that after fifty years of longing for a poodle, Nana deserved to have one."

Somehow, Toni wasn't in the least surprised that Brody had taken over the care of his grandmother's pet, and that he kept Fifi groomed and beribboned the way his grandmother would have wanted. "Fifi seems to have transferred her affections to you with no trouble," she observed.

Brody grinned. "Well, you said it yourself, she's a lady who's free with her favors."

"Brody—" She broke off, pulling her hand out of his, her eyes narrowing as she recognized Maurice weaving his way through the tables and the waitresses, heading in their direction. He came up to them, puffing and panting.

"Toni, thank goodness you're still here." Maurice forgot his French accent, a sign of serious trouble. "There was a phone call for you."

Toni was already rising to her feet. "Aunt Mary?" she whispered. "Was it about my aunt?"

"No, it wasn't. Gee, Toni, I'm sorry, I didn't mean to alarm you." Maurice reached into his trouser pocket and pulled out a sheet of notepaper. "The call was from a man who wouldn't leave his name. He said that you have to call him tonight. It's urgent, vitally important, and it's personal. This is his number where he can be reached." He cleared his throat. "Honest to God, Toni, he sounded like he was almost crying on the phone."

Toni looked at the number, which she didn't recognize. The area code seemed familiar, but she couldn't place it off the top of her head. "This call came through just now?" she asked, glancing at her watch. "At half past midnight? The guy must be frantic."

Maurice looked embarrassed. "He originally called at nine o'clock, right when you were getting ready to go out on stage, and he said it was urgent, but he didn't sound out of control, you know? And then he called again, a few minutes ago, and he sounded like he might do himself an injury if he didn't hear from you tonight." He flushed. "I'm sorry the first message got overlooked, Toni. Things got hectic tonight. You know what a madhouse it is when we're closing, and you didn't go into your office and check for messages like you usually do after your performance, so this one just sat on your desk. It wasn't until the guy called a second time that I realized you hadn't seen the first message. Thank God I knew where you were."

"Did he give you any clue what his problem is?" Toni asked, thinking Maurice's sense of drama might be causing him to overreact. The call had come through to the club, not to her home, which suggested it might easily be from a fan rather than someone she actually knew.

"Yeah, he said to tell you this was about your meeting

in the Hotel Maison de Ville last month." Maurice flashed
a dubious glance at Brody, obviously wondering how
much to reveal in front of him. "He said some, er, serious
problems have developed in regard to your meeting."

Toni looked down at the phone number and realized
why it looked familiar. This was the number of her ex-
husband's home in Shreveport. She'd called it almost four
weeks ago to let Dennis know that she'd spoken with her
brother and that Justin was confident he could take care
of the problems associated with the Henderson land deal.
Not surprisingly, Dennis had seemed relieved and pleased
that his name had been kept out of things. She wondered
what could have happened to get him so worried again.
She hoped to goodness he wasn't about to report fresh
trouble for Justin.

"I need to call him," she said, her alarm mounting.

"There'll be a phone inside," Brody said. "Go ahead,
I'll finish my coffee."

Toni hurried inside. "I need to make an urgent phone
call to Shreveport," she said to the woman at the cashier's
desk. "I have a credit card. Could you tell me which
phone I can use?"

"There's a pay phone in the hall outside the ladies'
room. It would probably be quieter there than if I let you
use this one."

"Thanks." Toni found the phone and dialed Dennis's
number. Her call was answered in the middle of the first
ring. "Dennis? This is Toni."

"Thank God! I thought you were never going to get
back to me."

"I'm sorry I didn't call earlier, but I just got your message. What's wrong?"

"The files on the Henderson transaction have been stolen," Dennis blurted out, obviously on the edge of full-
blown hysteria. "The FBI agents spoke to me right after

you called four weeks ago, and I never heard another word from them until this afternoon. Then today, three of them came to my office and asked for all the files pertaining to Shoreline Exploration's purchase of the Henderson property. So I agreed to hand them over, of course. But when I went to get them, they were gone! All of them!''

CHAPTER NINE

TONI HAD NO CHANCE to reply before Dennis launched into a catalog of his woes. "You told me Justin had taken care of this problem, and it's not true!" he wailed. "The FBI suspects me of conspiring with Justin to defraud the Hendersons. They're going to arrest me on charges of bribery and corruption and I'll lose my job and go to jail, and then what will happen to Cheryl and the kids? My poor kids…"

He was talking as if the FBI agents were waiting outside his bedroom door, handcuffs at the ready. Toni cut him off before he succumbed to complete hysteria. "Dennis, this is a problem but it's not a total disaster, for heaven's sake, at least not yet. And if anyone needs to worry, it's Justin. He's the target of the FBI investigation, not you."

"He was, but maybe he isn't anymore! With those files gone, I have no way of proving that I didn't take a massive bribe, right along with Justin!"

"But, Dennis, the whole point is that Justin didn't take any bribes, and neither did you!"

"Don't be so naive." Dennis suddenly sounded a lot more in control. "It makes no difference whether I actually took any bribes or not. Can you imagine what happens to a corporate lawyer if even a whiff of suspicion gets out that he's on the take?"

"Yes, but—"

"I'm dead meat," he said despairingly. "That's what

I am. Dead meat. If the president of Shoreline hears about this, he isn't going to stand behind me, saying I'm a great guy. He's going to kick my ass out of the company before I cause him any trouble with the stockholders. Do you know what it costs corporate America each year to defend itself from stockholder lawsuits?''

"Dennis, let's take this slowly, from the top." Toni was almost yelling to make herself heard above returning panic in her ex-husband's voice. "Did any of the FBI agents suggest they were about to arrest you?"

"No," he admitted. "But they told me they would be pursuing their investigation of the Henderson transaction and it would be in my best interest to find the missing files. You see, they don't believe they were stolen! They think I've gotten rid of them because they contain compromising material."

"How can you be sure the files were stolen?" Toni cut in ruthlessly. "Was your office broken into?"

"No, that's the worst of it. Nothing else is missing, and Security hasn't reported any break-ins, which is why the FBI doesn't believe the files are really stolen. They believe I destroyed them. The other files from the same month are all there, every damn one of them." His voice cracked. "You have to help me, Toni. I don't have powerful friends like your family does."

She soothed him as best she could, even though her own stomach was churning with anxiety. Justin's nomination had been on the brink of being sent to the Senate for confirmation, and this was a disastrous development.

"When did you last see the Henderson files, Dennis?" she asked.

"Last Tuesday. I went through them right after we met way back in July. And every week since then, I've double-checked that everything was in order and that I had all the documentation I needed to prove that Justin and I didn't conspire to do anything illegal. Everything was where it should have been last Tuesday.''

''At least they had an approximate time frame for when the files had gone missing. And you're sure Security hasn't reported any break-ins?''

''Positive. I checked as soon as I found out the files were stolen.''

''Then we know they must have been taken by someone who has access to your office,'' she said. ''Do you lock up your office when you're not there?''

''Only at night. Or if I leave the building at lunchtime.'' His voice became more thoughtful. ''During the day, I guess any member of Shoreline's management team would be able to walk into my office. Maintenance could always make a credible excuse, too. Even the clerical staff, in certain circumstances.''

''And your secretary wouldn't stop them from entering your office? Or go in with them?''

''Usually yes, sometimes no, depending on who it was and what excuse they gave her.''

''Assuming they managed to come up with a convincing excuse to get by your secretary, would it be difficult for an intruder to find the Henderson files?''

''Not difficult,'' Dennis said. ''But maybe time-consuming. I file strictly by date, so if the thief knew the dates of the Henderson deal, which I guess he did, it would simply be a question of finding the right filing cabinet, and then the correct drawer. Of course, the filing cabinets are kept locked, but it would be easy enough to get a duplicate of the key.''

His voice became morose again. ''How does this help, Toni? So now we've deduced that I'm getting screwed with insider help from one of my colleagues. Is that supposed to make it better for me and my family when I'm locked up in jail? To know somebody I work with on a daily basis helped send me there?''

"It helps because knowing how the files were stolen gives us a clue as to who might be behind all this.''

"Oh, that." Dennis dismissed the point as if it were of only trivial interest. "Toni, we don't have time to become detectives. What I need right now is to find a way to get the FBI off my back!''

"We always knew there was a risk that whoever wants to discredit Justin would turn nasty when they realized their schemes weren't working," she said, resisting the impulse to blame Dennis for not taking better care of protecting files that were obviously so crucial to proving both his and Justin's innocence. Obviously, he should have kept the Henderson files in a safe place, under lock and key, especially since the blackmailer had threatened all along to send the FBI a set of false documents. Still, it was always easy to criticize with the advantage of hindsight, and Toni bit back a harsh comment about her former husband's failure to think ahead.

"Dennis, I'll talk to Justin, explain the latest bad news and enlist his help. He's bound to have some good ideas as to how we should handle this." She hoped to God that was true. "In the meantime, what you need to do first thing tomorrow morning is check with your secretary and find out if she remembers letting anyone into your office without your knowledge.''

"I guess so." Dennis's voice radiated gloom. "It won't do any good, though. Whoever took those files will have destroyed them by now. Besides, Philip Delacroix is out to get me as much as Justin, I'm sure of it. Even if I find out who took those files, your uncle will just move on to plan B and find another way to destroy me.''

Toni frowned. She understood why Dennis was alarmed by the disappearance of the files, and she knew from their brief marriage that he was a man who tended to worry himself into a frenzy and then leap to conclusions that might or might not be rooted in the facts. Still, she couldn't understand why he was so firmly convinced that her uncle Philip was out to get him.

"Dennis, we don't know that my uncle is behind any of this," she said. "You're suspecting him on the flimsiest of evidence. After all, Philip is a respected lawyer and a state senator with an honorable career that stretches back fifty years. Why would he risk his whole reputation simply to prevent Justin being appointed as a federal judge? And if that isn't bizarre enough, it's totally weird to think he wants to get you into trouble. Why would he? He has absolutely no reason in the world to go after you."

"You're forgetting about the bribe Philip offered me all those years ago," Dennis said quickly. "Nobody else knew about that five thousand dollars and the fact that I'd taken Hamilton's papers. That's proof Philip is involved in all of this."

In Toni's opinion, it was light years away from being proof of anything, except Dennis's stubborn determination to accuse her uncle of wrongdoing. "Dennis, we can't afford to obsess about Philip's role in all this and then discover we've gone chasing off in completely the wrong direction. All we know for sure right now is that somebody threatened to blackmail you over an old land deal, and that the company files that would have helped prove your side of the story have gone missing. Why do you keep bringing my uncle's name into this? You have no valid reason to suspect him any more than a dozen other people."

The silence from the other end of the phone was suddenly fraught with tension. "Dennis?" Toni inhaled sharply. "Dennis, what haven't you told me?"

"Nothing." He sounded sullen. "You Delacroix are all

the same. You fight among yourselves and involve innocent bystanders in your battles. Philip was originally out to get Justin, not me. And now, because I'm trying to fight back, because I did the honorable thing and told you what was going on, you and your family are closing ranks, just like you always do, and I'm the person getting screwed.''

After fourteen years, it seemed that some of the fundamental things about her ex-husband's character hadn't changed. With an overwhelming sense of relief that she no longer had to cope with Dennis Carron's unpleasant habit of blaming other people for his misdeeds, Toni recognized one of his typical attempts at self-justification.

''Dennis,'' she said, sounding as weary as she felt, ''cut the recriminations, okay? We got divorced so that we wouldn't have to waste each other's time with this sort of garbage. Tell me exactly why you're so sure Uncle Philip is behind this attack on you and Justin, and I'll be more than willing to help in any way I can. Otherwise, I'm through. You have two seconds to start telling me the truth or I'm hanging up the phone.''

The silence continued.

''Goodbye, Dennis—''

''Wait!'' His breath hissed out in a frantic gasp. ''Don't hang up.''

''Then, start talking. And I want the truth this time.''

Dennis spoke, his tone of voice somewhere between resentful and ashamed. ''I know Philip Delacroix is behind this because he never attempted to hide that fact, at least from me.''

''You knew my uncle was behind this when you met me way back in July?'' Toni exclaimed.

Dennis gave a mumble of assent.

''Why didn't you tell me?'' she demanded furiously.

"Why in the world didn't you tell me this last month, Dennis?"

Once again there was silence on the other end of the phone. Fingers tapping against the phone book in frustration, Toni looked up and realized that Brody was standing at the end of the short corridor, watching her. He tipped his head in a silent question, turning his hands palms up in a gesture that asked if she was okay and at the same time offered her his help, support, sympathy—whatever she needed.

She felt a warm rush of relief at the knowledge he was there, waiting for her, ready to help if she wanted him to. She gave him a tiny smile, conveying her gratitude for his presence, then turned her attention back to the phone. Miraculously, the tension coiled in her stomach, like a snake waiting to strike, had unwound just a little.

"If you knew all along that my uncle was behind this, Dennis, why did you come to me with that red herring about Hamilton's files? Why didn't you tell Philip to go to hell, and then call Justin and let him know what was going on? Why involve me?"

"Your grandfather's files weren't a red herring. I wanted to return them," he protested quickly. "I... needed...to make you aware of what had happened at the end of our marriage."

"No." She knew that with sudden conviction. "My grandfather's old files were an *excuse* to involve me, not the reason. And the reason you didn't tell my uncle to get lost was because you were afraid of him and you hoped Justin and I would find a way to neutralize him. That way, he'd be off your back without you needing to take a stand. Which brings me right back to my question—what hold does Philip have over you, Dennis?"

"None." The denial was automatic and totally lacking in sincerity. Even Dennis seemed to recognize the limp,

defeated tone of his own voice. He gave a long, shudder-
ing sigh. "All right, if you want the truth, I've been...
helping...him."

"*How* were you helping him? Come on, Dennis, it's
one o'clock in the morning. Let's not drag out the sordid
details any longer."

"I was helping him with information," he admitted,
the confession coming in a rush once he decided to tell
her the truth. "The shares of Shoreline Exploration are
traded on the New York Stock Exchange, and since I
knew about every acquisition and merger, every new oil
well that came in, every important oil lease that was
signed, I could pass information about the company's financial position to Philip and he could buy or sell shares
in the company accordingly."

"Making a nice profit in the process," Toni said, feeling sick. "And what was your reward for selling confidential company information, Dennis? How much did
Philip pay you off with?"

"He didn't pay me off—"

"For heaven's sake, Dennis—"

"Ten percent," he said sullenly. "But I wasn't hurting
anyone with what I did, Toni. It wasn't like I stole money
from the company, or anything like that. Nobody was
hurt. Nobody lost a dime because of what I told Philip.
All I did was provide your uncle with the chance to make
a little extra money."

"It's called insider trading," Toni said dryly. "And
people go to jail for what you've been doing, Dennis."

"Oh, God, I know they do!" His voice shook. "I've
wanted to get out from under for years," he said, his
defiance collapsing. "I swear to you, Toni, that I didn't
want to be involved with your uncle. God, you can't know
how many times I wished I'd never stolen Hamilton
Delacroix's files, or taken that five thousand dollars Philip

offered me. That was just the beginning, and he's been after me ever since, dragging me down, sucking me in, deeper and deeper.''

She heard him draw in another shaky breath. ''Everything I told you last month was true, Toni, it just wasn't the whole truth. Cheryl has been begging me to stop giving in to Philip's blackmail ever since she found out what was going on. This latest demand from Philip to set up Justin was the last straw for both of us. Helping Philip with some snippets of information is one thing, falsifying company records is another thing altogether. Besides, Justin's a fine lawyer, and he was always good to me. I don't want to harm his career.''

She heard tears in his voice. ''Cheryl's going to leave me if I don't get this mess straightened out, Toni. I can't lose her, and the kids...my job, everything. Please, you have to help me. I need to get Philip off my back.''

''You could go to the FBI and tell them what you've told me.''

''But they'd arrest me!'' he exclaimed. ''Promise me, Toni, promise me that you won't turn me in to the feds.'' He was openly sobbing at the other end of the phone.

She felt an appalled sympathy, mingled with the realization that she had little choice other than to offer him the help he needed, since Justin's career was at stake, not to mention the unpalatable fact that she couldn't immediately see any method of bringing Dennis his just desserts without destroying his family, who'd done nothing to deserve the disgrace.

And then there was the whole knotty question of what she ought to do about Philip. She would have no compunction about seeing her uncle punished for what he'd done, but there was the rest of her family to think of, especially Aunt Mary. Mary's convalescence was going well, but there was no denying that she was frail. Seeing her brother arrested for bribery and corruption might easily be enough to bring on another heart attack. Not to mention how Charles and William would react. They both had such a strong sense of family pride, they would undoubtedly worry themselves sick if the Delacroix name was strewn all about the state as the focal point of a bribery scandal.

"All right, Dennis, I'll do my damnedest to help you," she said. "Although, God knows, I'm tempted—more than tempted—to leave you to stew in your own messy juices."

He started to thank her, but she cut him off. "I despise what you've done and I'd be quite willing to let you pay the price. But I don't see why Justin should lose his chance at becoming a judge simply because my uncle seems to be a crook, and you have all the moral backbone of pond scum."

"I'm really grateful, Toni." Dennis coughed and sniffed and blew his nose. "How are you going to stop Philip?" he asked, sounding slightly more in control of himself.

"I don't know yet. I need some time to think."

"You have to come up with a plan quickly. If Philip already has those files about the Henderson transaction in his possession, it isn't going to take him very long to destroy the originals and slip in a few pages where he's doctored the crucial details. And once he sends the phony files to the FBI..." Dennis's voice trailed away in misery.

He was probably right about the need for urgent action, Toni thought, which meant that she needed to consult with Justin as soon as possible. Should she drive to Bayou Beltane right now and wake him? Or was that being overdramatic? A phone call might suffice, but sometimes getting Justin on the phone was an almost impossible feat.

"Toni, are you still there?"

"Yes."

"What are you going to do? Do you think there's any way out of this mess I've made of everything?"

At least Dennis was finally willing to admit that he'd played a large part in creating the disastrous situation they found themselves in. "First, I'm going to consult with Justin," she said. "And this time I'm going to tell him exactly who and what we're up against. He needs to know that the campaign against him isn't being waged by vague, nameless political opponents, but by his own uncle."

"Are you going to tell Justin about me?" Dennis asked, his voice low and embarrassed.

"If I have to." Toni refused to let herself feel sympathy. "For what it's worth, I'll try to keep your name out of it, although I don't know why the heck I'm bothering."

"Thank you, Toni." Dennis sounded uncharacteristically humble. "I realize you're going to put Justin's needs first, and it's right that you should. I don't deserve your consideration."

"No, you don't. I'm doing this for Justin and your family, not for you."

He drew in an audible breath. "Toni, one more thing. I've dealt with Philip Delacroix for years now, and he doesn't give up easily. Don't think he's going to roll over without a fight. For some reason, he's determined to stop Justin's appointment as a judge, and you need to find out why. He never does things without a purpose, and he must have a real strong reason to go to this much trouble."

Did her uncle need more of a reason than the fact that he loathed his twin brother and had always felt a particular envy of Justin's success as a criminal lawyer? Toni was too tired and frazzled to speculate. "Justin and I will take care of this situation, Dennis, and I guess that's all I can say right at this moment. Except that you have my word that I'm going to do my very best to save your sorry ass."

Dennis launched into another tirade of thanks and warnings, and Toni hung up as soon as she could, unable to tolerate either his gratitude or his prophecies of doom.

She went quickly to rejoin Brody. He straightened from the wall where he'd been leaning and slipped his arm around her waist, leading her outside. She was grateful that he didn't ask any questions about the reasons for her lengthy call, and she gradually let herself unwind against him, absorbing his strength, not trying to find reasons why his arm around her felt so comfortable and supportive, or why she was so glad that he happened to be with her right now.

She realized after a couple of silent moments that they were heading back toward Chanson Triste. "Wait," she said. "Where are we going? I need to pick up my car, Brody. It's parked on Giramond. The owner of a bakery there rents me space."

"If you leave your car parked at the bakery overnight, will it be safe?" he asked.

"It would be safe, but I need it. I may have to drive to Bayou Beltane tonight." As she spoke, she recognized that she had no choice. "In fact, I'm sure I have to drive there."

"Then I'll take you."

It was overwhelmingly tempting to contemplate curling up in the passenger seat and letting Brody take charge. Tempting, but also inappropriate. Toni sighed, steeling herself to refuse. "Thanks for the offer, Brody, but I don't know when I'm going to get back into town, and this is the middle of the work week. You can't hang around waiting on my convenience. I'd better pick up my car and drive myself."

"I don't think that's such a great idea," he said. "You look wiped."

She grimaced. "Lie a little, Brody, could you?"

"You look beautiful," he said. "And wiped." He turned her to face him, his arms looped around her waist. "Toni, do you want to tell me what's going on?"

"Yes, I want to tell you, but there's no reason for you to get involved in this."

"There's one very good reason," he said. "*You're* involved. And that means I'd like to help out in any way I can."

She resisted for two seconds, then gave in to the temptation of sharing the burden she carried. "It's about Justin," she said. "Somebody's trying to make sure that his appointment as a federal judge doesn't win Senate approval. I thought everything was taken care of, but a new problem's just cropped up and I need to talk to him right away, to warn him about what's going on." She smiled wryly. "I guess that's the short version of the problem."

"You know that federal judges often face opposition during the nomination process, for party political reasons, and that their appointment is almost always confirmed in the end—" Brody broke off. "Yes, I can see you know that. How about giving me the long version of the problem to see if there's any way I could help? After all, Justin is one of my business partners, and I have a vested interest in seeing that his nomination goes through smoothly."

That was true, Toni reflected. She'd been so wrapped up in the personal aspects of the situation that she'd almost forgotten the serious implications the attacks on Justin's ethics and professional conduct would have for Delacroix and Associates. "I don't know if I can give you the long version, Brody. I promised to keep someone's name out of it."

"We have almost an hour's drive to Bayou Beltane. While I'm driving, you can tell me as much of the story as you can without betraying any confidences."

She didn't bother to protest anymore. Just the prospect

of confiding in Brody made the load Dennis had dumped on her seem less onerous.

The last time she'd sat in Brody's car, the rain had been coming down in a torrential stream, and she'd been tongue-tied. Tonight the sky was clear, and the words tumbled out of her. She explained everything, leaving her ex-husband's name out of it, although that was a wasted gesture on her part, as she soon discovered.

Brody drummed his fingers on the steering wheel. "I could pretend that I don't know who it is that Philip's been blackmailing," he said. "But the truth is, Toni, I don't have to be a genius to work out that the person who called you tonight is the same person who's being black-mailed by Philip. Namely, your ex-husband."

Startled, she twisted in her seat to look at him. "How could you possibly have worked that out? I didn't mention his name—"

"No, you didn't. But I knew Dennis Carron, your ex-husband, worked at Shoreline Exploration as their in-house counsel, and you said the name Dennis a couple of times when you were speaking on the phone, so it wasn't difficult to put two and two together."

"How in the world did you know that Dennis worked at Shoreline? And for that matter, how did you come to know the name of my ex-husband?"

Brody smiled slightly. "Your aunt Mary didn't just tell me that you were talented and beautiful," he said. "She also gave me a complete rundown of your life history. Among the many fascinating tidbits she passed on was the fact that you'd been married to a man called Dennis Carron, who'd treated you so badly that you'd been scared away from the institution of marriage ever since."

Toni was appalled at several different levels. "You do realize that my aunt's version of my life story probably bears only the most coincidental resemblance to the facts, don't you?''

He grinned. ''You mean you aren't the sweetest-natured child that ever lived, as well as a savvy business-woman, a wonderful employer and a loyal friend to everyone in the family, even though you pretend to keep your distance?''

''Aunt Mary said all that about me?'' Toni swallowed over a sudden lump in her throat. ''I'd make all sorts of modest protests, but you've been in Bayou Beltane for a couple of months now, so you already know that as far as my aunt is concerned, everyone in her family is close to perfect.''

''That's not true,'' Brody said quietly. ''I believe your aunt sees the members of the Delacroix family with exceptional clarity, their faults and foibles, as well as all their good points. She simply believes that the family is the best protective device ever invented, so she tries to keep all her relatives—good, bad and indifferent—inside the family fold, where she hopes they'll be safe, and guarded against their own worst instincts.''

He had an intriguing view of her aunt's character, Toni reflected, perhaps because he had the advantage of seeing the members of the Delacroix family from the perspective of an outsider. ''You could be right about Aunt Mary. Maybe she isn't determined to see us as perfect, the way I've always assumed. Still, she loves us all, and the family is the focus of her life. Which brings us right back to the problem of Justin and Philip. I don't want to do anything that's going to set back her full recovery.''

Toni stared gloomily at the twinkling lights of the bridge and the black expanse of lake water stretching on either side of the Twin Span. ''For the sake of my aunt's health, we have to find some way to handle this situation that isn't going to cause a huge eruption. Mary's going into the hospital on Thursday for a day of diagnostic testing. We simply can't let her come home to a major family argument, and a public scandal would be even worse. Honestly, Brody, if this situation isn't handled right, I think we could cause a heart attack that would kill her.''

"How do you think Justin will propose handling the situation?" Brody asked.

"I have no idea," Toni said. "Frankly, I'm hoping he has some better ideas than I do. All I can think of is going to see Uncle Philip, letting him know we're on to him and telling him to back off. Once he knows his involvement has been discovered, he might decide to cut his losses. I mean, it would be embarrassing for him if all his friends and colleagues knew that he was working to undermine his own nephew's appointment as a judge."

Brody snorted.

Toni sent a rueful look in his direction. "You don't think much of my plan, huh?"

"It sucks," Brody said. "In fact, as a plan for containing Philip Delacroix, it's worse than bad, it's dangerous. Basically, you're proposing telling him everything you know, and in exchange you're asking him to please play nicely. If Philip was a man who played by the rules, your brother wouldn't be in this mess in the first place."

"You seem to find it amazingly easy to believe that my uncle is behind a very nasty scheme to blackmail Dennis and falsify the record against Justin. You haven't expressed a single word of surprise at Philip's history of insider trading, or his threats to my ex-husband, or even the fact that he's quite willing to corrupt the judicial process in order to make sure Justin's nomination goes down to defeat."

"I haven't expressed surprise because I don't feel any," Brody said. "I've had a couple of unpleasant experiences of my own with Philip."

"You have? What about?"

Brody shrugged. "You were the person who warned me that your uncle wasn't likely to take well to the idea of competition, if you remember. Although, I didn't need the warning by the time you gave it. I'd already found out the hard way that Philip wasn't willing to see Delacroix and Associates moving into the areas of commercial law that he'd previously considered his own personal territory."

"What did he do?" Toni asked. "Find out who you were negotiating with and undercut you with potential clients?"

"Nothing that subtle. I was warned off in no uncertain terms over a month ago. Before I had the pleasure of meeting you, in fact."

"By Uncle Philip himself?"

"By his surrogates," Brody said, after a tiny pause.

"That sounds ominous."

"I'm sure Philip intended it to be." Brody smiled grimly. "However, your uncle obviously hadn't done his homework properly where I was concerned. He knew my father, of course, and I guess he'd gotten hold of my résumé. He probably saw that I'd studied music at Northwestern and that I'd taken my law degree at Yale, and he jumped to the seemingly obvious conclusion that I was a preppie wimp who'd go to pieces at the sight of a couple of thugs waiting for me in the alley near my house."

"Thugs?" she said faintly.

"Yeah." Brody's smile expanded into a cheerful grin. "Wish you could have seen those poor little tough guys when they discovered that I knew how to fight twice as hard as they did, and at least three times as dirty."

Toni jerked against her seat belt. "My God, Brody, are you saying Philip actually tried to hurt you *physically?*"

"According to you, he's willing to devastate the lives

of your brother, Dennis Carron and both your families. Why would you be surprised that he might be willing to rough me up a little?''

''Well, for heaven's sake, Brody, where did he find these thugs who attacked you? Did he hire them from a rental company? You're making him sound like a...like a real criminal. How can you be sure he was the person who set the thugs on you? They could have been burglars, drug addicts...anything.''

He shook his head. ''They were Philip's boys, I'm sure of it. I wasn't supposed to find out who was behind the attack, but when you've dealt with as many fly-by-night oil companies as I have, you learn to be really smart at discovering exactly who's pulling the strings.''

Toni's heart was pounding. With fear for Brody, she realized, as well as shock at her uncle's behavior. ''You went ahead and opened the new law office in New Orleans, anyway.''

''But of course.''

She turned to him, stomach churning. ''Damn it, Brody, don't you realize yet that my uncle Philip will keep coming after you until you give up?''

Brody gave a throaty, full-bodied laugh. ''Then he's going to be coming after me for a long time, honey. You should know me well enough by now to realize that I'm not going to be scared off by a bully who's been cock of the dung heap for far too long. Hell, I opened up the offices in New Orleans a month earlier than I'd planned simply *because* Philip tried to scare me off.''

Far from joining in Brody's laughter, Toni was rapidly becoming a bundle of nerves. ''Brody, street fighting when you were a kid may have made you great with your fists and quick on your feet, but that's not what my uncle is about. He won't make the mistake of underestimating you again.''

"And I won't ever underestimate him," Brody said.

"But Philip obviously doesn't play fair, and he won't care what means he has to use to get back at you. Everything that's happening to Dennis and Justin only confirms what I've always suspected about how ruthless he is. Justin has a professional record that's as close to blameless as you could ever expect to find in the real world, and yet my uncle has found the one tiny weak spot in my brother's résumé and exploited it. Don't treat Philip's opposition lightly, Brody. I'd hate to see you get hurt, and I don't just mean physically. Philip could devastate your career."

Brody stretched out his hand and rested it on her knee. "Don't worry, Toni. Philip isn't going to hurt me, and that's another promise you can take to the bank. Anyway, right now, I'm not the issue. We need to focus on making sure that he doesn't harm your brother, either."

Toni frowned in concentration, watching the dark mass of water give way to the approach of land without really registering what she was seeing. The problem that had been niggling in her mind for the past couple of hours moved front and center.

"You know, Brody, my uncle's behavior doesn't make a lick of sense. In order to keep Justin off the federal bench, he's set up an elaborate scheme involving Dennis Carron that must have cost him time, effort and money to put in place. Plus, he's running risks at every step of the way that something will backfire and he'll be the person who ends up in trouble. He put pressure on Dennis and then had to hope Dennis wouldn't crack or rebel. And basically Dennis has done both, leaving Philip exposed in exactly the way he must want to avoid."

"You're right. He seems to be operating under tremendous pressure, and he's miscalculating."

"But why?" she asked. "Why is Philip doing this? For

a while, I assumed this whole elaborate deal was just one more round in the ongoing feud between him and my father. But that's ridiculous. Something more has to be at stake than a stupid family squabble and a desire to frustrate Justin. Surely there has to be a huge potential gain involved for him to be willing to take all these risks?''

"A huge potential gain. Or a huge potential threat," Brody said.

She twisted around to look at him. "You said that as if you know something I don't."

"I don't know anything that I could prove in a court of law. But I have a theory and a few shreds of proof to back it up."

"Are you willing to share your theory?"

"When we get home," he said.

"Home?" She gave another glance out of the window and realized they were heading not toward Bayou Beltane and Riverwood, but toward Covington and Brody's house. "Why are we going to your place, Brody?"

He smiled into her accusing eyes. "I'd like to say it's so we can get started on that wild, uninhibited sex you were talking about earlier tonight. Unfortunately, I guess it's because I have a couple of ideas I want to discuss with you before we wake Justin, and I'm getting tired of driving around."

The trouble was, spending the next few hours in Brody's house having wild, passionate sex seemed a much more appealing way to pass the night than discussing Uncle Philip's attempts at blackmail. Toni was still pondering the significance of her feelings when Brody drove into his garage. They went in through the kitchen, just as they had done on the night of Mary's party.

"Where's Fifi?" Toni asked, realizing that no bundle of yapping white fur had come to greet them.

"I had to kennel her," Brody said. "That's the only

problem I'm finding with my commute back and forth to the city. Fifi spends more time than I'd like in a boarding kennel." He flashed a quick grin. "Still, I've found a place where the staff realize she's a princess and treat her accordingly."

He went to the fridge and pulled out two bottles of flavored mineral water. He popped the tops with his thumbs and handed one to her. "Shall we sit on the porch?" he asked. "It's screened, so the bugs won't attack us."

She followed him onto the porch and stretched out in a wicker rocking chair with thick cushions and a padded footstool. Brody sat at her feet, on the stool. She sipped her drink, yawned, then stretched lazily, oddly content to be here in the warm night, feeling the solid warmth of his thigh pressing against her toes.

"I think this chair might have been a mistake," she said, giving him a drowsy smile. "I'm in serious danger of falling asleep, but I'm too comfortable to wake myself up by moving."

"Don't move," Brody said huskily.

Her sleepy smile faded when he leaned over her and pushed her hair away from her face with a hand that wasn't quite steady. Then he braced himself against the arms of the rocker, holding her trapped beneath him, his eyes never leaving hers as he slowly closed the gap between them.

His kiss was long, gentle and altogether devastating. The other times they'd kissed, she'd felt instant hunger, followed by a quick, sharp thrill of desire. With all the sexual tension that had been simmering between them tonight, Toni would have expected an even greater urgency, more razzle-dazzle from this kiss. Perhaps that was why the searching tenderness of it disarmed her so completely.

She lifted her hands to Brody's shoulders, then combed

her fingers through his thick hair, stirring languidly beneath him. The tactile pleasure set her heart thudding against her ribs and intensified the ache that had been growing inside her for days.

When he finally deepened the kiss, her lazy pleasure changed instantly to dark excitement. And yet, buried inside the sharp, hot rush of desire, Toni acknowledged the presence of other, far more complex emotions. For the first time since the disaster of her marriage to Dennis, she found herself wondering what it would be like to have a lover who was also a friend, a man who filled the empty corners of her life as easily as he met the needs of her body.

And then, finally, desire took over and she didn't want to think anymore. Cradling the weight of his body, she let herself surrender to the sheer sensuous enjoyment of what was happening between them.

"Toni." He gave a quiet groan and dragged himself away from her, returning to his earlier seat on the footstool. But his eyes stayed on hers, and the look in them made her long for his return.

She reached out her hand and he took it, lacing his fingers with hers and drawing their linked hands to his mouth so that he could kiss the tips of her fingers. "This wasn't supposed to happen," he said hoarsely. "I didn't bring you back here tonight to have sex."

Desire arced through her, but there was something sweeter and even more urgent fused with the physical yearning. "I'm glad, because I don't want to have sex with you," she said. "But I'd like very much for you to make love to me, Brody."

His grip on her hand tightened, crushing her fingers. He murmured her name just once before he slammed his mouth across hers, raining kisses over her face, along her throat, down to her breasts. All the fire that had been absent earlier flared between them, an instant bonfire of desire. But the tenderness and sweetness of their previous kiss lingered, a sustained chord that echoed and reverberated through the dazzling high notes of passion.

"Do you want to go inside?" he asked against her mouth, and she shook her head.

"I like it out here. We can see the stars."

He pulled her to her feet and led her to the wicker sofa, tossing an extra cushion at one end to make a pillow for her head. The night air was warm and soft, caressing her skin as Brody unfastened the buttons of her dress and pushed it from her shoulders. A puff of breeze danced across her breasts, and he kissed her hardened nipples while she tugged at his shirt and stripped it from him.

Her thoughts skittered and unraveled, unable to take clear shape, but her senses seemed to have become more acute. She heard the flutter of wings as a mockingbird landed in a distant magnolia tree, and smelled the faint tang of Brody's cologne mingled with the heat of his skin and the scent of the geraniums in stone planters at the foot of the porch steps.

They quickly slipped free of the rest of their clothing, and her body felt alive to his touch, responsive in a way that was new to her. Wrapped in Brody's arms, she was aware of wonderful new feelings unfurling inside her, carrying her toward a climax that seemed different in kind from anything she'd experienced in the past.

Desire rippled and flowed in response to the caress of his hands, a melody drifting across water, rising toward the ultimate crescendo of pleasure. The bird flew away from its temporary perch in the magnolia tree, and the ensuing silence was broken only by the sound of Brody's voice whispering her name. Toni was edging higher, closer to the peak, and she knew that at any moment he would push her over the edge.

She kissed him with fierce need as heat coiled and scorched in the pit of her belly. Suddenly, the intensity of what she was feeling seemed too powerful, too different, more than she could handle. She stiffened, pulling away from him, jerking her head to the side, gasping for breath.

Brody grasped her chin and turned her head back, holding her mouth steady beneath his. "Don't fight it, Toni. Let it happen."

"I can't. I'm scared."

"Don't be. I'm here for you." He slipped inside her as he spoke, and the spurt of panic turned back to pleasure. Intense pleasure that erupted deep inside her and spread with molten speed to the farthest extremities of her body. His eyes held hers, no longer a warm brown, but black and fathomless as the night around them. Slowly, he penetrated to the deep warm depths of her, and she felt herself rise to meet him until they moved together, gathering speed as they pressed on toward the inevitable end.

Desire spun tighter and tighter. When everything inside her seemed to break apart, she gave an astonished gasp and let Brody take her over the edge.

CHAPTER TEN

LATER, THEY MADE LOVE again in the spaciousness of
Brody's bed, finding new ways to give each other pleasure. He'd known many exciting women in his life, Brody
reflected, but he'd never before felt the combination of
tenderness and desire that Toni aroused in him. A couple
of years ago, he'd come close to marrying one of the
junior partners in his firm. Jill had been fun, sweet-natured
and easygoing, with a relaxed attitude to life that had
seemed a perfect foil to his own intensity. He'd asked her
to marry him, and she—thank God—had been smart
enough to say no. Given his strong sense of family obligation and Jill's willingness to compromise, they'd have
stayed faithfully married for life, growing more and more
aware of what they were missing as the years passed.

Toni stirred, turning toward him and reaching out to
touch him while she was still sleeping. Brody's stomach
constricted with a rush of emotion. Their bodies were in-
tertwined, but he took her hand and kissed her fingers,
needing the extra sensation of contact. Her fingers uncurled, resting briefly against his cheek, and her eyelids flickered open.

"Hi." She smiled at him sleepily. Her eyes were big
and drowsy, her body languid and flushed with the after-
glow of good sex.

"Hi yourself." He stroked the tangled mass of her
honey blond curls spread out across the pillow. "I'm
sorry, I didn't mean to wake you."

"Didn't you?" He saw the sleepiness in her eyes turn into laughter. Her hand glided across his stomach and came to rest on the hardness of his erection, and he shuddered with pleasure at her touch.

She sighed, and her laughter faded as she moved into his arms, reaching up to kiss him. "Hold me, Brody," she whispered. "Make love to me."

"My pleasure, ma'am." He cupped her breast, rubbing his thumb over her nipples and watching her cheeks flush with desire. "My grandpa taught me that a gentleman always accommodates a lady's wishes."

THE MIST OF EARLY MORNING still hung in the air as they showered and made their way downstairs to the kitchen. While he measured water and ground beans for their coffee, Brody watched Toni, who was pacing restlessly, as if eager to get out and grab the day by its throat. The first rays of early morning sunlight streamed into the kitchen, setting fire to the tawny highlights in her hair. She was barefoot, her cheeks were pale, her eyes were shadowed with fatigue, and she wore no makeup. She wasn't as conventionally pretty as Jill had been, but Brody didn't think he'd ever seen a more beautiful woman. He sure as hell had never seen one he desired more. Even now, after a night filled with making love, he wanted her.

He'd learned over the past few weeks that Toni was a woman who needed space for her restless, creative energies, so he let her pace until the coffee was ready. Then he put a steaming mug into her hands, dragged out a chair and pushed her into it. She took the coffee gratefully, but she'd barely drunk half of it when she uncoiled herself from the chair and started pacing the kitchen again, occasionally bending over and peering under pieces of furniture.

"What are you doing?" he asked mildly.

"Looking for my shoes." She found them by the porch door and thrust her feet into them, adjusting the straps around her heels impatiently. "We don't have time to hang around, Brody. We need to get to Riverwood. Justin often leaves for his first meeting by seven-thirty, and it's already six o'clock."

Bayou Beltane was, at most, a twenty-minute drive from his house, but he could see she wasn't ready to listen to that sort of logic. Brody put his arms around her and sat her down again in the chair, knowing she wasn't going to like what he was about to suggest. "Honey, I don't think we should go to Riverwood right now. In fact, it would probably be better not to go there today."

"Not go?" She stared at him blankly. "But that's why we drove over here! We have to tell Justin that the Henderson files have been stolen from Shoreline's offices."

"It's not the smartest idea for us to involve Justin in this," Brody said. "I believe we can take care of the situation without bringing your brother into it."

She stood up and stared at him in amazement. "How can we do that? This whole situation is about him."

"Not really. I'd say this is much more about Philip than about Justin."

"In practical terms, that's the same difference," she said, tugging at his hand and already halfway out of the door. "Come on, Brody. We need to let Justin know what's going on."

Brody stopped her progress toward the garage by the simple process of picking her up and carrying her outside to the porch. He deposited her on the sofa where they'd made love only a couple of hours earlier, and sat down next to her, his arm clamped around her waist so that she couldn't leave.

"Toni, you're not thinking this through. If you go storming over to Riverwood and pour out details of Philip's illegal activities into Justin's ears, you're going to put him in an impossible position. He's been nominated as a judge, an officer of the court. He can't just sit back and ignore the fact that you've reported a series of crimes and planned crimes to him. When he takes office, he's going to have to swear a solemn oath to uphold the law without fear or favor to any individual. How can he possibly swear to that if he knows his nomination was only confirmed because he suppressed evidence that Philip Delacroix is guilty of blackmail, conspiracy to commit fraud, insider trading and a host of other illegal activities?"

"Oh, my God." Toni stared at him in dismay. "It never occurred to me that Justin would be morally obligated to report what I tell him about Uncle Philip to the authorities."

"It's more than a moral obligation," Brody said. "If he doesn't report what he knows, he's complicit in your uncle's crimes. And if he does report everything he knows, I can guarantee there will be a major scandal. If Philip's activities become known, he's going to become the prime target of a police investigation and the Delacroix name is going to be plastered over every newspaper in the state. As for Dennis Carron, there would be no chance of keeping him out of the picture. He's going to be toast. I don't think you want to put Justin in that kind of a lose-lose situation, do you?"

"Of course I don't. *Damn!*" Toni scowled at a frog that had hopped onto the porch steps and was flicking its tongue in hopeful search of breakfast. "What are we going to do, Brody? What *can* we do?"

"Fortunately, I'm not about to become a judge, which means I've got a lot more room to maneuver than Justin has. And I'm more than willing to play hardball with Philip."

"I appreciate the offer, but what can you do? As I see

it, the problem is that right now my uncle is holding the bat, the ball and the rule book. How are you going to play hardball against a man like that, Brody?''

"Philip doesn't have nearly as much going for him as you think," Brody said. "I believe your uncle is in deep trouble and that's why he's lashing out, trying to contain a situation that's running out of control."

"What sort of trouble? Financial trouble? He always seems to have more money than he knows what to do with."

"Money isn't always about material possessions. Your uncle likes luxury, but he craves the power that money can buy even more. That's a dangerous mind-set for a lawyer. I'm guessing that when he started out in his profession, he was careful to operate strictly within the letter of the law, even if not the spirit. But for someone who's power hungry, the temptations of the legal profession are enormous. Add in a political career, as your uncle did, and you're just about doomed unless you have a rock-hard core of ethics. Before you know what's happening, you wake up one morning and realize that you're not a lawyer anymore, or a democratic representative of the people. You're a crook with a law degree."

Toni shivered. "Is that what you think my uncle has become? A crook with a law degree?"

Brody hesitated, then decided to give it to her straight. "Yes."

She got up and walked over to the screen window. Brody came and stood behind her, just in time to see the frog hop away into the bushes. He wondered if it had gotten its breakfast.

Toni turned around and looked up at him, her eyes a vivid blue against the pallor of her face. "I realized last night that you obviously know a lot more about my uncle's activities than I do. Stop beating around the bush,

Brody, and tell me everything you know about him. Somebody in my family needs to face up to the facts before my uncle causes real harm.''

He hated to hurt her, but there was no way he could think of to cushion the truth. ''Your uncle is drowning in illegal campaign contributions,'' he said. ''He's been a state senator for the past twenty years, and he has allies in every major power center in the state, so he has a lot of people willing to send him a check for a thousand dollars, just to keep on his good side.''

''But there's nothing illegal about doing that, is there?'' Toni asked.

It was her uncle they were talking about, and Brody could see that her desire for the truth was battling with her desire to hear that maybe her uncle hadn't done anything too terrible. ''There's nothing illegal about taking money from your political supporters, providing you comply with all the reporting laws. Although Philip's accepted money from some very unsavory people and organizations, having scum bags as your allies isn't illegal, either. The real temptation for Philip has been the fact that he chairs the Environmental Oversight Committee in the state Senate. Sounds innocuous and civic-minded, and Philip's certainly taken advantage of that aspect of his chairmanship.''

''I've noticed that he seems to have had his picture taken in front of every restored wetland in the state,'' Toni said.

''Yes, he's spent a lot of time and effort encouraging the voters to believe that he's out there fighting to keep Louisiana ecologically pristine. Meanwhile, the big land developers know the truth. Nobody gets to develop any sizable piece of property without a nod from his committee, and getting a favorable vote from his committee can cost a builder several hundred thousand dollars. All channeled through phony groups and organizations into Philip's campaign funds, of course, so nobody has to mention anything sordid like the word *bribe*."

Toni flinched. "Aren't there strict limits as to how much money one person or organization can give to a politician's reelection campaign?" she asked.

"Yes, and Philip has found a dozen creative ways to extend those limits."

"How do you know all this, Brody? Do you have proof of anything you're saying?"

"Some proof, and I can get more. Until Philip made the mistake of getting too aggressive in his attempts to warn me off, I had no interest in him or his activities. But since he set those thugs on my tail, I've been hot on his heels and I've uncovered a lot that's incriminating. Even so, I doubt if I've sorted out the specifics of half of what your uncle's involved in. Still, it's obvious from what I've checked already that he stepped completely over the legal line at least five years ago. What he's doing now isn't just fudging his campaign finance records, he's selling his vote outright in return for money and favors."

Toni shuddered. "The worst of it is, I have only a tiny bit of difficulty believing you. It's all of a piece with the way he's behaved toward Justin and Dennis. There's something not quite…genuine, I guess is the word…about my uncle. I've always despised the way he switches that fake Southern charm off and on."

She stopped abruptly, her brows drawing together in a frown. "His blackmail of Dennis and his campaign against Justin don't surprise me, but I don't see how Philip benefits. Even if he's swimming in a sea of illegal bribes, how does Justin's nomination to the federal bench threaten that?"

"Justin has always been an outspoken champion of campaign finance reform," Brody explained. "And if Justin's nomination is confirmed, he'll be the judge presiding over the trial of one of Philip's cronies who got caught with his hands so deep into the developers' pockets that even his friends in high places couldn't manage to cover up what had been going on.''

"Does that mean there's a risk this trial will dish the dirt on my uncle?''

"Possibly. Justin can't be bribed, and Philip, of all people, must know that. He's running scared—terrified that this case will take the lid off a can of worms that he desperately wants to keep locked up in a dark cellar.''

"And preventing Justin's nomination is going to make that much difference?'' Toni asked, her voice doubtful.

"No other potential judge in this state has Justin's reputation for integrity, combined with opposition to sleazy politics. I'm guessing Philip doesn't just want Justin's nomination to fail. He wants to sling the sort of mud that will be so messy and cling so tightly that Justin's reputation will be totally destroyed. Which, from Philip's point of view, will have the highly desirable effect of neutralizing Justin's efforts to clean up the scandalous campaign finance situation in this state.''

"Leaving Philip free to continue floating at the top of his cesspool of dirty money,'' Toni said. She wrapped her arms around her waist, bending over as if she were physically in pain. ''Philip's done a real number on us, hasn't he? If we report him to the authorities, then all the sordid details of how he's been taking bribes is going to come out. He might even be sent to prison. If we don't report him, he's going to do his damnedest to see that Justin's publicly disgraced. Either way, it's going to kill Aunt Mary. And Dad…''

She swallowed hard. ''Dad and I have never been close, but I've always admired him, you know? He has a really old-fashioned sense of honor, and he's fought all his life to uphold the integrity of his profession. How in the world is he going to react when he's forced to listen to garbage like this about his twin brother? Or watch Justin's nomination crash in flames? God, he'll *hate* that. He's so proud of Justin.''

Brody took her into his arms and cradled her head against his chest, stroking her hair and using his thumbs to brush away the tears that glittered on the ends of her lashes. When she had herself under control again, he dropped a quick kiss on her forehead, then held her at arm's length.

''Okay, before you get too upset, I have a good news, bad news scenario to bring to your attention here. The good news is, as I told you a while ago, I have a plan. The bad news is that even if my plan works perfectly, Philip isn't going to be punished for what's he's done. We're not going to be able to stop him from hauling in thousands of dollars more in illegal campaign contributions, and the world isn't going to be made permanently safe for democracy.''

She wrinkled her nose and managed a wry laugh. ''I have to say, Brody, that doesn't sound like much of a plan.''

''But you didn't let me finish. The good part is, Justin gets to be a judge, and the people in your family that you care about don't have to confront the unpleasant truth about what Philip's done. As a side bonus, if you insist on it, I can probably save Dennis Carron's worthless hide.'' He touched his forehead to hers, wishing he could offer her more. ''In the real world, honey, I guess that's about as good as it gets.''

''It sounds pretty good, given what we have to work with.'' She pushed her hair out of her eyes, her energy returning. ''To be honest, I don't see how you can achieve even that much.''

"There's only one way," he said. "I have to convince Philip that he'll lose more by continuing his campaign against Justin than he will by allowing Justin's nomination to go through."

She grimaced. "I hate to criticize, Brody, but isn't that basically another way of saying that you're going to ask Philip to please play nicely?"

"No." Brody's grin was quick and confident. "The difference is I intend to get every bit as low-down and dirty as your uncle. I'm sure I'll soon persuade him to see things my way."

She directed a worried glance toward him. "Brody, you're a lawyer. Aren't you just as much obligated to report Philip's illegal activities as Justin?"

"Maybe. It's not something I'm going to lose sleep over." He shrugged. "Life is full of risks and compromises, and this is one compromise that won't trouble my conscience at all."

"But it's unnecessary for you to put your professional integrity on the line," she said. "Brody, I'm not a lawyer, I have nothing at stake. Let me be the person to put the screws on Philip."

"It wouldn't work, Toni," he said.

"Why?" The color came and went in her cheeks, momentarily distracting him. "Step out of your macho mode for a moment, Brody—"

"This has nothing to do with machismo or my ego," he said. "Philip is only going to back off if he believes our threats, and I can deliver those threats more effectively than you can. It's as simple as that."

She gave a frustrated sigh, tacitly acknowledging his point. "There must be something useful I could do, Brody. I can't just sit around here waiting for you to come back and say it's all taken care of. Or not."

"There is something you can do," he said. "Call Philip

at his home and tell him you need to see him urgently. If I try to set up a meeting, he'll probably decide to give me the runaround, and by the time I actually get to see him, it might be too late. He's got less reason to be worried about you, and that means he's less likely to try to avoid you."

"If I arrange the meeting, Brody, he'll expect me to turn up for it."

"That's not a problem," he said. "We'll go to the meeting together and you can wait outside while I—"

"Don't even suggest it," she said, shaking her head. "Once I'm there, Brody, I'm coming in with you. This is my brother's career on the line, and it's my uncle who's causing the trouble."

"Okay, you win. But leave me to do all the talking, that's essential." Having won the war, he was prepared to concede her a small victory in terms of the truce. He took her into his arms, smiling ruefully. "Did anyone ever mention to you that you're one hell of a stubborn woman?"

"Nobody," she said. "I guess you bring out the best in me, Brody."

CHAPTER ELEVEN

PHILIP DELACROIX CAME out of his office, his feet making no sound on the thick midnight blue carpeting. "Antoinette, my dear, this is certainly an unexpected pleasure. I don't believe I've ever had the privilege of entertainin' you in my offices before." Her uncle's voice was thick with Southern charm. He took her hand into his, patting it with every appearance of kindly affection.

"No, I've never had any reason to come here before," Toni said. She extricated her hand from his clasp and stepped sideways just as Brody appeared at the end of the short hallway. "I believe you know Brody Wagner, Uncle Philip. He worked most recently for Blake Shawcross in New York, and he's the newest partner in my father's firm."

Philip's smile congealed into a grimace. "Mr. Wagner and I met at Mary's birthday party." He turned to his secretary, his anger barely concealed, all trace of charm vanishing in a flash. "You didn't tell me that my niece had brought anyone with her. Why not?"

"She didn't know," Brody said, stepping forward to the visible relief of the secretary. "Shall we continue this discussion in your office, Mr. Delacroix?"

Philip ignored him, turning to Toni as if he'd never spoken. "Antoinette, what is this all about? I agreed to see you as a personal favor because you're my niece—"

"Toni has retained me as her legal counsel," Brody said. "I suggest we step inside your office, Mr. Delacroix.

The business we've come to conduct would be better dealt
with in private."

Philip turned on his heel and stalked into his office,
leaving his door open, although he didn't acknowledge
either of them directly. Toni realized they'd just achieved
their first victory. Her uncle would never have agreed to
speak with Brody unless he was a bit afraid of what they
had to say.

They followed him into his office, which was a huge,
ostentatious room with paneled walls and a bookcase full
of leather-bound law journals, too pretty to have seen
much use. The eight-foot-high picture window looked out
onto an enclosed courtyard with a fountain spurting water
into a small pool lined with black marble. Corruption obviously paid well, Toni reflected grimly.

Brody closed the door as Philip went to stand behind
his desk, an oversize walnut affair, decorated with an an-
tique pewter inkwell and gold-embossed leather trays that
held neat stacks of documents. For a seventy-nine-year-
old man, he stood very straight and made a commanding
figure. Physically, he still looked a great deal like her
father, Toni reflected. It was curious that even as a child,
she'd always been much more aware of the differences
between the two men as opposed to the similarities. For
all his inability to express his emotions, and for all their
battles during her adolescence, she'd never doubted that
her father was basically a good, honest person.

"I have an important meeting starting in ten minutes,"
Philip said coldly, neither sitting nor suggesting that they
should sit. "I understood that you had an urgent personal
matter to discuss with me, Antoinette, which is why I
agreed to squeeze you into my extremely busy morning
schedule."

"Yes, Uncle Philip, I do have something important to
discuss with you," she said, putting down the briefcase

she'd carried in for Brody. "I want to talk to you about Justin's nomination to the federal bench."

Philip's left eyebrow rose in a token gesture of surprise, but Toni noticed that his fingers closed abruptly around the handle of the paper knife he'd been toying with. "Other than to offer him my congratulations on his imminent confirmation, I can't imagine any contribution I could make to such a discussion."

"You underestimate yourself," Brody said. "Which I'm sure must be a novel experience. We're not so much concerned with Justin's nomination, which you presumably tried—and failed—to get quashed before it was ever announced. What we'd like to talk to you about today, is the routine background check the FBI always conducts in regard to anyone who has been nominated to a high federal office."

Philip's expression remained bored. "I have even less to contribute on that subject."

"Really? Toni, however, has a great deal to say to you concerning the false evidence you've constructed purporting to show that her brother Justin defrauded an elderly couple who were his clients."

"I have no idea what you're talking about."

"I'm talking about the Henderson land deal with Shoreline Exploration," Brody said. "And your plans to pass false information relating to this deal to the FBI."

"I still have no idea what you're talking about, except that your attitude so far has been insulting and your remarks slanderous."

"You're a lawyer, Mr. Delacroix, so you should know that truth can never be deemed slanderous." Brody braced his hands on the edge of the desk and leaned forward. "So, since you're such a busy man, why don't we both save ourselves a lot of time and skip right over your protestations of innocence and get to the point of the deal I plan to offer you. A deal you would be very smart to accept."

Philip finally condescended to look straight at Brody. "I don't find you amusing, Mr. Wagner. In fact, I should warn you that this conversation is being recorded, and what you just said sounded remarkably like a threat to me."

"Not a threat, Mr. Delacroix, simply a statement of intent."

"I think you'll find that your behavior this morning has been less than wise, young man, given that you're new in town and somewhat short of influential friends."

Toni made a small involuntary sound, although she'd sworn to Brody that she wouldn't interfere in any way with his conduct of the meeting. Neither Brody nor Philip spared her a glance.

Brody straightened, his gaze locked with Philip's, his expression almost amused. "Mr. Delacroix, you've already tried to intimidate me by a wide variety of methods, including sending two thugs to beat me up in my own backyard. Since you know that all those previous efforts at intimidation were unsuccessful, you should surely recognize by now that I'm not likely to be driven into a state of major panic by the knowledge that you're taping our conversation." He paused, then added, "In fact, in the interests of full disclosure, perhaps I should tell you that I'm taping it, too."

"Is that really necessary?" Philip asked.

"Yes." Brody's one-word response hung in the air with unexpected menace.

Philip coughed. "Enough, Mr. Wagner. Shall we consider the preliminary skirmishes over and get to the point?" The mildness of his tone implicitly acknowledged that his scare tactics hadn't worked. He put down the letter opener he'd been holding and walked over to the window, lifting up the edge of the draperies to reveal an electronic keypad fixed to the wall. His finger hovered over a red button. "In recognition of the fact that Antoinette is my niece, I'm willing to turn off my recording equipment."

"But I'm not willing to turn off mine," Brody said.

"Why not?"

Brody's mouth stretched into a cold smile that was so completely unlike his normal open friendliness that Toni felt as if she were looking at a stranger. A somewhat dangerous stranger who was used to getting his way.

"Experience suggests that people doing business with you need to keep their own records so that there's no confusion about exactly what was agreed upon," he said. "Your records have a strange habit of mutating their sub-clauses, Mr. Delacroix."

Philip's lips tightened angrily. He let the drapes fall back into place without switching off his recording equipment and returned to his desk. "Your precautions are excessive, Mr. Wagner, since I can imagine nothing on which we are likely to reach agreement."

"We're going to reach an agreement about how you can save yourself from prosecution on charges of bribery and corruption," Brody said. "You're a man who's lived long and comfortably, Mr. Delacroix, and I'm sure you don't want to spend your final years in a federal prison. Negotiate a deal with me today, and you won't have to."

If Philip was nervous, Toni could detect no signs of it. His only visible reaction was to pull back the stiffly starched and monogrammed cuff of his shirt and look at his watch. "That suggestion is too absurd to dignify with a response. Now, if you'll excuse me, I believe I must get to my next appointment. My secretary will show you out."

He reached for the intercom and Brody leaned forward, laying his hand over Philip's wrist, preventing him from picking up the phone. "If you really have an appointment, tell your secretary to cancel it. Otherwise, I suggest you stop playing games and listen to what I'm offering you."

Toni saw the first faint flicker of fear in her uncle's eyes, but Philip was much too experienced to cave in without seeing his opponent's full hand. "It seems that unless I have you bodily thrown out, you're determined to make your offer. So say your piece, young man, and then get out."

"Listen up, Mr. Delacroix, because this is a one-time offer. No refunds or exchanges allowed." Brody's voice was clipped, confident and implacable. "You will cease and desist in your efforts to derail Justin's nomination to the federal bench. You will return to me the files on the Henderson land deal that you arranged to have stolen from Shoreline's offices. You will refrain from making anonymous accusations and submitting false documentation regarding the Henderson case to the FBI agents in charge of checking into Justin's personal and professional background. You will also cease and desist your blackmail of Dennis Carron. And in exchange…"

"And in exchange?" Philip demanded softly. "Exactly what favor do you propose selling in return for that long laundry list of ridiculous demands?"

Brody leaned forward, spacing each word precisely. "In exchange, Mr. Delacroix, I will refrain from informing the authorities of your many and varied criminal activities. Grab the offer and run with it. It's a good one."

Philip laughed, but Toni noticed that he'd stopped talking about leaving for another meeting. "You have nothing on me, Mr. Wagner. You're all bluff and no substance."

"No bluff is involved in this deal. Trust me."

Philip's voice lowered to a scornful softness. "This is Louisiana, Mr. Wagner. Half the law enforcement agencies in this state owe me favors. You'll get nowhere with your accusations.''

"I won't be stupid enough to report you to the state authorities," Brody said. "You're not going to be able to buy yourself out of this problem, Mr. Delacroix. If we don't reach an agreement, I'm going straight to the feds.''

"And why would they bother to listen to you stringing them a series of fairy tales about one of Louisiana's most revered public figures?''

"No fairy tales. Documented accusations." Without taking his eyes from Philip's, Brody bent down and picked up the briefcase Toni had brought into the office. He put it onto the desk, flipped the locks and swung it around, lid open.

"Help yourself, Mr. Delacroix. Pick any sheet of paper at random. Naturally, I don't have to tell you that I have copies of every piece of information contained in this briefcase.''

Her uncle was old enough that it was possible his hand always had a slight tremor, but Toni almost found it in her heart to feel sorry for him as he reached into the briefcase with hands that shook so hard he seemed to have trouble picking up the papers. He sat down, giving away the advantage of meeting Brody eye to eye, and read a page at random.

She couldn't read the details upside down, but Toni recognized a list of donations made to a registered nonprofit foundation called the Committee to Save Our Wetlands. Brody had done the laborious cross-referencing necessary to demonstrate that the organizations receiving money from the committee were fakes—nothing but financial fronts for her uncle.

Philip put the page down and picked up another, a similar listing for the Baton Rouge Nature Conservation Group, and so on through at least a dozen more sheets, leading to the final page, which showed all the organizations making contributions to Philip's reelection campaign. After five minutes of silent reading, he turned and reached for the crystal jug of iced water standing on his credenza and poured himself a glass. Finally, he swung his chair around again and looked up at Brody.

"Where did you get this information?" he asked. "How did you know where to look? Did Joanna set you on the trail? Am I being betrayed by my own daughter?"

"Joanna has nothing to do with this," Brody said. "This is personal, strictly between you and me. You shouldn't have sent your hired help after me, Mr. Delacroix, and if you decided to have me beaten up, you should have paid for experts, a couple of real pros who weren't going to tell me everything they knew when their attack didn't go quite like they'd planned."

Philip started another denial, but Brody cut him off. "You made a bad mistake when you went after me, Mr. Delacroix. The problem is, I'm not a fine southern gentleman like you, and I get downright mean and ornery when people start using their fists to tell me how to conduct my business. I had no interest in you or your law firm until your hoodlums made me realize that you were the person behind all my lost clients and deals that suddenly went sour."

"You have absolutely no way to prove that I initiated any attack on you," Philip blustered.

"I have proof," Brody said coldly. "You've been king of your local dung heap so long, you've gotten careless. For a man like me who's spent the past eight years dealing with a bunch of international operators who are selling oil leases one week and ballistic missiles the next, finding out which dirty pies your fingers had been stuck into was too easy to be amusing."

Philip crumpled the sheet of paper he was holding.

"You'll need more convincing proof than this to convict me," he said, but his voice shook, sounding old and tired.

"I don't have to provide evidence that would stand up in a court of law," Brody said. "Based on the information I can give them, the federal authorities will get warrants to examine your bank accounts, your tax returns and every financial transaction you've made for the past ten years. And if that doesn't put the fear of God into you, Mr. Delacroix, think about your cronies and friends, the slimy bunch of co-conspirators you've gathered around you over the years. Once they hear that their names are on lists that have been handed over to the feds, they'll be running for cover so fast you won't even have time to wave as they pass by. They'll be so busy saving their own skins by selling yours that they'll have the flesh stripped off you quicker than a pond full of piranhas."

Her uncle started to look so unwell that Toni finally intervened, alarmed that he might have a stroke, or even a heart attack like his sister. "Uncle Philip, I don't want to see you in jail. In fact, that's almost the last thing I want. But Justin has worked long and hard to become a judge, and he deserves to have his nomination go through. You need to back off and stop opposing him. Otherwise, you're going to wake up in jail one morning and realize that you've paid an unbearably high price for the dubious privilege of keeping Justin off the bench."

"You are both fooling yourselves if you believe these accusations could be made to stick," Philip said with a final burst of shaky defiance. "You would never get an indictment, much less a conviction."

"Do you really want to put your theory to the test?" Brody asked. "Be reasonable, Mr. Delacroix. Surely I don't have to warn you not to allow your personal dislike of Justin to get in the way of your own best interests."

Philip was silent for a few brooding seconds. Then he

gathered the papers scattered over his desk and flung them in the direction of the briefcase. "Take your damn lists and get out," he said.

"Does that mean we have a deal?" Brody asked.

"Yes, damn you." Philip stared straight ahead.

"Then I need the Henderson files that you arranged to have stolen from Shoreline," Brody said. "Just as a token of your sincerity, you understand."

"I don't have them yet." Philip sounded pettish. "You'll have to wait."

"I'm not willing to wait," Brody said. "The deal's off, Mr. Delacroix." He shut the lid of the briefcase, snapped the locks and started to walk toward the door. Caught off guard, Toni could only scramble in his wake.

"Wait!" Philip said.

Brody paused, hand on the door, and glanced back over his shoulder. "I asked for the Henderson files and you lied. You told me you didn't have them. I don't offer second chances, Mr. Delacroix."

Philip scowled. "Once I give you those files, I've got no leverage. How do I know that you won't walk straight out of here and into the arms of the feds?"

Brody's gaze was cool. " Because we agreed to a deal and I've given you my word."

Philip gave a wintry smile. "You won't be surprised to hear that I don't place a great deal of faith in a man's word, Mr. Wagner."

Toni decided it was time for her to intervene again. "You have more to count on than our promises," she said. "It's not in our interests to go to the FBI or anyone else who might prosecute you. We don't want to stir up any scandals if we don't have to. You're my uncle, my father's twin brother. I have no desire to drag the Delacroix name through the mud unless you force me to."

"But don't get any ideas," Brody drawled. "Even if

Toni might prove too softhearted to turn you in, trust me, Mr. Delacroix, my heart is made of concrete, reinforced with steel. I'll turn you in without a split second's hesitation."

"And that, unfortunately, I do believe," Philip said dryly.

"This is your last chance," Brody said, his voice intimidating in its soft clarity. "I'm about to leave these offices and I won't be back. The choice is yours, Mr. Delacroix. You can hand over the files you stole from Shoreline, or you can watch me drive straight from here to the FBI office."

"I'll give you the files, damn you." Philip walked slowly to the wall of bookshelves. He opened the flap on the spine of one of the law books and a panel glided open, revealing a wall safe. Philip dialed the combination and brought out three slim manila folders. "This is what you're looking for," he said, holding them out. "Shoreline's records of their negotiations for the Henderson property."

Brody didn't move and neither did Philip. The deal was done, but apparently Philip wasn't prepared to lose any more face by walking across the room and meekly handing over the files. Brody, meanwhile, was asserting his dominance as the victor and had no intention of relinquishing his post by the door.

Recognizing the makings of one of those male power rituals that caused world wars and never made much sense to a woman, Toni simply stepped forward and took the files. While Brody and Philip were still blinking with shock at the resolution to their standoff, she flipped through the folders, seeing that many of the pages inside were headed up with the Shoreline logo and that the name Henderson appeared several times. She handed the collection to Brody.

"As far as I can tell, these are the files we're looking for," she said.

Brody didn't read them, just clicked open his briefcase and pushed the folders inside.

"Aren't you going to check that I've given you the right files?" Philip asked.

"You'd better hope that you have," Brody said, and gave one of his smiles that sent chills racing up and down Toni's spine. "Thanks for your time, Mr. Delacroix. Have a good day."

Toni could recognize an exit line when she heard one. Waving her hand at her uncle, she followed Brody out of the office.

She managed to contain her glee until they reached the parking lot where Brody had left his car. "You did it!" she exulted, flinging her arms around his neck.

"*We* did it," Brody said, letting the briefcase drop to the ground. Laughing, he wrapped his arms around her waist, scooping her up and swinging her high into the air.

She grinned down at him. "Hey, you know what? Remind me never to get on your bad side. You're a pretty scary man when you go into attack mode, Brody."

He did a bad imitation of James Cagney. "You ain't seen nuttin' yet, babe." For a moment, he held her poised above him, the joy of their success like a current passing back and forth between them. Then the laughter faded. Brody's arms relaxed their hold, and she slid slowly down the length of his body, until her toes touched the ground again and her breasts were pressed against his chest, heartbeat thudding against heartbeat, her breath mingling with his.

"Toni..."

She leaned back in his arms. "Yes?" The look in his eyes made her yearn. Not just for sex, but for something intangible, something she couldn't quite define.

"I'm falling in love with you," he said, his voice husky. "And it's only fair to warn you that I plan to do my damnedest to make you feel the same way."

She felt her legs go wobbly at the knees, and it took her a moment before she could breathe again. Brody caught her hands and pulled her close, holding her when she would have jerked away. "Does it scare you to hear me say that?" he asked.

"A little," she admitted, hearing the tremor in her own voice. "In my family, love isn't a word we say often or easily."

He framed her face with his hands. "Don't be scared," he said. "We can take this as slowly as you want."

"I'm not scared. Not of you, anyway." She hesitated. "The truth is, I'm afraid of myself, and what you can make me feel. I don't have a great track record where relationships are concerned, and I'm worried that we could do each other some serious damage."

"Then we won't have a relationship. For now, let's just agree to spend some time together, as lovers as well as friends."

A smile tugged at her mouth. "Isn't that the same thing as having a relationship?"

"Not unless we say it is." He kissed her softly, lingeringly. "Whatever happens between us will happen because we're both sure we want it."

She drew in a steadying breath. "I guess I can handle that."

"Then let's go home," he said.

CHAPTER TWELVE

BRODY HELD OUT HIS HAND to Toni. "Ready?" he asked.

She shut the car door. "Ready as I'll ever be." Scowling, she looked at her aunt's house. "Remind me why I agreed to do this."

"You've decided that you want your family to know that we're dating."

She glared at him, determined to be annoyed. "No, *you* decided that we ought to tell them we're dating and I let myself be persuaded."

Brody seemed unperturbed by the accusation. "Trust me, you won't regret this."

Toni's scowl deepened. "Families are a royal pain in the you-know-where."

"True. They also happen to be one of the greatest institutions ever invented." Tucking her hand through his arm, he bent down and kissed her.

Forgetting that he was an infuriating man and that she was justifiably angry with him, Toni kissed him back until she realized that anyone walking out onto the veranda would be able to see them. She pushed away, flustered. "Brody, stop. Someone might see us."

He looked down at her, his gaze amused but sympathetic. "Would that be so terrible?"

She sighed. "Don't try to make me behave rationally about this, Brody. Yes, it would be terrible."

"Honey, there's no need to be so uptight." He spoke

with fake solemnity, but his eyes were alight with laughter. "I'm going to be there for you, honey. All the way."

"You're loving every minute of this," she said accusingly. "You think this is no big deal."

"You're wrong," he said. "I know it's a big deal for you, and that means it's a big deal for me, too. A very big deal. I'm honored that you're finally willing to appear with me in public."

She turned to him, dismayed. "Brody! I never meant... Surely you never thought that I was trying to keep our relationship a secret?"

"Only from your family. And only because you want their approval so badly."

"I don't give a flying fig for their approval."

"If you say so."

Her irritation returned in full measure. "If there's one thing I can't stand, it's a patronizing man."

"Especially if he's right?" Before she could explode, Brody dropped a swift kiss on the tip of her nose and looped his arm around her waist, keeping it there as they scrunched up the crushed shell driveway leading to Aunt Mary's house.

Although it was late September, almost two months since Mary's fateful birthday party, summer still lingered and the midday heat was intense. Toni pushed open the front door and walked inside, gulping down a welcome breath of cooled air. They were probably the last guests to arrive, since she'd already lost her nerve twice this morning. Brody had finally threatened to lift her bodily into the car if she didn't stop procrastinating. The hum of voices and laughter coming from the parlor almost made her lose her nerve for the third time, but she dredged up her courage and walked doggedly down the hallway until they reached the parlor door.

Her hand reached for the old-fashioned latch, then

stopped. The members of the Delacroix family were assembled in full force on the other side of the door, celebrating the specialist's recent pronouncement that Mary was now fully recovered from her heart attack. Toni could brave an audience of a thousand fans and critics with no problem, but the prospect of being scrutinized by the assembled Delacroix clan was enough to dissolve her into a mass of melting Jell-O.

Brody saw her hesitation and recognized its cause. "Go for it," he said softly. "Three deep breaths and then just do it."

Steeled for the worst, she pushed the door open and stepped into the parlor. A few family members waved and smiled, but the hum of cheerful chatter continued unabated. So much for her vastly overinflated ego, Toni thought with rueful self-mockery. Only Aunt Mary seemed to find anything at all noteworthy about the fact that her niece had just arrived, hand in hand with Brody Wagner.

Aunt Mary was seated by the hearth in her new recliner, a welcome-home gift from her family. She had been leaning back against the smoky blue cushions, her feet elevated on the built-in footrest, but at the sight of Toni walking across the room with Brody, she pressed the electronic button, lowered her footrest and sat up very straight, feet planted firmly on the floor in front of her. At the merest whiff of an impending romance, Mary's sensors always went on full alert.

"Antoinette, my dear!" In the past few weeks, Mary's voice had recovered all its former strength. "How nice that you were able to come in time for lunch. And I see you've brought Brody with you. This is a most unexpected pleasure."

Brody stepped forward and shook her hand. "It's good to see you looking so well, Miss Mary. I hope you'll forgive me for crashing your party, but you did say Toni could bring a guest.''

"You know you're always welcome at any time, Brody."

Toni bent down and kissed her aunt. "I'm sorry we're a little late, Aunt Mary." Her father was standing on the opposite side of the hearth, and she turned to him quickly, before her aunt could ask any awkward questions "Hello, Dad. How are you?"

"Well, thank you. And how are you, Antoinette?" Her father made a small half movement toward her, then stopped and stepped back again to his previous position.

It was the sort of tepid welcome she'd received from him all her life. But for some reason, this time Toni understood that his reticence wasn't caused by disapproval of her appearance or her behavior, but by uncertainty about her reaction to him. Seized by a surge of unfamiliar emotion, she leaned forward and put her hands on his shoulders, tugging him gently forward so that she could kiss him. Her father stiffened, but in shock rather than rejection, she realized.

He pressed a swift kiss against her cheek, then backed away almost at once, seeming unsure of what to say next. His gaze traveled over her distractedly, coming to rest on Brody's arm. Which, Toni realized, was locked firmly around her waist.

"I wasn't aware that you and Brody were such good friends," he said finally.

"Toni and I have been dating for quite a while," Brody said. "I hope you approve, sir?"

"Humph." Her father's gaze became openly speculative. "Antoinette is a grown woman. She doesn't have to get my approval before she chooses her dates. Or even her husband."

He cocked his head to one side, waiting. In hopes that

she was going to announce her engagement to Brody Wagner, Toni realized. Instead of being irritated by her father's curiosity, she felt an unexpected wish to give him the news he wanted to hear.

Instead of reacting with stiff politeness, she smiled as she answered him. "If Brody and I decide to get married, you'll be the first to know, Dad."

"And how long might I have to wait?"

"Stay tuned," Brody said easily. "Story and pictures will be scheduled eventually."

"This is wonderful news," Mary said. "You see, Toni, I told you all along that Brody was the perfect match for you, and I never make a mistake about these things. How splendid that the two of you are planning to become engaged."

"But we've never discussed getting engaged!" Toni protested, sending a frantic glance in Brody's direction and too disconcerted to remind her aunt that Brody was merely the last in a long line of disastrously unsuitable men that Mary had picked out as prospective husbands. "We're just dating," Toni continued hurriedly. "We haven't made any definite plans for the future at all."

Remy passed by. "Did I hear Aunt Mary say the two of you are engaged?" he asked. He grasped Brody's hand and pumped it enthusiastically. "That's terrific news! Congratulations."

"Remy, listen up," Toni said through gritted teeth. "Brody and I are *not* engaged. We're just good friends. Although that state of affairs may not survive this party."

"Oh, sure," Remy said. "I understand." He grinned and gave Brody's arm a friendly punch. "Take my advice, man, and elope. A full-scale Delacroix family wedding requires more organization that Operation Desert Storm."

Remy strode off, whistling. Toni unclenched her jaw.

"You see?" she hissed at Brody. "I warned you something like this would happen."

"But, honey, nothing's happened."

Just like a man to bury his head in the sand and refuse to acknowledge reality. "Nothing's happened?" Toni's voice was spiraling upward and she forced it back under control. "If you're not careful, Brody Wagner, by the time we get out of here we'll be an engaged couple!"

He turned her around so that they were standing face-to-face and took her hands into his. "Sounds like a great idea to me," he said quietly. "How about you?"

Acutely aware of her father and her aunt listening to every word, Toni contemplated murdering Brody. "Is that supposed to be a proposal of marriage?" she snapped. "If so, it could use some work."

"Yes, it was a proposal," he said. He carried her hand to his lips, and the expression in his eyes sent Toni's stomach swooping. "I could work on some improvements and do it again when we're alone."

"Do that," Toni said. "In the meantime, you'd better take yourself somewhere very far away or you won't live to have a second chance at proposing."

"Toni! Brody!" Shelby came and hugged them both. "What's this I hear about the two of you getting married?"

Toni wondered if she really had fire coming out of her nostrils or if it only felt that way. Brody laughed, kissed her breathless while Aunt Mary looked on approvingly, and walked off arm in arm with Shelby. "I need your protection to get me out of here," he said. "I think my life hangs by a slender thread."

Her father was actually smiling as he watched Brody retreat. "A fine young man," he said. "I'm very happy for you, Antoinette."

"We're not engaged!" This time Toni didn't even attempt to lower her voice. She yelled, full throttle.

"Quite right," Aunt Mary said. "Every woman is entitled to the pleasure of a proper proposal. Don't say yes, my dear, until Brody offers for you in style."

Toni counted to ten. Suddenly, she saw the funny side of things and started to laugh. Her father joined in. Then, as William and Philip approached to speak to Mary, he drew her aside, where they could talk in reasonable privacy.

"I meant what I said, Antoinette. Brody's a fine man and I believe he'll make you a wonderful husband. I'm very happy for you."

Toni gave up on the attempt to maintain the illusion that she and Brody were merely friends. "Why do you think he'll be a good husband?" she asked. "Because he's a lawyer?"

"No, of course not. Because you're head over heels in love with him. And he with you."

Were her feelings for Brody that obvious? Toni wondered. How strange that she'd barely realized herself how much she loved him, and yet everyone else seemed to consider their relationship not only established, but almost inevitable. Still, she needed to provide a note of caution. "Dad, you're jumping the gun. We haven't agreed to get married. In fact, we haven't agreed to any sort of a permanent relationship."

"Do you love him?" Charles asked.

"Well, yes..."

"Then, I'm not sure how much else there is to discuss," her father said. "Surely the rest is all details."

"I've heard you say a hundred times that the devil is often in the details," Toni pointed out. "Brody and I are both ambitious people, and we have two very different careers to mesh."

"Brody Wagner is ambitious, but he's also a sensible man. He's not going to quibble over details if he's lucky enough to persuade you to marry him."

Toni stared at her father, too astonished to speak. Was he actually suggesting that Brody would be lucky to get her? She would have expected him to find the advantages of the marriage all on the other side.

Her father filled the silence. "I'm not a person who finds it easy to express my feelings to the people I care about, Toni. Once, when I was a young man, I imagined myself passionately in love, and I behaved very foolishly as a consequence. So foolishly, that ever since I've been wary of deep emotion. Frightened of it, to tell the truth."

He cleared his throat, speaking again before she could respond. "I wasn't a good father to you, Toni, although I tried to be. I saw the passion in you, the fire and the talent, and instead of helping you learn how to discipline that passion, I tried to stamp it out. Fortunately, I didn't succeed. I hope that one day you'll be able to forgive me for the mistakes I made, and accept that I made them with the best possible intentions. All I ask is that you don't repeat my mistakes. Don't deny what you feel for Brody because you're frightened to take a chance on love. Of all the mistakes we can make in this world, I believe that one's the biggest."

Toni knew precisely how much it had cost her father to make such an admission. She swallowed over the lump in her throat, wishing that she could fling her arms around his neck and wash away old hurts in a storm of hugs and tears. Unfortunately, she was more of her father's child than he knew, and she could no more cling to him and cry than he could sweep her into his arms in an effusive bear hug. Instead, she reached out tentatively, taking his hand and holding it between hers.

"I would never have become such a strong person if I

hadn't had you to fight, Dad. You know you have my respect and deep admiration. You always have."

"Thank you." The smile he directed at her was wryly self-mocking. "I've spent the last sixty years striving to be a respectable and admirable person. Isn't it ironic that now, when it's too late, I find that what I really want is to be loved?"

From a long way away, she heard herself say the words, "I do love you, Dad. I love you very much."

He touched his hand to her face, and when she felt the wetness of her tears against his fingertips, she realized that, after all, she was crying. Her father spoke softly. "I don't deserve your tears, Toni, but I thank you for them."

He left the room while she was still rummaging around in her purse for a tissue.

Toni was still dabbing her eyes when Justin found her. "Toni, I'm glad to catch you alone for a—" He broke off abruptly. "Damn, you've been crying. What's the matter? If you and Brody have had a tiff—"

"No, it's nothing to do with Brody. In fact, Brody and I seem to be quite amazingly compatible. It was just an unexpected attack of sentiment, that's all." She closed her purse and turned to face him. "Why did you want to speak to me, Justin?"

"Well, if you're sure nothing's really wrong…"

"I'm positive."

"Then, I wanted to let you know that my nomination has just now been approved by the Senate Judiciary Committee. It's going to be sent to the full Senate next week for confirmation."

"Justin, I'm so glad. Congratulations! This is terrific."

"Isn't it? This seems to be a day for sharing good news. I'm really happy for you and Brody, Toni."

For a bunch of lawyers, her family seemed determined

to jump to unfounded conclusions. "Well actually, Justin, we're not engaged."

"Not officially, maybe." Justin dismissed her protests with a wave of his hand. "I may not know you as well as I should, Toni, but I know you well enough to be quite sure that you'd never have brought Brody to one of Aunt Mary's family parties unless you'd already decided to marry him."

She was beginning to wonder if her family didn't understand her better than she understood herself. In retrospect, Toni was well aware that she would never have made such an issue of coming to Aunt Mary's party with Brody if she hadn't known all along exactly what that gesture implied. And Brody had doubtless realized days ago what she was so uptight about.

Toni hooked her arms through Justin's. "So give me the rest of the scoop on your confirmation as a judge, big bro'. Presumably nobody on the Judiciary Committee raised any questions in regard to the Henderson deal?"

"None. Their name never came up. But that's not surprising, considering that the official FBI report summed up the whole incident in three sentences."

"Yes, that whole episode turned out pretty well, all things considered."

He sent her a searching look. "One interesting tidbit of information did surface during my conversations with the FBI."

"Oh, what was that?"

"The person at Shoreline they were dealing with in regard to the Henderson deal was the in-house legal counsel. In other words, Dennis Carron, your former husband."

"Oh," she said. "Fancy that."

"Yes, indeed. Fancy that." Justin gave her a quick hug. "Thanks, Toni, for passing on the word. And thanks to

Dennis, too. I owe you both big time. The Henderson land deal could have developed into a nasty situation if I hadn't been forewarned.''

Little did he know how nasty the situation had been, or that Brody had really been his savior. ''You're welcome,'' she said. ''I'm glad it all worked out for you, Justin. I'm sure you'll be a great judge and make all of us Delacroix proud.''

Brody came back into the parlor. ''Hi, Justin. Hi, Toni. Ready to come and get some lunch, honey? Your father's waiting to propose a toast to Aunt Mary, and he says the longer he waits, the longer his speech is going to be.''

''Coming,'' she said.

Justin walked out, leaving the two of them alone. ''Wait!'' Brody said when she was on the point of following her brother out of the room. He crossed from the shadow of the doorway into the sunlight that streamed in through the window. Oddly, the brilliance of the light obscured his expression, making it hard for her to know what he was thinking. ''Toni, things got a bit out of hand just now and I'm sorry. You shouldn't feel pressured to change the status of our relationship just because your family seems to have decided that I'd made an okay husband for you.''

''Do you want to *change the status of our relationship?*''

''Only if that's what you—'' He broke off, his clenched fist pounding into his hand. ''Hell, yes, I want to change it,'' he said. ''I want to marry you. I want to share my life with you for the next hundred years or so. I want you to be the mother of my children. I want it all, but only on one condition—''

''What's that?''

''You have to love me,'' he said.

''I do love you,'' she said. ''I love you more than I

thought it was possible to love anyone. So will you please marry me, Brody Wagner?''

"Yes," he said, and swept her into his arms.

DELTA JUSTICE

continues with

LETTERS, LIES AND ALIBIS

by Sandy Steen

Rancher Travis Hardin is determined to right a sixty-year wrong and wreak vengeance on the Delacroix. But he hadn't intended to fall in love doing it. Is his desire for Shelby greater than his need to destroy her family?

Available in October

Here's a preview!

CHAPTER ONE

"YOU'RE TEMPTING me."

Travis looked straight into her eyes. "That's the whole point, darlin'."

Exactly when they had ceased talking about food, Shelby wasn't sure, but the conversation had definitely taken a more personal turn. "Maybe I should stick to what I know is good for me."

"Possibly. But it's a whole lot more fun when you don't. Besides, you don't strike me as a strictly-by-the-rules kind of woman."

"Oh, but I am." Shelby smiled. "Particularly when they're my rules."

Travis leaned across the table. "You are direct, aren't you?"

"Afraid so."

"Well, I can't argue with that. I usually play by my own rules, too." He leaned back. "So what's it going to be? Indulge or deny yourself?"

"Indulge...moderately."

After Travis devoured his pie and Shelby consumed half of hers, they drove back into town. By the time they reached the park, darkness had fallen and the landscape lights were on, illuminating the walkways with soft dots of light. Only a few shops were still open, and for the most part everyone had left "downtown" Bayou Beltane.

"Not much happens here after dark," Shelby commented. "At least, not in public."

"Yeah, it's the same in Comfort."

"Not that it prevents people from talking about everything that does happen, and embellishing as they go."

"Gossip and small towns are joined at the hip."

"I suppose. For instance, by tomorrow morning, you and I will be the topic of conversation over everyone's coffee. The fact that no one knows who you are will only add fuel to the gossip flames. I wouldn't be surprised, by the time they've finished, to hear that you and I were making mad passionate love on this beach."

"And you wouldn't like that."

"What? Being gossiped about—"

"Making mad, passionate love with me."

Shelby's heart hammered against her ribcage, and for a second she held her breath. "You're pretty direct yourself, cowboy."

HARLEQUIN PRESENTS®

HARLEQUIN PRESENTS
men you won't be able to resist
falling in love with...

HARLEQUIN PRESENTS
women who have feelings
just like your own...

HARLEQUIN PRESENTS
powerful passion in
exotic international settings...

HARLEQUIN PRESENTS
intense, dramatic stories that will keep you
turning to the very last page...

HARLEQUIN PRESENTS
The world's bestselling romance series!

PRES-G

LOOK FOR OUR FOUR FABULOUS MEN!

Each month some of today's bestselling authors bring
four new fabulous men to Harlequin American Romance.
Whether they're rebel ranchers, millionaire power brokers
or sexy single dads, they're all gallant princes—and
they're all ready to sweep you into lighthearted fantasies
and contemporary fairy tales where anything is possible
and where all your dreams come true!

You don't even have to make a wish...
Harlequin American Romance will grant your every desire!

Look for Harlequin American Romance
wherever Harlequin books are sold!

HAR-GEN

HARLEQUIN SUPERROMANCE®

...there's more to the story!

Superromance. A *big* satisfying read about unforgettable characters. Each month we offer *four* very different stories that range from family drama to adventure and mystery, from highly emotional stories to romantic comedies—and much more! Stories about people you'll believe in and care about. Stories too compelling to put down....

Our authors are among today's *best* romance writers. You'll find familiar names and talented newcomers. Many of them are award winners—and you'll see why!

If you want the biggest and best in romance fiction, you'll get it from Superromance!

Available wherever Harlequin books are sold.

Look us up on-line at: http://www.romance.net

HS-GEN

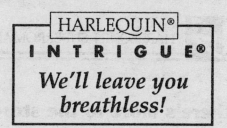

HARLEQUIN®
I N T R I G U E®
We'll leave you breathless!

If you've been looking for thrilling tales of
contemporary passion and sensuous love stories
with taut, edge-of-the-seat suspense—
then you'll *love* **Harlequin Intrigue!**

Every month, you'll meet four new heroes
who are guaranteed to make your spine tingle
and your pulse pound. With them you'll enter
into the exciting world of Harlequin Intrigue—
where your life is on the line
and so is your heart!

THAT'S INTRIGUE—DYNAMIC
ROMANCE AT ITS BEST!

HARLEQUIN®
I N T R I G U E®

INT-GENR